New

in

Lakewood Med

Book 3 of the Lakewood Series

TJ Amberson

NEW IN LAKEWOOD MED
Book 3 of the Lakewood Series
by TJ Amberson

Text ©2021 TJ Amberson
Cover design ©2021 Maria Spada and TJ Amberson
All rights reserved

ENGLISH TRAILS PUBLISHING, LLC
ISBN 978-1-7366513-0-8

While every reasonable effort was made to ensure a product of the highest quality, minor errors in the manuscript may remain. If you have comments, please email englishtrailspublishing@gmail.com.

For healthcare workers and first responders.

Books by TJ Amberson

Love at Lakewood Med
Back to Lakewood Med
New in Lakewood Med

Fusion

The Kingdom of Nereth
The Council of Nereth
The Keeper of Nereth

One

I cannot believe I'm doing this.

I've never considered myself an outdoorsy person, so I have no idea what possessed me to take a detour through Yellowstone National Park during my cross-country drive.

Don't get me wrong, it's not that I don't like nature. I enjoy leisurely walks, listening to chirping birds and ocean waves, feeling the wind against my face, and watching sunsets and falling snow. I even managed to grow snap peas last year.

However, I'm definitely not one of those intense "outdoor enthusiast" types. I simply don't see the allure of climbing up a mountain with nothing but a rope to stop you from plummeting to your death. Or spending the night in a claustrophobia-inducing sleeping bag while suffocating within a hot tent. Or voluntarily going to a place where one has to use leaves for toilet paper and worry that drinking the water will cause giardiasis.

Yet here I am, sitting behind the wheel of my eleven-year-old Toyota, in a lineup of about fifteen other vehicles, waiting to cross the south entrance into Yellowstone.

"Well, what else was I going to do with my time?" I ask aloud, though there's no one else in the car with me. After several days of driving alone, I've become quite adept at conversing with myself. "Since I can't move into the apartment for a couple more days, I might as well do some sightseeing while I pass through this part of the country, right?"

I shrug in agreement with myself, and I toss the wrapper of the granola bar I just consumed onto the floor in front of the passenger seat. The wrapper lands on top of a growing pile of evidence that my road trip eating habits haven't exactly been admirable. Cookie boxes, energy drink bottles, crumpled napkins from various fast-food establishments, and remnants of vending machine purchases are only some of the proof of my penchant for junk food. It's a miracle I'm as tall and wiry as I am. I thank good genetics for that.

In my own defense, though, I do normally keep my diet and exercise patterns pretty responsible. As a fourth-year medical student, I've certainly gained an appreciation of the benefits of a healthy lifestyle. Not to mention, I realize it's important to practice what I preach about healthy living—or, rather, what I *will* preach after I graduate from med school in a few months to become Quinn Meyers, MD, and I begin taking care of patients as a brand-new emergency medicine resident.

But road trip eating is different. Road trip calories don't count, kind of like holiday calories don't count. On a road trip—especially when there's nothing to see for hundreds of miles except antelope—sometimes a gal needs a candy bar. Or three. And maybe one of those unexplainably delicious hot dogs that are sold in gas stations.

The vehicles in front of me creep nearer to the park's entrance, and I inch my car forward along with them. Sitting up taller, I can see that traffic bottlenecks down to one lane up ahead as each car passes through an open gate to enter the park. The gate is flanked on both sides by little log cabins that have peaked roofs and cute windows framed in white.

The procession comes to another stop. I place my foot back on the brake and turn on the radio, but there's nothing except static to accompany my wait. So I shut off the radio and check my phone; it's not getting reception either. I blow a strand of my long, curly brown hair from my gray eyes and focus out the windshield once more.

"At least there will be WiFi in the hotel," I point out to myself. "I won't be completely cut off from the world while I'm here."

I luckily managed to snag a last-minute reservation at Old Faithful Inn for the next three nights while I explore the park. Obviously, a hotel was a must; there was no way I was going to camp. Though I intend to enjoy the glorious outdoors by day, I also fully intend to take a hot shower and sleep in a king-sized bed at night. So it's probably a good thing I'm visiting in the latter part of March. I bet getting reservations at any of the park's lodging during busier times of the year is nearly impossible, especially on the type of short notice I had.

I actually wasn't expecting to visit Yellowstone at all on this trip. My original plan was to drive across the country without doing any sightseeing along the way. However, a few days into my journey, I received an unexpected call that forced me to change my schedule. The call came from the landlord of the apartment I'm renting through the end of April; he informed me a pipe had burst in the unit above mine, and a few extra days were needed to clean up before I could move in. So somewhere between South Dakota and Wyoming, I decided to add a detour through Yellowstone to my itinerary. I figured a few days surrounded by nature would be a welcome reprieve from all the driving, especially before I found myself working in a hectic emergency department once again.

Not that I mind working in an emergency department. I love it, in fact. Last summer, I did my first-ever emergency medicine rotation at my own med school, and from the moment I walked into the department, I was hooked. Somehow, I knew emergency medicine was the right specialty for me. I—

Motion yanks me from my thoughts. The cars in front of mine are again rolling closer to the park's entrance. So I lift my foot from the brake and let my car do the same. Once the lineup comes to another halt, I stop my car and resume peering out the windshield. I note that every driver is stopping to speak with someone who's inside the tiny cabin on the left side of the open gate. The person inside the cabin then reaches out a window to hand a map to each driver before he or she proceeds into the park. Basically, if you replace the map with a venti-sized cup, it looks like we're going through a coffee shop drive-thru.

My mouth waters. I could really use a hot chocolate. And maybe a pastry to go along with it. And perhaps one of those—

There's more movement in line, and I guide my car forward another foot or two until I have to come to another stop. I take my hands off the steering wheel and rub them together, and then I turn up the heat in my car. The afternoon is growing late, and the bitingly cold temperature here in Wyoming is taking hold.

Once my car returns to being comfortably toasty, I glance over my shoulder at the backseat, eyeing the bright red cooler that's sandwiched between my two mammoth suitcases and strategically positioned so it's within arm's reach. I contemplate opening the cooler to retrieve another granola bar, or maybe some yogurt-covered pretzels, but I manage to resist any more snacking. At least until I get to the hotel.

Facing forward again, I drum my fingers on the steering wheel and start trying to figure out what I would like to see and do here in the park. I soon realize, however, that I actually don't have much knowledge about what there is to do in Yellowstone other than viewing Old Faithful. I've frequently heard Yellowstone is amazing, but that's really about all I know.

"Then it's a good thing I've got two full days to explore the park and learn more about it," I reassure myself.

I release the brake so my car migrates another short distance, and I continue mulling over what the next few days might bring. The more I think about it, the more excited I become about this little adventure. I may not be a hardcore outdoor fanatic, but I'll definitely enjoy relaxing in nature before I resume the long drive to the apartment.

I was thrilled when I found the listing for the apartment online. Enticingly advertised as "cozy" and "fully equipped with amenities," the apartment seemed particularly ideal when I mapped its location and saw it was only a couple blocks from Lakewood Medical Center, the huge hospital with the nationally renowned, extremely busy, high-acuity emergency department where I'll be doing an emergency medicine rotation for the month of April.

As for why I'm leaving my hometown and my own med school, and heading all the way across the country to do an elective rotation at Lakewood, I suppose there are a couple reasons. The first reason is simply that one of the perks of being in the fourth and final year of med school is having the opportunity to choose from a variety of elective rotations, including rotations at other locations around the country. When I learned Lakewood had an opening for a visiting med student to rotate in their famous ED, I eagerly signed up.

The other reason I decided to do a rotation at Lakewood is that—I'm immensely excited to say—I'll be starting my three-year emergency medicine residency there this summer. Since I've only been to Lakewood once before, and that was just for a day when I interviewed for the residency program, I figured doing an elective rotation at Lakewood before med school was over would be a great way for me to become familiar with the facility prior to starting residency.

A few months ago, like all fourth-year med students, I went through the exciting, stressful, and slightly frightening residency interview process. After doing an immense amount of research about emergency medicine residency programs throughout the country, I narrowed down the options to the eleven programs that appealed most to me. After I submitted my application, all I could do was wait and hope those programs would offer me an interview.

Of all the programs I applied to, I kept my fingers crossed most tightly for Lakewood. I was convinced Lakewood's fast-paced, high-volume emergency department would be a phenomenal place to train. I figured if I could handle practicing emergency medicine at Lakewood, I could handle working in an emergency department anywhere.

Needless to say, I was overjoyed when I received the invite to interview at Lakewood. A week or so later, I flew there for one long, jam-packed day. The morning kicked off with interviews with some of Lakewood's current emergency medicine residents—I met with a third-year, Henry Ingram, and a first-year, Elly Vincent. Admittedly, I was a bit awestruck by them both.

As if meeting residents wasn't intimidating enough, I had to keep my wits about me for interviews with some of the emergency department's attending physicians. I met Wes Kent, the director of the med student ED rotation; Jesse Santiago; Wilma Fox; and the director of the emergency medicine residency program himself, Gary Priest. Each attending struck me as wise, extremely knowledgeable about emergency medicine, and passionate about teaching. Meeting them only reaffirmed how much I wanted to get into the program.

After interviews, the other applicants and I were given a tour of Lakewood's emergency department. The place was loud, chaotic, and crowded with high-acuity patients . . . in other words, exactly the type of place where I wanted to train. Observing how the doctors, nurses, and other ED staff were skillfully caring for patients was even more inspiring when we were reminded that the area had recently experienced a major earthquake and some of the ED remained shut down from the damage. During the tour, we were informed that construction of Lakewood's new emergency department had recently received approval to accelerate its timeline, so the hospital would soon be opening a brand new, state-of-the-art emergency department.

When the interview day concluded, I flew home hoping more than ever that I would be accepted into the program. In subsequent weeks, I interviewed with the other programs I applied to, but Lakewood remained my top choice. When the time came to submit my rank list—a list of all the programs I interviewed at in order of where I most wanted to train—I didn't hesitate to put Lakewood first. Meanwhile, I knew Lakewood and all the other residency programs were submitting their own rank lists, rating every applicant they had interviewed in order of who they most wanted in their programs.

Once my rank list was submitted, it was the most torturous "hurry up and wait" period yet. Everything hinged on the results of a third-party software program running its mathematical algorithm to match interviewees to the residency program they ranked most highly. A match wouldn't be made, however, unless that residency program ranked the interviewee high enough on its list to fill one of its limited number of spots.

It wasn't until earlier this month, the infamous Match Day that happens in March, when every fourth-year med student across the nation finally learned the results of the match. I received an email that simply stated I had matched at Lakewood Medical Center for my emergency medicine residency. Though the email was brief, it was all I needed. I was elated, and that same day, I checked online to see if Lakewood offered visiting med students a chance to rotate in their emergency department. When I saw an opening for April, I signed up.

A honk from the car behind me snaps me to attention. It's finally my turn to enter the park. I tap on the gas pedal, advancing my vehicle so it's parallel to the window of the small cabin on the left side of the road. I crank up the heat another notch before I roll down my window, and then I shift in my seat to view the person inside the cabin.

The person—a guy—has his back to me while he puts something into the top drawer of a desk behind him. I can see he's wearing a long-sleeved shirt that's a color I can't quite name; it's like brown, green, and gray all mixed together. Anyway, whatever color it is, it seems very appropriately nature-like and Yellowstone-ish. The guy has a similarly colored hat on his head, which has a black band above the hat's straight, circular brim. Based on his outfit, I'm guessing this guy is a park ranger. I nearly snicker aloud as images of the old Yogi Bear cartoon suddenly pop into my mind. I wonder if—

"Good afternoon. Welcome to Yellowstone Park," the guy says in a deep, commanding voice. He turns to face the window.

I do a double take, and then I stare at the guy, my ability to speak suddenly gone. This park ranger looks nothing like what I've seen on television. Not even close.

This park ranger is the hottest guy I've ever seen in my life.

Two

Seconds pass while I continue staring at Hot Park Ranger in my stunned stupor. He peers right back at me with his bright green eyes and stern, no-nonsense expression. As best as I can tell, he's a couple years older than I am—probably in his upper twenties. His chiseled features include a straight nose, strong cheekbones, and a well-defined jaw. He has short brown hair, which is just visible under the edge of his hat. An olive green tie is resting over the button-down, color-of-no-name shirt of his uniform, which happens to fit noticeably well on his extremely muscular frame. There's a badge pinned above his shirt's left breast pocket and a nametag pinned over the pocket on the right. I stealthily attempt to read his nametag, but the writing is too small. I put my eyes on his face once more.

Hmm. Maybe I'll convince myself to become an outdoor enthusiast after all.

"Miss?" he prompts, breaking the silence.

I emerge from my daze. "What? I mean, hi. I mean, thanks. I mean, I'm here to visit the park." I blush as I state the obvious.

His deadpan expression doesn't change. "I need to see your *America the Beautiful Pass*, please."

"My what?" I check the rearview mirror. The lineup of cars behind mine is getting longer. I hastily refocus on the park ranger. "I need a pass?"

The corners of his mouth curve downward slightly. "You don't have an *America the Beautiful Pass*, miss?"

I fidget with my seatbelt. I have no idea what he's referring to. I need a pass? Am I the only person in this entire lineup who didn't know a pass was required to enter the park?

"No, I don't have a pass," I admit. "May I get one here?"

Hot Park Ranger glances at the waiting cars before shaking his head. "No. You can't purchase the pass here."

My stomach drops. Have I come all the way out here only to learn I won't be able to enter the park? Will I need to drive two hours to return to Jackson and buy a pass? If so, I won't make it back here until well after dark, and I'm not particularly excited about the prospect of driving unfamiliar, remote park roads at night, especially since bears or bison might be hanging out along the route.

Hot Park Ranger turns away from me and picks up something from the desk behind him. When he faces the window again, I see he's holding a clipboard in his left hand. I also happen to observe he isn't wearing a wedding ring.

"If you're only planning to visit Yellowstone, you can use a credit card to purchase a limited, seven-day pass for the park here," he states.

"Really?" I break into a relieved smile. "That's great. Yes, I'll by one of those limited-use passes, please."

I reach over to the seat beside me to grab my purse, but I stop as my heart lurches with alarm. My purse is gone. Did it fall out at a rest stop? Did someone steal it while I was getting gas? Could I have—

Then I remember: I stuffed my purse into one of my gigantic suitcases when I stopped for a vanilla milkshake about six hours ago. At the time, I figured if I hid my purse, it would reduce the likelihood that I would make any more impulsive stops for junk food before I reached the park.

Twisting around as best as I can so I'm facing the backseat, I stretch out my arm in an attempt to reach the suitcase that has my purse inside. However, not only do I quickly realize I would make a lousy contortionist, I also realize I won't be able to unzip my suitcase and retrieve my wallet from where I'm seated.

I hurriedly face forward again and unbuckle my seatbelt. "My wallet is inside one of my suitcases," I explain to Hot Park Ranger as I heave open my door and hop out of the car. "It'll only take me a second to find it."

"Miss," Hot Park Ranger barks.

"Yes?" I jump and spin his direction.

Hot Park Ranger and I are now standing only a few inches apart on opposite sides of the cabin's open window. As the wind rustles the nearby trees, I catch a whiff of his woodsy-smelling cologne. A little tingle runs down my spine.

Hot Park Ranger clears his throat and gestures to a pull-out spot just inside the park. "I'm going to ask you to drive over there to look for what you need."

I glance in the direction he's indicating. "No problem."

I dive into my idling car, tug the door closed, and maneuver through the open gate to officially enter Yellowstone. I drive only a few feet more before steering into the large, graveled pull-out area at my right.

I turn off the engine. Leaving my keys dangling in the ignition, I push my hair from my face and take a couple seconds to collect myself. Between thinking I was going to have to drive all the way back to Jackson to buy a park pass, fearing I had lost my purse, and coming face-to-face with a ridiculously hot park ranger, my pulse has definitely ticked up a notch or two. The jury is still out as to which of those factors has affected my pulse the most.

I peek at my car's side mirror and find Hot Park Ranger in the reflection. His naturally commanding presence is impossible to ignore, even as he just reviews people's park passes and directs traffic through the open gate. I continue enjoying the view until, without warning, Hot Park Ranger suddenly looks across the road, and our eyes meet in the mirror. I yelp and sit back fast.

I allow several seconds to pass before I get out of my car and shut the door. I shiver as I'm hit by the biting cold. My v-neck t-shirt and leggings were comfortable for a long day of driving, but they're certainly not adequate to fend off the cold around here this time of year.

With my teeth chattering, I open the driver's-side back door so I can access my suitcase. As soon as the door is released, however, everything that's jammed in the backseat unexpectedly shifts my way and starts toppling out of the car. With a gasp, I lunge forward with my arms extended in a clumsy attempt to stop my enormous, bright pink suitcase from crashing to the ground. I manage to wrap my cold fingers around the zipper, but this only causes the suitcase to unzip as the bag continues sliding past me with increasing momentum. The bag opens, flinging its contents into the air. Before I can let go, my foot slips on some gravel. I emit a shriek as I stumble to the ground. The bag lands beside me with a thud.

I blink a few times, and then I push myself to my knees, brush off my hands, and raise my head. And I groan. Everything that was inside my suitcase is now scattered all over the gravel— and, of course, it had to be the suitcase that contained my bras, panties, pajamas, and hygiene products.

"Miss, are you all right?"

I freeze when I hear Hot Park Ranger's deep voice. I think he's standing right behind me. Maybe if I don't move, he'll go away.

"Miss?"

Still on my knees, I see the park ranger's olive-colored pants and hefty black boots appear into view as he comes around to stand in front of me. He reaches down a hand.

Despite the fierce cold, my cheeks are uncomfortably warm as I place my hand in Hot Park Ranger's grip and let him assist me to my feet. His touch causes an electric sensation to rush up my arm, and the thrilling sensation lingers even after he lets me go.

I lower my arm while I raise my eyes. Hot Park Ranger is observing me with an expression that's impossible to decipher.

"Are you all right?" he asks.

"Yes, I'm fine. Thank you." I glance at the ground, and my face reignites. Basically, my entire collection of colorful underwear is on display. "It will only take me a few moments to clean this up and find my wallet. Please don't let me keep you from your work."

Hot Park Ranger's striking features are being highlighted by the waning sunlight as he looks over my shoulder to view the vehicles waiting at the gate. He then concentrates on me once more.

"You're sure you don't need assistance with your . . ." Hot Park Ranger trails off when his gaze drifts to my underwear that's all over the ground. He snaps his eyes back to mine. "Bag?"

"I'm sure." I'm also sure it would be impossible for my face to get any more painfully warm than it is at this moment. I motion toward the cabin. "Please don't let me delay you. I'll be over with my wallet in a moment. Thanks again."

Hot Park Ranger studies me a second longer before he strides off in the direction of the gate.

I sigh and look over my shoulder, watching while Hot Park Ranger crosses the road and re-enters the cabin. I then crouch down and begin tossing my things into the suitcase. When I locate my purse in the heap, I spring up, open the driver's door, and toss the purse onto the front seat so I won't lose track of it again. Shutting the door again, I return to my knees and resume cleaning up the mess.

Once I have everything repacked, I zip shut the bulging suitcase. Getting to my feet, I heave the monstrous bag onto the car's backseat, barely managing to cram it in beside the cooler, the other oversized suitcase, my emergency travel supplies, and whatever else I packed before I left home. I actually have to lean against the door to get it to close, but I finally hear a click that indicates the door is successfully shut and locked.

I shake out my arms and then reach to open the driver's door so I can retrieve my purse.

The door doesn't open.

I jiggle the handle again. The door still doesn't budge. I cup my hands around my eyes and peer through the window. I can see my keys hanging from the ignition and my purse on the front seat. With a growing sense of unease, I shift my eyes from one door to the next.

I've locked myself out of my car.

Forget everything I said about becoming an outdoor enthusiast. I'm not cut out for this.

I turn around and look across the road. Hot Park Ranger continues speaking with drivers and using his muscular arms to wave cars through the entrance with sharp, concise movements. Shifting my eyes, I peek at the cabin on the other side of the road, praying there's another park ranger here whom I can ask for assistance. But the other cabin is dark and empty.

With another resigned sigh, I walk to the edge of the road that separates the pull-out area from where Hot Park Ranger is working. The motion seems to catch his attention, for he promptly holds up a hand to stop traffic, and he looks across the road. He gestures for me to cross.

I dash forward, showing an appreciative smile to the folks who are waiting in their cars as I pass in front of them, and I charge up to the cabin's window.

Hot Park Ranger picks up the clipboard from the table behind him. "It's thirty-five dollars for the pass."

"Okay." I cough. "I'm happy to pay, of course. But I've . . . locked myself out of my car, and my wallet is inside."

His expression goes blank.

I peer past him, trying to look around the interior of the cabin. "You don't happen to have a lockout tool I could use to open the car door, do you?"

His eyebrows rise. "Do you break into cars often?"

"Yes. I mean, no. No, of course not." I shake my head, causing my curls to bounce against the sides of my face. "That is, I've broken into a car before . . . a few times, actually . . . but it was always mine."

Hot Park Ranger is watching me so intently that I'm convinced he's making a mental note of my face so he can put a sketch of it on one of those old-fashioned *Wanted!* posters, which he'll post all over the park. At this point, I couldn't entirely blame him.

"Miss, go ahead and return to your car," Hot Park Ranger says. "I'll be over to assist you."

Without waiting for my reply, Hot Park Ranger raises an arm again, signaling the drivers not to advance. Taking the cue, I sprint across the road to my vehicle. I wrap my arms around myself and jog in place, trying to stay warm.

Within moments, I see Hot Park Ranger step out of the cabin again. To my relief, he's holding a lockout tool, which basically looks like a long, thin strip of aluminum. He jogs across the road with athletic strides, and when he gets to my side, he proceeds to slide the tool between the driver's window and the rubber seal around it. Slipping the tool farther down toward the lock, he makes a couple small motions with his wrist, and then I hear the recognizable sound of the door unlocking. Hot Park Ranger uses his free hand to open the door while he removes the tool.

"Thank you." I lean past him to reach inside the car and grab my purse. "I'm sorry to have caused so much trouble." I open my wallet. "I've got my credit card right here, and—"

"Don't worry about it, miss." Hot Park Ranger pulls a park pass and a map from his back pocket, and he holds them out to me. "Drive safely in the park."

I take the items from him, and before I can say anything else, he turns away and jogs toward the cabin. I watch after him, until a frigid gust of wind hits me. With another shiver, I slide into my car, shut the door, start the engine, and crank up the heat. As the car warms up, I buckle my seatbelt, click on the dome light, and take a look at the map. To my pleasant surprise, it's both detailed and user-friendly; I have no doubt I'll be putting this to good use while I'm here.

I put away the map, hang the park pass from my rearview mirror, flip off the dome light, and turn on the headlights. Pulling forward, I merge onto the two-lane road and begin driving deeper into the park. But I can't resist casting a final glance in the rearview mirror, taking a last look at Hot Park Ranger before he disappears from view.

Three

I confirm the keys are securely in my grip before I shut and lock my car. Stashing the keys into a side pocket of my bright yellow backpack, I start making my way across the large, nearly empty parking lot.

Overhead, the sun is drifting lower in a cloudless blue sky, and the air remains cuttingly cold in these early days of spring. So for this, my second full day in Yellowstone, I've kept myself bundled up in a black sweatshirt and red puffy jacket, a pair of long johns under my jeans, thick green socks to go with my hiking boots, and a royal blue beanie cap pulled down low over my curls. I realize I basically look like a walking color wheel, but it's the warmest outfit I could put together from what I had in my suitcases.

Mismatched outfit aside, spending a couple days in Yellowstone has proven to be even more enjoyable than I anticipated. Yesterday, I kicked off the morning with a hearty breakfast of sizzling sausage and scrambled eggs. I then only had to step out the door of my hotel to join the crowd of early rising tourists who were waiting for the next eruption of the iconic geyser, Old

Faithful, which sat atop a small incline only yards away. It wasn't long before the geyser came to life, shooting gallons of boiling-hot water and steam straight up over a hundred feet into the air. The sulfur-scented eruption lasted over two minutes before the geyser fell quiet once more.

As soon as the eruption was done, most of the tourists put away their cameras and dispersed toward the parking lot. However, I took some time to stroll the planked pedestrian walkways that snaked across the surrounding area. I hadn't known there were other active geysers dotting the landscape—each one erupting on its own schedule, and some of them spewing water more frequently and even higher into the air than Old Faithful—so getting to see them was an unexpected bonus.

After my walk, I circled back, joining a fresh batch of vacationers to watch Old Faithful erupt again. I then hopped into my car and set off to spend the rest of the day exploring the southern part of Yellowstone. I had a fantastic time driving and hiking around some of the park's most amazing sights, including Yellowstone Lake and the West Thumb Geyser Basin. When the afternoon finally grew late and the sun began to set, I returned to my hotel, enjoyed a robust dinner, took a shower, and crashed to sleep.

This morning, I got another early start and ventured into the north half of the park. The Mammoth Hot Springs area was a highlight, though perhaps the most memorable moment occurred while I was driving and unexpectedly came upon a lineup of slow-moving cars. I soon discovered that the reason traffic had been forced nearly to a standstill was because a humungous bison had emerged from the forest and decided to start meandering down the middle of the road. The mighty beast didn't seem bothered in the slightest by the cars of picture-taking tourists . . . probably because Mr. Bison knew he outweighed every vehicle in his path.

Now with my tour of the northern part of the park complete, since I still have a little time before it gets dark, I've decided to return to a place I visited earlier today and fell in love with: the south rim of the upper falls of Yellowstone's own Grand Canyon. While the scenery throughout the park is nothing short of breathtaking, and it's made even more so because it's so unique and varied, I think this place is the most gorgeous spot of all.

I direct my course toward the main lookout, passing through a wide patch of shade that's being cast by the tall, densely packed trees. I shiver from the chill and zip up my jacket all the way under my chin. Yes, it's definitely getting colder as the sun drifts lower in the sky. However, I think it's worth enduring the cold that comes with this time of year to enjoy the park when it's less busy. Both yesterday and today have been blissfully peaceful, and I've relished being able to move at my own pace and appreciate the scenery without being surrounded by huge flocks of tourists.

A breeze stirs the trees, adding a soft whisper to the pleasant quiet, which is otherwise disturbed only by the occasional sounds of the few other sightseers who are still mingling about. I see an older couple—a woman in a pink overcoat and a man with a tweed cap on his head—strolling not far from the main lookout. Farther down a wooded path, a mother and father are trying to get their young children to hold still for a photo. Otherwise, the area is empty.

Reaching the main lookout, I lean against the waist-high wall and begin taking in the stunning vista. I think the sight is even more beautiful than it was when I first saw it, thanks to the vibrant glow of the late-afternoon sunlight. From my vantage point, I can see all the way across the wide, forested canyon, which has a sparkling river cutting through the base of it. On the far side of the canyon is the majestic waterfall itself, endlessly pouring over the cliff with a roar while causing a cloud of mist to rise up from the base of the canyon far below. There's something both awe-inspiring and perfectly serene about this place.

It's not until I notice how low the sun has dipped that I finally push off from the wall and start meandering down a pathway that leads into a thickly forested area. Since I don't have much daylight left, I want to explore as much as I can before heading to the hotel.

I grow lost in thought as I continue making my way farther into the forest. I'm vaguely aware of the path narrowing and changing from concrete to dirt beneath my feet, and I sense the trees steadily closing in around me. Soon, all I hear are the sounds of my footsteps upon the terrain, the wind, and the distant roar of the waterfall. By the time I stop to peer around, I'm alone in the middle of what feels like a dense wilderness. Thankfully, the sound of the waterfall provides constant orientation like a compass, and I walk a little farther until I find a gap in the trees that gives me another view of the falls.

A gust of wind prompts me to shove my hands into the pockets of my jacket and glance around at the elongating shadows. It's probably time for me to return to the hotel. I'm thinking a bowl of hot soup will really hit the spot for dinner. And perhaps a—

"Miss, you're in a prohibited area of the forest," I hear a man behind me say in a deep voice. "Please return to the designated pathway."

I jump in surprise and spin around. And I freeze.

Hot Park Ranger is standing only a few feet away from me.

As our eyes meet, I send up a silent plea to the Universe that Hot Park Ranger won't remember me—more specifically, that he won't remember my colorful underwear scattered all over the road. But when I see his eyebrows rise with a look of recognition, I know Hot Park Ranger is recalling every humiliating, bra-and-panty moment of the other evening. I groan inwardly while my cheeks flush.

For another beat, we keep staring at each other. Despite how flustered I am, I can't help noting Hot Park Ranger somehow looks even more handsome than the last time I saw him . . . I wouldn't have thought that could be possible. He's again in uniform, complete with the round-brimmed hat, and this time his uniform also includes an olive-green coat with the emblem of the National Park Service over the left breast. He has a gun belt on his hips, and there's a walkie-talkie clipped to a side pocket of his pants.

And he's watching me with his penetrating gaze and unreadable expression.

"Prohibited?" I squeak out. "This area is prohibited?"

He nods once. "This area is known for rockslides. Not to mention, wildlife come to feed around here at dusk."

"I didn't realize that." I fix him with a more pointed look. "If this area is dangerous and off-limits, perhaps it would be wise to post a sign about that somewhere."

Hot Park Ranger stares at me for a long moment. Then, without a word, he shifts his gaze to my left. I slowly follow his line of sight to a large sign that's staked in the ground nearby. The sign warns, "*STAY OUT OF AREA*" in colossal font on both sides, and overlying the words is a red circle with a diagonal line through it to further emphasize the point. I then notice there are four more identical signs strategically positioned in conspicuous places along the route I took from the lookout.

"Ah." I clear my throat and look at Hot Park Ranger once more. "I guess I missed the sign . . . all of the signs, actually."

Though I can't be sure, I think the corners of his mouth twitch upward. Quickly, though, his serious expression returns. He flicks his eyes across the darkening wilderness before putting his concentration back on me.

"Miss, are you out here alone?"

I nod in the affirmative.

His brows draw together. "You shouldn't be out here by yourself, especially not when it's nearly dusk."

"You're right," I admit. "I was actually about to go to my car."

To prove my point, I take a hurried step in the direction of the parking lot, but my foot slips on some loose rocks I didn't see in the expanding darkness. I let out an awkward screech as I stumble and start to fall.

The next thing I know, Hot Park Ranger has caught me in his arms.

Neither of us moves. I'm not even sure I'm breathing. Suddenly, the quiet of the forest around us feels very charged and very intense.

The moment passes, and I manage to collect myself enough to gather my footing and slip out of his embrace.

"Thank you." I glance at his name, which is stitched on the outside of his coat. "Ranger Gillespie."

He lowers his arms to his sides while his eyes remain on mine. "You're welcome. Please—"

"Help! Someone help!"

A woman's distressed shout echoes through the forest. I whip my head in the direction from where it came: the main lookout.

Ranger Gillespie puts a hand on his gun belt and begins sprinting toward the lookout. "Miss, get to your car!" he shouts to me over his shoulder.

I hike my backpack higher up on my shoulders and run after Ranger Gillespie, straining to see in the shadows while dodging tree roots, branches, and rocks in my path. Though I'm a decent runner, I soon discover I'm no match for Ranger Gillespie's long, athletic strides. He continues charging through the woods ahead of me, and I have to pick up my pace even more just to keep him in view. I'm breathing hard with exertion, and my chest is burning from the cold. I have no idea if I'm running toward danger or away from it—in fact, visions of a woman getting attacked by a bear are already plaguing my mind—but Ranger Gillespie is right: I have a better chance of finding safety in my car than I do wandering alone in the forest this time of evening.

I finally emerge from the trees near the main lookout, and I anxiously scan the scene. For a brief moment, I feel relief; there's not a bear in sight. However, when I spot Ranger Gillespie, I'm filled with alarm of a different kind. He's down on one knee beside the elderly man with the tweed cap whom I saw earlier. The elderly man is seated on the ground and hunched forward at the waist. His respirations are labored, and he has a hand clenched to his chest. The woman in the pink coat—undoubtedly the source of the panicked shout for help we heard—is standing beside them, crying and wringing her hands.

In an instant, my mind shifts into work mode. With the familiar feeling of adrenaline starting to pump through me, I dash across the lookout and drop down onto my knees directly in front of the elderly man. Out of the corner of my eye, I see Ranger Gillespie snap his head my direction, but I keep my concentration on the man who's working hard to breathe.

"Sir, my name is Quinn Meyers," I tell him, making sure to speak clearly. "I'm a fourth-year medical student. I'm not a doctor yet, but I'm willing to try to assist you in any way I can. May I ask what's going on?"

Still in the periphery of my vision, I notice Ranger Gillespie open his mouth as if to interject, but he then shuts it again. Instead, he gets to his feet, unclips his walkie talkie from his belt, and moves a few steps away while speaking into the walkie talkie in a low voice.

I return my complete focus to the elderly gentleman who's seated before me. By the glow of the lights coming on across the parking lot, I see the man is pale, his eyes are wide and panicked, and the hand he's holding to his chest is trembling.

"I'm . . . having chest . . . pain," the man says.

I look over at Ranger Gillespie, who immediately stops talking into his walkie talkie to return my gaze.

"Do the park's EMS crews transport patients out of here by road or air?" I ask.

"Typically by ground," Ranger Gillespie replies. "When roads are open, it's as fast, if not faster, to transport patients to Jackson by ground rather than waiting for a chopper for medical evac." He tips his head toward the walkie talkie in his hand. "I'm having the park dispatcher send a unit our way."

"Great." I resume eyeing the elderly man. "Sir, when did your chest start hurting?"

"Earlier this afternoon," his wife interjects, still crying. "I've been telling him for hours that he should get seen in one of the park's clinics, but he kept insisting he was fine. I knew he wasn't fine, though."

I give the wife a nod. My worry for her husband is mounting by the moment, but I maintain my composed demeanor as I resume addressing the man:

"Do you have any heart problems, sir?"

"I've had . . . two heart attacks," he replies between labored breaths. "My last heart attack was three years ago. They put . . . a couple stents in with that one."

"Does the pain you're currently experiencing feel like your prior heart attacks?" I reach out and palpate the pulse in each wrist. His heart rate is a little low, but at least his pulses are symmetric.

"Yes," the man answers. "The pain feels . . . exactly the same."

The woman moans and drops her head in her hands. "I knew it. I just knew it."

"Any other symptoms?" I inquire.

The man shakes his head.

"Do you have any other medical history?"

"They've kept me on . . . medications for cholesterol and blood pressure . . . since my first heart attack."

"Any allergies?"

He shakes his head again.

Ranger Gillespie strides toward us while clipping the walkie talkie to his pocket. "A transport crew will be here soon." Looking at me, he adds, "I'll be right back."

Ranger Gillespie sprints for the parking lot. I peer over my shoulder to watch him, and I realize he's heading for a white Chevy SUV that's parked nearby; the SUV has a dark-green stripe along its sides and the National Park Service emblem on the doors.

I face the man and his wife once more. "Do either of you carry aspirin?"

His wife lets out another groan. "We have some, but it's at our hotel. He does take a baby aspirin every morning."

I hear the sound of a car door being opened, and I glance behind me again. Ranger Gillespie is reaching into his SUV. He pulls out a small bag with one hand and an automatic external defibrillator with the other. Appearing as unruffled as ever, he runs back across the parking lot and rejoins us. He gets down on one knee beside me, sets the AED on the ground, and opens the bag.

"We have full-strength and baby aspirin in our kits," Ranger Gillespie states, like he somehow overheard the conversation I was just having with the elderly man and his wife.

I ask the patient, "Sir, did you take your baby aspirin today?"

"Yes. I . . . always do."

I turn to Ranger Gillespie. "Please get out three baby . . ."

I trail off. Ranger Gillespie already has three of the tiny, circular baby aspirin tablets in his hand. He meets my curious stare for only a moment before handing over the medication to the man.

"Please chew those up, sir," Ranger Gillespie instructs before I can say the same thing.

The man puts the aspirin into his mouth and starts chewing as directed. To my relief, I begin hearing an ambulance siren somewhere in the distance. The wail of the siren steadily gets louder, and then a white ambulance marked with the emblem of the National Park Service comes flying into the parking lot with siren wailing and lights flashing.

The ambulance is brought to a stop at the closest curb. Two men and a woman hop out; they're all dressed in uniforms similar to what Ranger Gillespie is wearing. One of the EMTs is carrying a defibrillator, and another is holding a kit of medical supplies. As the two of them jog toward us, the third member of the crew opens the back door of the ambulance to pull out the stretcher.

The lead crew member reaches Ranger Gillespie's side. "What do we have?"

I'm retreating to give the crew room when Ranger Gillespie unexpectedly motions my way and replies:

"This is Quinn Meyers. Fourth-year medical student. She'll provide report."

If her dropped jaw is any indication, the lead EMT is as surprised as I am. She shoots Ranger Gillespie another perplexed look, but he only tips his head my way again. So while her partner starts assessing the patient, the lead EMT turns my direction. And she waits.

I wet my lips, extremely aware the lead crew member isn't the only one who's staring at me. Ranger Gillespie is watching me, too. Trying not to get rattled, I begin giving the lead EMT my report:

"This gentleman has a history of two prior MIs. His most recent MI was three years ago, and two stents were placed at that time. Today, he has been experiencing chest pain that feels like his prior MIs. No associated symptoms. Past medical history otherwise unremarkable. He takes meds for blood pressure and cholesterol management. He also takes a daily baby aspirin; he had his dose this morning, and he received three more baby aspirin here."

The lead crew member breaks into an appreciative smile. "Great. Thanks."

She spins around and joins her teammates in preparing the patient for transport. Meanwhile, Ranger Gillespie is speaking with the patient's wife, explaining what's happening and the anticipated plan for care. I have to say, I'm impressed by how fluently Ranger Gillespie speaks medical lingo. Park rangers must get some really solid basic medical training so they're able to assist with emergencies in the park.

Once the crew has the patient on their stretcher and hooked to the portable cardiac monitor, they hurriedly push the stretcher to the ambulance. While the crew works fast to get the patient loaded inside their rig, Ranger Gillespie and the patient's wife follow behind. The wife is still listening intently to what Ranger Gillespie is saying to her. I then overhear her decline his offer to drive her to the hospital. She tells him she prefers to drive herself to the hospital in Jackson where her husband is being taken for care.

Two crew members stay in the back of the ambulance to continue caring for the patient; the other crew member gets into the driver's seat. The doors of the ambulance are swung shut with resounding slams. The engine roars to life. There's a deafening chirp from the siren, and the lights begin flashing against the dark sky. The ambulance is driven away, and soon the sound of the siren fades, and everything becomes still once more.

Alone on the curb, I keep peering in the direction the ambulance went while mentally debriefing what happened, like I always do after any adrenaline-inducing encounter with a patient. I may be in the middle of a national park, but for a few minutes, it felt like being in the emergency department. That patient was certainly high risk, yet I think he'll get to the hospital in time to receive the care he needs.

A gust of wind pulls me from my thoughts. Overhead, the sky is black and starry. All I hear is the mighty waterfall on the far side of the canyon. Once again aware of how cold it has gotten, I blow into my hands and rub them together while I peer around.

Ranger Gillespie is escorting the woman to her vehicle. I watch as he opens the door for her, and after she's settled behind the wheel, he says something else before he shuts the door. The woman drives away, vanishing into the night. Now the only cars left on the premises are Ranger Gillespie's SUV, which isn't far from where I'm standing, and my car at the opposite end of the parking lot.

Ranger Gillespie seems to pause, and then he turns his head and sets his eyes on mine. I feel a little skip inside my chest. The pattering in my chest gets stronger when he starts striding my way.

A phone rings, shattering the quiet. Ranger Gillespie stops in the middle of the parking lot, pulls the ringing phone from his coat pocket, and puts it to his ear. After a moment, he shifts the other direction and begins speaking into the phone in a voice too low for me to hear.

A sigh escapes me as I turn away from Ranger Gillespie and trek to my car. Sliding my backpack down one arm, I remove the keys from the side pocket and tap the key fob. My car lets out a welcoming chirp, and the dome light comes on. I open the door and slide inside. Moving fast against the cold, I shut the door, put the keys into the ignition, and crank up the heater as high as it will go.

While the car warms up, I toss my bag onto the passenger seat. I pull off my beanie cap, shake out my curls, and buckle myself in. Thankfully, the temperature in here has risen to something slightly higher than Arctic by the time I flip on the headlights and commence driving toward the exit.

Before I pull out onto the main road, a motion in the side mirror catches my eye. In its reflection, I see Ranger Gillespie striding to his SUV; he still has his phone to his ear. Unexpectedly, he halts and looks over, and our eyes meet in the mirror. My breathing hitches as I find myself wondering if he's going to come over here and say something. But he doesn't. Instead, Ranger Gillespie resumes talking on the phone and gets into his vehicle.

I look out the windshield and exit the parking lot, telling myself I have no reason to be disappointed about what happened—or, rather, what didn't happen—with Ranger Gillespie. He may be handsome, gentlemanly, intelligent, and a bit mysterious, but none of that matters. Because I'm in love with someone else. While it's true Chad and I are currently in yet another "off" phase of our on-again-off-again relationship, it doesn't mean I'm going to give up on him. After all, love is about patience, devotion, and forgiveness, and so I owe it to Chad—I owe it to *us*—to see if we can work things out.

Right?

Four

"Code Blue. ETA ten minutes. Code Blue. ETA ten minutes."

I jump skittishly when the announcement blares out from the speakers overhead. Forcing myself to a halt, I inhale some slow breaths, trying to calm my heart, which has begun rattling. I can't help it. This is my first day working in Lakewood Medical Center's emergency department, and I'm not even through the doors yet, and it already sounds as though this shift is going to be wild one.

I step up to the emergency department's main door and wait for it to slide open. As I cross the threshold and enter the gigantic waiting room, I'm flooded by sound: screaming babies, adults coughing, a woman gasping loudly as she sobs, phones ringing, people engaged in tense conversations, and the echoing of more overhead announcements. Adding to the chaos is the droning narrative of an infomercial, which is playing on an ancient television that has been mounted to the wall and has its volume cranked to maximum. Topping off the cacophony of noise, someone from environmental services is cleaning the floors with an industrial-sized machine that looks like one of those things they use to resurface the ice in a hockey rink.

I flick my widening eyes around the room. I note cracks and large patches of peeling paint on the walls. Water stains mar the ceiling. The lights are sputtering as if they're on the verge of going out. The magazines on the tables are so outdated that the covers are faded. And I don't even want to guess how old the furniture might be. All together, the dilapidated condition of this place makes a striking contrast to the rest of the hospital, which is beautifully renovated to give it the appearance of a high-end hotel . . . with operating rooms. Anyway, it's evident that construction of the new emergency department was long overdue.

What's also striking about this place is the number of people who are crammed in here. The emergency department affiliated with my med school back at home—the place where I did two ED rotations last summer—is busy, but I've never witnessed anything like what's going on here at Lakewood. This is the biggest waiting room I've ever seen, yet it's completely packed, and it's not even nine in the morning. I can only imagine how busy this place must get as the day progresses.

My nerves spike. This is a far cry from what I'm used to. Am I cut out for this? Will I really be able to handle working at Lakewood?

I'm starting to feel queasy as I continue scanning the people who fill the waiting room.

Over in a corner, three guys are shaking an old vending machine in an attempt to get it to drop a candy bar . . . whether or not they actually paid for the candy bar is anyone's guess. There's a man seated against the far wall who has a bloodied cloth wrapped around his hand. Beside some empty fish tanks, a man and a woman are arguing about who's going to move their car out of the drop-off zone. A lady seated by the door is attempting to rock a fussy infant while feeding crackers to a toddler. A guy with the hood of his sweatshirt pulled up over his head is making loud retching noises as he vomits into an emesis bag. There's a man pacing and yelling into his phone about how "the coach doesn't know diddly-squat about a full-court press" while a teenage girl in a basketball uniform is seated nearby, keeping her swollen foot and ankle propped up on a tiny table.

Looking from one patient to the next, my stomach knots up even more. What have I gotten myself into? Am I—

I realize the nurse who's staffing the triage room is watching me through a window of bullet-proof glass. I manage to show her something like a smile before I head toward the locked double doors that lead into the treatment area of the ED. I can feel the collective stare of every person in the waiting room settle upon me as I go.

I reach the double doors and stop again. I need to get a handle on my nerves—something I'm usually pretty good at doing, but I'm finding it to be nearly impossible today. How could I be calm, though? I'm about to start working in Lakewood's emergency department. I'll be caring for extremely sick patients. My skills and knowledge will be tested more than ever before. Plus, I'll be making a first impression on the attendings, residents, nurses, techs, and other members of the ED team—and they're people I'm not just working with for the month—they're people with whom I'll be working for the next three years.

No pressure.

On top of all that, adding to the stress is the fact that I'm coming off a whirlwind past few days and still trying to get my feet on the ground.

Only two nights ago, I finished my cross-country drive to reach the rental apartment. At first, I wasn't sure I was in the right place because the building's graffiti-covered exterior didn't exactly match the "lovely ambience" described online. So after I pulled into the pot-hole-filled parking lot, I had to check the address twice before I convinced myself I really was in the correct spot.

Unfortunately, things only got worse from there. The parking lot, with its broken lights and collapsed chain-link fence, definitely didn't strike me as a "safe and secure" location for my vehicle. Meanwhile, the thick bars over the building's windows weren't conveying the vibe of a "quaint and cozy abode located in a charming area of town." I probably would have described the vibe more along the lines of "needs to be condemned" or "located where no one without training in some form of martial arts should walk alone at night."

Anyway, as I sat in my car, warily eyeing the building and glancing around to make sure no one was lurking in the parking lot, I contemplated my options. It didn't take me long, however, to realize I didn't really have any other options. It was late at night, I was exhausted, I was hundreds of miles from home and in a place where I knew no one, and I didn't have the funds to go live in a hotel. In other words, I was stuck.

So I texted the landlord, Mr. Utteley, to inform him I had arrived. About an hour later, he met me in the parking lot to give me the keys. Mr. Utteley proved to be a short, balding man with an apparent penchant for sweater vests. He assured me the leaking pipe in the apartment above mine had been repaired, but then he mumbled something about the building's elevator being broken, and he added another comment I couldn't hear before he scurried away.

Alone again, I approached the building and used the keys to unlock its not-even-remotely-a-deterrent-to-burglars outside door. Stepping into the dimly lit lobby, I was greeted by the smells of mildew and artificial cheese. The main door hadn't even finished shutting behind me with a loud squeak before I concluded the building's interior was as bad as the outside.

Like Mr. Utteley had warned, the lobby's elevator was broken—and from the looks of things, it had been broken since I was in high school. So I hauled my monster suitcases, cooler, and all my other belongings up three flights of stairs and down the narrow hallway to my apartment. Ever the optimist, I remained hopeful things wouldn't be so dire inside my actual living quarters, but once I opened the door and saw unidentifiable stains on the carpets and cigarette burns on the furniture, I knew my "one-bedroom, fully furnished accommodations" weren't going to be as "charming" as I had been led to believe.

Nothing about the place was "quiet," either. Road noise was heavy outside, and music coming from the apartment above mine rattled the light fixtures. Nonetheless, I managed to fall asleep that night . . . but not before I pulled off the discolored bedspread, peeled away the sheets, and covered the lumpy, stained mattress with a pile of my sweatshirts and scrub pants.

Yesterday morning, I was jarred awake by what I thought was a bomb drop. Turned out it wasn't the apocalypse; it was a garbage truck rumbling down the street and emptying dumpsters. Regardless, it was clear I wasn't getting back to sleep, so I wearily pulled myself out of bed to start tackling my to-do list.

I first bought a bus pass. I next hit the nearby grocery store to stock up on food and other essentials. (Other than crime-scene tape blocking off the bread aisle, I didn't find the grocery store to be *that* bad.) Only after returning to the apartment with my groceries did I discover a sticky note from Mr. Utteley inside the refrigerator that explained the fridge worked "most of the time."

Once grocery shopping was done, I headed to Lakewood Medical Center for my orientation meeting with Lynn Prentis, the coordinator for the emergency department. The meeting was in her office, which she shares with Dr. Kent, on an upper floor of Prescott Tower. (Mercifully, the elevators of Prescott Tower were working.)

Lynn was immensely helpful as I filled out the required forms for a visiting med student. Once the paperwork was completed, we visited the IT department so I could receive my computer log-in information, have my photo taken, and get issued a temporary employee badge.

Lynn next took me on another tour of the ED. This time, she focused on explaining things that would help me with day-to-day work, like what computer stations I should use and where lac repair carts were located. As I followed Lynn and observed the non-stop activity swirling around us, that was when the reality struck me fully: I wasn't there simply to take a tour. The next day, I would be taking care of patients, too. And I knew that once my first shift began, ED staff members would be observing me and formulating opinions about whether or not I was good enough to be part of the incoming residency class. I also knew that if I failed to impress everyone, my reputation at Lakewood could be destroyed before residency even started.

With such heavy thoughts weighing on my mind, it took a long time falling to sleep that night.

The next morning—this morning—I was again woken by noise. It wasn't garbage trucks this time, though. As best as I could tell, someone in the apartment above was bowling. I rolled out of bed and downed a smoothie. I put on blue scrubs and my short white med student coat, and I managed to tame my curls enough to cinch my hair into a low bun. I packed my work bag with the typical essentials: stethoscope, phone loaded with medical reference apps, pens (the clicky kind), lip balm, water bottle, snack bars, wallet, and keys. Once my bag was packed, I threw on a jacket and made the walk to the hospital.

So now here I am, staring at the locked, windowless doors that lead into the treatment area of the ED while still trying to process that this moment has actually come. In many respects, this ED rotation will be even more important than the ones I did last summer at my own med school. Now everyone will be watching me. Now I have an expectation to live up to. Now staff members will form opinions of me—good or bad, right or wrong, fair or unfair—that will follow me throughout residency.

I shake my head. Why, exactly, did I come here this month? What was I thinking? By doing this rotation, I'm only exposing myself to extra scrutiny before residency begins. I'll be scrambling to prove myself while working in an unfamiliar ED that's far busier and higher in acuity than anywhere I've worked before.

I'm starting to wonder if I'm going to puke like the guy in the waiting room.

I touch my badge to the scanner that's mounted on the wall to my left. The scanner beeps. The double doors clunk loudly and begin swinging out toward me. Once the gap is wide enough, I slip between the doors to enter the treatment area of the emergency department. As the doors slowly shut behind me with a resounding thud, I force down a swallow. Though I was here twenty-four hours ago, everything feels completely different today. Today, I'm expected to care for patients. Everything I say and do will be judged. And I have to prove I deserve to be here.

I peer around, trying to absorb every detail of the scene before me. It's impossible not to first notice that this gargantuan, brightly lit department is absolutely packed with patients. Every exam room has its curtain drawn closed to indicate there's a patient inside, and every corridor is lined with patients on chairs or stretchers. Nurses and techs are dashing from one patient to the next. EMS crews keep entering through the ambulance-bay doors at my right, wheeling in even more patients who need to be seen. Secretaries are racing to get patients registered, answer phones, scan paperwork, and send out pages to consultants. Attending physicians and residents are speaking with patients, performing exams, doing procedures, taking phone calls, and charting at their workstations. Meanwhile, the noise is relentless: more announcements over the PA system, phones ringing, a man in one of the exam rooms screaming profanities, pagers going off, someone crying, and the rumble of a portable x-ray machine as a radiology tech wheels it across the department.

As I soak in the scene, my breathing hitches with unexpected emotion. In only a couple months, I'll be starting residency here. I'll have "MD" after my name. Instead of being on an elective rotation, I'll be working as an intern—a first-year resident. This place will become my emergency medicine training ground. Though I'll still be under the supervision of an attending physician, I'll be handling much more responsibility. I'll laugh here, and I'll cry here. I'll see amazing things, and I'll see awful things. Staff members who are strangers to me today will become my colleagues and, hopefully, my friends. The course of my life will be shaped by the years I spend here at Lakewood. I—

"May I help you find anything?"

I realize someone just addressed me, and I spin toward the source of the voice. A gal who appears about my age is coming my way. She's wearing hospital scrubs, and she has on a short white coat, so I'm guessing she must also be a med student. She's a couple inches shorter than I am. Her thick, dark red hair is pulled into a ponytail, and her big green eyes are sparkling warmly.

"Hi." I smile at her. "I'm Quinn Meyers. I'm a visiting fourth-year med student who's rotating here this month, and—"

"Oh, you're Quinn! Lynn Prentis told me you would be here!" Her smile widens, and she reaches out a hand. "I'm Danielle. I'm also a fourth-year, and I'm rotating in the ED this month, too. I'm excited to work with you!"

I shake Danielle's hand with both gratitude and relief. It will be great having another med student in the ED this month. It's always nice to work alongside someone who understands the stress you're going through. A fellow med student is someone you can bounce questions off of without feeling stupid. Or someone you can roll your eyes with when a resident or attending chastises you for no good reason. And someone to commiserate with after a difficult day. So I'm thankful Danielle will be here, especially since she seems so friendly and welcoming.

I glance at her ID badge, but it's flipped over so I can't read it. "Are you also a visiting student?"

"Nope, I'm local. I go to med school here." Danielle steps closer to make room for a tech to pass by with an ECG machine. "I did an ED rotation last July, too, so feel free to ask me any questions. I'm happy to try to help." Her eyes dart around the department, and she shakes her head. "I understand how overwhelming this place can feel at times."

"Thanks," I tell her. "So if this is your second ED rotation, does it mean you're going into emergency medicine?"

"Gosh, no. I like it down here, but I definitely couldn't do this all the time." Danielle laughs and adjusts the stethoscope she has around her neck. "I'm going into OBGYN, and I'm rotating through the ED this month for my elective in emergency OBGYN care. So I'm here specifically to help manage any OBYGN patients who present to the ED."

"That's great. Where did you match for your OBGYN residency?"

"Here at Lakewood." Danielle's eyes sparkle again. "This residency program was my number-one choice. Also, I've lived in the area my entire life and really wanted to stay. Even more importantly, my boyfriend's job will keep him in the region for the foreseeable future, and I obviously didn't want to have to move away from him." She sighs. "In other words, for about a million reasons, I was hoping to match here, and I was thrilled when I got the good news on Match Day."

"That's wonderful," I reply sincerely, though I'm also pricked with remorse. Chad and I will be living on opposite ends of the country for the next several years as we do our respective residencies, and though we're broken up at the moment, it's hard to think about living so far away from him.

"What about you?" Danielle peers at me inquisitively. "Where did you match at?"

"I also matched here at Lakewood. I'm going into emergency medicine." I have to pause while my own words replay in my head. It's still surreal to envision myself as a soon-to-be resident. "I'm doing this elective to give myself some experience here before residency."

"You're starting your EM residency here this summer? Are you serious? That's awesome!" Danielle is beaming. "My best friend, Savannah, is part of the incoming emergency medicine class, too! I can't wait to introduce you to her! And our friends, Rachel Nelson and Tyler Warren, also matched here in emergency medicine, so we'll make sure you meet them while you're in town."

Before I can reply, there's a clamor in the ambulance bay behind me. I spin around. An EMS crew is racing through the doorway, and one crew member is driving a stretcher that has a woman lying motionless upon it. Another crew member is doing compressions on the patient while the third EMT is bagging the patient to provide oxygen into her nose and mouth. Without slowing, the crew flies past Danielle and me and pushes the stretcher into the nearest resuscitation bay, where members of the ED team are waiting to take over.

I stare into the resuscitation bay, watching in awe as the ED team bursts into action to take over running the code. As the lead EMT begins giving report, I realize that in a few months, the resident who's running the code could be me . . . actually, the resident *will* be me. I'll be running codes here at Lakewood. I'll be carrying that immense responsibility on my shoulders. The thought causes my insides to churn again.

I finally pull my stare from the resuscitation bay and turn back to Danielle. As I do so, something far behind her catches my eye: a glimpse of a tall, well-built guy in dark green scrubs who's stepping into an exam room. A split-second later, he's lost from view behind the room's curtain. I blink as I process what I just saw. That guy looked like Hot Park Ranger. The resemblance was uncanny.

"I should probably go meet up with my team for rounds, and I'm guessing you need to go find your attending," Danielle says. "It was great to meet you, Quinn. Good luck today, and I'll see you soon."

I refocus on her and smile. "Thanks. I'll talk to you soon."

Danielle dashes away. I glance at the clock on the wall, and my throat suddenly feels parched. My shift starts in three minutes. My first day at Lakewood is about to begin.

I scan the department, looking for the charge nurse's station. Yesterday, Lynn told me that's where I should meet the attending who's going to be my supervisor for the next four weeks. When Lynn explained this to me, though, she was still reviewing the ED doctors' schedules and hadn't assigned someone as my attending yet, so I have no idea who I'll be working with this month.

But I'm about to find out.

I tug on the hem of my white coat and start heading in the direction of the charge nurse's station. I soon halt, however, and I stand up straight, trying to appear as put-together as possible, because Dr. Jesse Santiago, one of the ED attendings who interviewed me last winter, is walking toward me.

I groan inwardly. Of all the attendings in this department, why did I have to get paired with someone I previously interviewed with? Presumably, Dr. Santiago had positive things to say about me after my interview, and his feedback would have helped me rank higher on Lakewood's match list. While that's all well and good, it also means I have nowhere to go but down in his estimation. Making a great impression during an interview is one thing. Making a great impression through patient care in the emergency department is another thing entirely. As Dr. Santiago supervises my every move in the ED this month, what if I don't live up to his expectations? What if he winds up regretting that he ranked me highly?

I can't let that happen. I have to prove I deserve to be here. I have to prove to Dr. Santiago that I'll be as strong of an addition to the incoming residency class as he believed.

Dr. Santiago strides closer. He's dressed in navy blue scrubs, and he has his stethoscope draped around his neck. His dark hair is combed, and his dark eyes convey the same wit and sense of humor I detected in him when we met. If I had to guess his age, I would put him somewhere in his mid-thirties.

"Hi, Quinn," Dr. Santiago greets me once he's close enough that I can hear him over the din. "Welcome back to Lakewood. I'm looking forward to working with you this month."

"Good morning, Doctor Santiago." Thankfully, my voice stays steady. "I'm looking forward to working with you, too."

"Call me Jesse." Dr. Santiago motions to my bag, which I've got hanging from one shoulder. "How about we get you situated at one of the workstations and let you start seeing patients?"

"Okay," is all I can say because my mind is racing so fast that I can barely put together a sentence. I'm still trying to convince myself this is truly happening. I'm about to start seeing patients in Lakewood's emergency department.

Dr. Santiago tips his head toward the center of the department. "I'll show you where I'm working, so you can get set up nearby."

I follow him toward the workstations that are in the middle of the ED. While Dr. Santiago appears as though he's strolling through a park on a summer day, I undoubtedly look like I'm maneuvering a minefield in the middle of a warzone. I dart around techs who are carrying splinting supplies, nurses taking medications into patients' rooms, and secretaries scrambling to get patients registered. I'm so distracted by everything, in fact, I nearly crash into Dr. Santiago when he comes to a stop beside one of the large computer desks that, as I recall from my ED tour, is designated as a workstation for the attendings.

"This is where I'm working for the shift," he tells me. He points to a workstation close by. "No one is using that spot today, so please feel free to get settled in there."

"Thanks." I set my bag on the floor beside what will be my home base for the shift.

"Take your time getting logged into the computer." Dr. Santiago sits at his desk. "Once you're ready, we'll get you seeing your first patient."

I manage something like a smile. "Great."

I'm actually experiencing palpitations as I sit at my workstation and wiggle the mouse to wake the computer. A log-in window appears on the monitor, and I commence with the process of accessing the hospital's computer system for the first time. I update my computer username, reset my temporary password, reset my password again because my previous password wasn't strong enough, log into the computer with my new username and password, install a hospital-based app on my phone, enter a security code that's sent to the app, log into the hospital's software program itself, reset my username and password for the software program (and they can't be the same username and password I used for logging into the computer), enter another security code from the app, click the *enter* button . . . and then I'm in.

I'm surprised it didn't require a retinal scan.

The software program opens to show the emergency department's tracking board, which is set up like a spreadsheet. All the ED patients are listed in the left column, followed by columns containing the patients' chief complaints, lengths of stay, status of pending studies, and any free-text comments made by the care providers. My eyes get bigger and bigger as I keep scrolling through the names of the patients to reach the bottom of the list. The department is even busier than I thought.

"It appears you were able to get logged in all right," I hear Dr. Santiago remark.

I look up. Dr. Santiago has turned in his chair so he's facing my direction. With a grin, he adds:

"However, the real question is: how many passwords were you required to create in the process?"

I actually laugh. "It was definitely like breaking into Fort Knox."

"Well, now that you're in, you'll see they put a new patient in Hallway Nineteen. If you're feeling ready, you're welcome to go see her."

"Yes, I'm ready," I completely lie.

"Great. I'll let you get to it. When you're done, we'll talk about how you would like to care for the patient."

Without another word, Dr. Santiago returns his focus to his computer and begins typing a note in a patient's chart. I stare at the back of his head for a few seconds while yet another daunting realization strikes me: Dr.

Santiago isn't going to treat me like a med student this month. He's going to treat me like I'm already a resident. He's expecting me to function more independently than I ever have before. In other words, his expectations of me are as high as I feared.

So I can't let him down. I can't cause him to regret ranking me highly on the match list.

My hands are trembling as I sling my stethoscope around my neck, put a pen and a piece of paper into one of the large pockets of my white coat, and slip my phone into the back pocket of my scrubs. Turning to the computer, I use the mouse to click the patient's room number on the tracking board; my initials appear in the column next to the room number, indicating I'm taking care of the patient. Reading the info that's available on the tracking board, I learn my patient is a fifty-three-year-old woman named Wendy Eccles. Her chief complaint is listed only as, "*Other.*"

I stand up straight and take in a determined breath. This is it. I'm about to go see my first patient at Lakewood Medical Center. From here on out, my reputation is on the line.

I scan the department until I spot a sign—which is nothing more than a piece of paper with *Nineteen* written upon it—taped to one wall of a long hallway. Below the sign, there's a woman seated on a stretcher.

I glance Dr. Santiago's way a final time. He's on the phone, and it sounds as though he's talking to a neurologist about a patient who presented after several hours of stroke-like symptoms. I don't even think he notices that I'm watching him. This is for real. I'm on my own. I need to start acting like a resident.

My heart is pattering as I begin maneuvering across the department. Despite how intimidating this place is, it's a little reassuring to discover many of the strange sights and bizarre sounds—and even the smells— remind me of the emergency department at home. I guess some things in emergency medicine, including the odors, are universal.

Still making my way toward the hallway where the patient is located, I start passing in front of a curtained entrance into an exam room. Just then, there's an overhead announcement asking for a physician to come to Resuscitation Bay Two. Almost immediately, the curtain of the room I'm walking in front of is thrown back from the inside, and a guy steps out. I jump aside so we don't collide. The guy doesn't see me before he hurries off toward the resuscitation bay.

For a long moment, I stay right where I am. That was the guy in the dark green scrubs. The guy who looks like Hot Park Ranger. Exactly like Hot Park Ranger.

I slowly turn toward the resuscitation bay, attempting to get another look at him through the crowd, but all I see is a flash of his green scrubs before the guy vanishes into the commotion.

I shake my head. Okay, obviously that guy wasn't really Hot Park Ranger. What's also obvious is that I need a good night of sleep. The exhaustion of the past several days is clearly catching up with me, considering I've begun hallucinating that Hot Park Ranger is walking around Lakewood's emergency department.

I straighten my white coat and resume making my way to Hallway Nineteen. I fix my attention on the short woman who's seated on the stretcher. Her long, frizzy brown hair is hanging loosely around her shoulders. She's wearing a velour track suit, and she has a huge purse resting on her lap. I note that a manila envelope stuffed with papers is sticking out of the top of the purse.

"Good morning, Ms. Eccles." I reach the stretcher and show a businesslike smile. I'm doing my best to speak loudly enough that she can hear me above the commotion, yet quietly enough so she has some privacy despite the fact that we're conversing in a hallway crammed with patients. "My name is Quinn Meyers. I'm a fourth-year medical student, and I'll be assisting you while you're in the emergency department today. Would you please tell me what brings you in?"

She keeps an unblinking stare on me. "I need x-rays."

I glance over her again, but I don't see any part of her body that appears to be bleeding, bruised, deformed, or otherwise injured. I meet her undeviating gaze with an inquiring one.

"Please tell me a little more. What do you feel you need to have x-rayed?"

"My entire body," she replies in monotone.

My smile vanishes. "You want x-rays of your entire body."

"Yes."

"I see. Could you help me better understand why you think you need x-rays of your entire body?"

"Because I want to sue someone."

"Is there any particular reason you feel the need to sue someone?"

"No."

"Is there anyone in particular you're intending to sue?"

"Not yet."

I massage my forehead, which is starting to ache. "To make sure I'm totally clear, Ms. Eccles: you don't have any injury, and there's no specific incident you want to pursue litigation over. Yet you would like to have x-rays of your entire body so you can sue someone."

"That's correct."

I drop my arm to my side. I can already see my reputation swirling the drain.
So much for demonstrating to Dr. Santiago and the rest of the ED staff that I'm able to engage in complex medical decision making and take excellent care of critically ill patients.

With a silent, resigned sigh, I motion to the manila envelope that's poking out of the patient's purse. "I'm assuming you've brought in some forms you would like me to review?"

"Indeed."

Ms. Eccles tugs the bulging envelope from her purse, turns it upside down, and proceeds to shake out its contents. I can do nothing but watch as the papers spill all over the stretcher and onto the floor.

"These are the results of my prior radiology studies." Ms. Eccles motions to the mess. "After you review them, please put your detailed medical opinion about each one in my chart. Also, I need you to provide a copy of all these studies to the radiologist who will be reading the x-rays you'll order for me today, so he or she can have them for comparison purposes."

I glance up and down the hallway, certain I'm going to catch staff members laughing as they watch the visiting med student flounder. Thankfully, though, the ED is so hectic that no one seems to be noticing the little catastrophe that's unfolding here at Hallway Nineteen.

I bend at the waist and start picking up one piece of paper after the next. I discover they're dictated reports of MRIs, CT scans, x-rays, myelograms, nuclear med studies, and other types of imaging I've never even heard of. As best as I can tell, Ms. Eccles has literally been scanned from head-to-toe via multiple imaging modalities, and every report indicated nothing abnormal was found.

"These reports certainly seem to suggest you're in excellent health." I adopt another smile, trying to put a positive spin on things.

Ms. Eccles sighs despondently, and her shoulders slump. "I know. They never find anything wrong with me." Her expression evolves into a scowl. "*How am I supposed to sue someone if nobody can find anything wrong with me*?"

I stuff the papers into the envelope. "I'm no attorney, but I would assume that without abnormalities noted on imaging, and without any sort of inciting event, it would be hard for you to successfully pursue litigation."

With a huff, she crosses her arms. "That's precisely why I need you to order new x-rays today. I need you to find something wrong with me, otherwise I'm not going to be able to sue anyone."

I return the envelope to her purse. "Ms. Eccles, are you experiencing pain or any other symptoms?"

She rolls her eyes. "Of course not. *As I've been trying to explain*, there is apparently nothing wrong with me, and that's my problem."

I remove my stethoscope from around my neck. "Would you allow me to perform a basic exam, so I can make the most informed decision for you as possible?"

"Why on earth would I let you do that?" She's staring at me as though I'm insane. "How many times do I have to explain that *I'm totally fine* and that's why I *need new x-rays*?"

I give up.

"Ms. Eccles." I slide my stethoscope into the pocket of my white coat. "I won't order any radiology study—or any test, for that matter—if there's no medical indication to do so."

Her face gets red. "That's what all the doctors have been saying lately! Everyone is refusing to help me!"

Ms. Eccles slings her purse over her shoulder and springs off the stretcher. Though she's only about five-one, from the look in her eyes, I'm convinced she could cause *me* to need x-rays if she put her mind to it. I back up a step.

"You know what? You're the worst!" Ms. Eccles bellows, pointing right at me. "You. Are. The. Absolute. Worst."

The other patients in the hallway go silent and turn to stare at me. Out of the corner of my eye, I see a few nurses, a tech, and a couple secretaries also looking to see what the commotion is about.

This is a complete disaster.

It takes everything I have to act unfazed as I address my patient. "Before you go, Ms. Eccles, would you please wait to speak with my attending physician?"

"I'm not waiting for anybody!" Ms. Eccles turns to the other hallway patients, and like a leader rallying a coup, she points at me again while shouting, "Don't let this woman near you! She's the worst! She is the very worst in the entire world!"

Ms. Eccles finishes her tirade and storms down the hallway. She slams open one of the double doors that lead to the waiting room and charges out of the department. The door shuts behind her with a resounding clang.

I close and reopen my eyes. Ms. Eccles, one. My reputation here at Lakewood, zero.

"That looked like it went well," I hear someone behind me say in an amused tone.

I turn around. To my surprise, I see Elly Vincent—one of the residents I met on interview day—walking my way. She stops beside the stretcher and shows me a grin.

"Hi, Quinn. I heard you would be in the department this month. It's great to see you again."

"Thank you." I'm not sure whether to be thrilled Elly is taking the time to talk with me or humiliated she witnessed what happened with my patient. "It's great to see you again, too."

Elly's gaze flicks to the exit. Her smile widens. "Let me guess: Ms. Eccles was requesting more x-rays?"

I do a double take. "Wait a second. This wasn't her first visit?"

"Oh, no. She's a regular," Elly chuckles. "While not the most intellectually challenging case, I suppose she was a good way for you to start getting familiar with some of Lakewood's frequent fliers, and . . ."

Elly trails off when her eyes shift over my shoulder. Following her gaze, I see she has begun watching a guy who's coming our way. The guy has black hair and strikingly blue eyes, and he's dressed in scrubs. Peeking at his ID badge, I discover his name is Grant Reed, and he's also an ED resident. So he's yet another person I need to impress this month. As he draws closer, Grant glances at Elly for a long moment, and then he looks away and continues past us.

Elly refocuses on me. Her furrowed brow relaxes. "I need to go assess a patient, but it's great to see you again, Quinn. Please come find me if there's anything I can help you with."

"I will. Thanks."

Elly hurries away. My eyes shift to the vacant stretcher of Hallway Nineteen, and I sigh. Short of conjuring up a patient, there's nothing I can do but tell Dr. Santiago what happened. I have a sneaking suspicion he won't be too impressed when he hears my patient hated me so much she attempted to start a mutiny.

I dejectedly head toward the workstations. Dr. Santiago is again on the phone, and as I get closer, I overhear him speaking to someone about admitting a patient with acute renal insufficiency. Since he's tied up in the call, I take a seat at my desk, open the chart for Ms. Eccles, and begin typing a note about my encounter with her. However, considering I don't have much to write other than she demanded x-rays of her entire body and tried to lead a revolution before leaving the ED, I doubt I'll impress Dr. Santiago with my charting skills, either.

"So how did it go?" Dr. Santiago hangs up the phone and faces me.

I stop typing. "Well, my patient . . . left."

"She left?" Dr. Santiago arches an eyebrow. "What happened?"

Here goes nothing.

I slowly turn his way. "The patient wanted x-rays of her entire body so she could sue someone. She didn't have anyone in mind to sue, though." I pause, acutely aware of how ridiculous I sound. "The patient denied symptoms, and she refused an exam. When I wouldn't order the x-rays for her, she left."

Dr. Santiago doesn't reply at first . . . probably because he's busy contemplating how he's going to word his letter to the hospital administration when he advises having me removed from the incoming residency class. He then unexpectedly says:

"So Ms. Eccles was here again, huh? Gotta love the morning hallway patients around this place." He seems totally unruffled as he flicks his eyes around the department. "I'll go check on one of my admits, and then we'll see if we can get you another patient—preferably one who doesn't want her entire body unnecessarily radiated."

Dr. Santiago walks away. I watch him go, and I gradually relax. Though I didn't impress my attending, at least I didn't completely obliterate my reputation. I'll thankfully have another chance to prove I can fit in around here.

"Hey, Quinn?"

Checking to my right, I see Danielle coming toward me with her phone in her hand. She plunks herself down on a chair near my workstation.

"Are you working this Friday evening?" she asks, scooting her chair closer.

I shake my head. "Nope. I have this first weekend off."

"Perfect." Danielle types a text on her phone with lightning-fast speed. "If you're available, Savannah and I would love to have you over to our place for dinner."

"Really?" I smile. "I would love that."

Danielle smiles in return. "I can't wait for you to meet Sav. The two of you will get along great." She gestures to her phone. "Would you mind giving me your number? I'll text you our address and other details, once Sav and I sort them out."

I tell Danielle my number, and she rapidly enters it into her phone. A moment later, I hear a ping from my own phone, confirming I received a text from Danielle so I have her number, too.

Danielle stops texting and peers at me. "Do you have any food allergies, or are there any types of foods you don't like?"

I snort a laugh. "I think you'll find I'm a connoisseur of just about everything. No allergies, either."

"Good. Because I was thinking about making something really comfort food-ish, like lasagna for dinner and chocolate cake for dessert." Danielle stops and glances around, suddenly appearing sheepish . . . almost guilty. Lowering her voice, she leans toward me and goes on. "That is, if you're down with splurging occasionally. If not, that's totally okay. We'll eat something healthier."

I laugh again. "I wish I could say I was regimented one hundred percent of the time, but I'm definitely not opposed to an occasional splurge."

"I knew I liked you." Danielle giggles and gets to her feet. "Oh, I was also toying around with the idea of inviting a few more people, but I wanted to see what you thought about that." She leans her hip against the desk. "I would include my boyfriend, Joel, who's over all the time and practically a third roommate, anyway, and Savannah's boyfriend, if he's available. And my brother, too." She fixes a worried look on me. "Or is that too many?"

"No, it's not too many at all. Feel free to invite as many people as you would like," I reply. "I'll look forward to getting to know everyone."

"Great. You can invite your significant other, too, if you have one." Danielle stops, and her cheeks turn crimson. "Hang on. That's not what I meant. What I meant is that you're welcome to invite your significant other if you want to . . . but you don't have to . . . because you don't need a significant other at all, of course . . . that is, I just didn't want to inadvertently leave someone out if . . ." she trails off and throws up her hands. "I think I'm making this awkward."

I manage a laugh. "No worries. I'm not dating anyone, so there's no one for me to bring, anyway. My ex-boyfriend and I . . . well, we very recently broke up. It's complicated, but the short version of the story is that I came out here alone."

"You just broke up with your boyfriend?" Danielle claps a hand over her mouth for a moment. "That's terrible! I'm so sorry. In that case, we can make Friday a girls' night instead. We'll watch a bunch of cheesy movies and eat chocolate."

I snicker. "Normally, I wouldn't turn down a night of cheesy movies and chocolate, but please invite anyone you want. Honestly, I'm looking forward to meeting people."

Danielle doesn't seem convinced. "Are you sure?"

"I'm sure."

"All right. I'll . . ." Danielle's attention shifts past me. A grin appears on her lips. "Hmm. I should probably let you go. I think your next patient has arrived."

Before I can ask what she means, the sound of a man screaming all sorts of interesting profanities hits my ears. Tracing Danielle's line of sight, I spin around in my chair to see who she's looking at.

"Ah, yes," I remark in a sage-like way. "That patient definitely looks like someone who will be assigned to a visiting med student."

Danielle and I continue observing the patient—a middle-aged man—who's being wheeled in on a stretcher by an EMS crew. The man is dressed in a superhero outfit, complete with spandex, mask, and cape. Based on what I can discern from his extremely colorful language, he's upset that he wasn't allowed to jump off the top of Prescott Tower to prove he can fly. As the EMS crew drives him past where Danielle and I are seated, the potent aromas of alcohol and marijuana hit my nostrils, so I'm guessing some recreational morning substance use has led to our superhero's current state.

I stand up, watching the man as he starts flapping his arms to demonstrate his "magical flying abilities." Soon, I hear someone behind me say:

"Uh, Quinn?"

I look over my shoulder. Dr. Santiago is approaching, and he's clearly trying not to smile.

"As much as I would like for you to have a chance to tackle a more medically complex patient," Dr. Santiago continues, scratching his head, "it appears the next patient in the queue will be . . ." He lets his eyes drift to the man on the stretcher, who has begun singing the theme from "The Greatest American Hero."

"No problem. I'm on it." I tell Dr. Santiago with a smile. I turn to Danielle. "Thanks again for the invite. I'll look forward to Friday." I tip my head in the direction of the intoxicated patient. "In the meantime, I should probably go introduce myself to Mr. Remarkable."

Danielle salutes. "See you soon."

As I start heading toward the new patient, I glance back to give Danielle a final wave, but I stop short. Through the open door of the resuscitation bay, I catch another glimpse of the guy in dark green scrubs. A moment later, he's gone.

Five

I'm standing beside my bed, analyzing the outfits I've got laid out on top of the pile of sweatshirts I'm still using as a mattress cover. I'm trying to decide what to wear to Danielle and Savannah's apartment tonight, and my options are pretty limited. When I packed to move out here for the month, I included mostly hospital attire and loungewear, figuring that between spending the bulk of my time in the ED and not knowing anyone in the area, I wouldn't do much in the way of socializing.

Not to mention, your boyfriend dumped you, a voice in my head adds.

Stung by the truth, I push aside thoughts of Chad and resume concentrating on my outfit choices. Ultimately, I select my pink cable-knit sweater paired with dark jeans and ankle boots. Hopefully, the ensemble will strike the right balance. I don't want to look too underdressed or too overdressed, especially since I'm not entirely sure what tonight will entail or even who will be there. So I think sticking to something middle-of-the-road is probably the safest thing to do.

I change and head into the bathroom to finish getting ready. The mirror is so badly warped that it looks like it belongs in a carnival funhouse, but at least I'm able to discern my curls are being reasonably cooperative tonight. I'll take that as a win; I never quite know how my hair is going to behave from one day to the next.

I jump when deafeningly loud music begins radiating down from the apartment above mine. I raise my gaze to the ceiling with a sigh. In the few days I've been here, it has become abundantly clear that whoever lives upstairs is a huge fan of eighties bands. At the moment, a Def Leppard song is shaking the mirror. Last evening, Motley Crue nearly caused my dinner plate to rattle off the table.

I apply my makeup, which is no small feat when using a contorted mirror that's shaking in time to a song's bass line, and then I return to the bedroom. As I start searching through the closet to find the one purse I remembered to pack, above the music from upstairs, I hear my phone start ringing. I freeze when I recognize the ringtone.

Chad is calling.

A flood of emotions crashes down on me, and a million thoughts fly through my mind in an instant. Do I want to talk to Chad? I'm not sure. I'm still immensely hurt about what happened the night before I moved out here. On that evening, Chad took me out to eat. At some point during the entrée course, he blindsided me by saying he wasn't "feeling right about the long-distance thing," and that he had decided "breaking up was best for both of us."

Getting dumped unexpectedly was brutal, and what made it even worse was that Chad didn't seem particularly upset about our relationship ending . . . again. I, however, was devastated. I felt so betrayed. I had only agreed to rekindle our relationship months before because, at that time, Chad vowed he was truly ready to commit. Cleary, he wasn't.

Chad's ringtone keeps playing. With a lump forming in my throat, I stare at the rickety nightstand that has my phone sitting upon it. The part of me that wants to ignore Chad's call is the same part of me that wants to get off the emotional roller coaster I've been riding for years because of him. It's the part of me that, when I'm being totally honest with myself, thinks it would be best if I never interacted with him again.

Yet the other part of me can't deny how much I care about Chad. How could I not care about him? We've been through so much together. We know each other better than we know anyone else. For good and for bad, our lives are intertwined, and it's not like I can simply turn off those feelings, forget all those memories, and pretend I don't care.

Nonetheless, the on-again-off-again nature of our relationship has been exhausting, and it's certainly not the type of relationship I ever wanted to be in. When Chad and I met during the first quarter of med school, we hit it off immediately, and it wasn't long before we were dating exclusively. I thought things were going great, but near the end of our first year, Chad shocked me by breaking up with me. He explained it had been a hard choice, but he felt the rigors of med school were making it too difficult to give an exclusive relationship the dedication it deserved.

I was crushed, yet I couldn't entirely disagree with Chad's reasoning. The demands of med school *did* make it hard to find the time to nurture a relationship, and Chad and I both knew our second year was going to be even more grueling. So as first year came to a close, we officially broke up.

Chad and I remained friends, however, and through study groups, class parties, and mutual acquaintances, we continued spending time together. Midway through second year, Chad confessed he continued to have feelings for me, and I told him I did, too. So we decided to give our relationship another try.

Our renewed relationship felt stronger and more grounded than ever. Chad and I remained together as second year concluded and our third year of med school began, heralding the conclusion of classroom studies and the start of clinical rotations. The work was hard, and our schedules were tough, but I found Chad's companionship to be a great support, and I hoped I provided the same type of support to him.

In December of our third year, however, while Chad and I were Christmas shopping, he dropped the breakup bomb on me for the second time. Like before, Chad attributed his decision to external circumstances, saying he felt it wasn't possible to maintain an exclusive relationship while managing the brutal hours and stresses of clinical rotations.

I was caught so off-guard that I just stood in the middle of the mall's food court, staring at Chad while pathetically holding a peppermint hot chocolate in one hand and a bag of presents in the other. Eventually, after I finished processing the fact that Chad had broken up with me, I realized I was single again. Just in time for the holidays. I left the mall alone, too distraught to realize I was carrying a bag of presents for Chad that I would need to return. Once my emotions died down, I vowed I would never get back together with Chad, no matter how much I cared about him. Chad's fear of commitment and propensity to run away whenever times got hard were more than I could take. I deserved better.

Of course, my vow was one thing, and making my feelings for Chad go away was entirely another. Though I still cared about him, however, I remained determined to get Chad out of my heart and mind. I took up new hobbies in what little spare time I had. I dated other guys. I even kept a Christmas decoration in my apartment to remind myself of that day when Chad dumped me at the mall. Yet I still wondered if things might have played out differently had the demands of med school not interfered. And I wondered if the heartache I felt would ever truly go away.

This past summer, during the short gap between third and fourth year—about the time I began researching residency programs—Chad unexpectedly showed up on my doorstep. In an almost desperate way, he professed he didn't want to be without me any longer. He promised he was ready to commit. He insisted that no matter what fourth year would bring, he wanted nothing more than to be with me. He begged me to give him another chance.

And I did. I let Chad back into my life. I trusted he was ready to commit. I also knew I couldn't completely fault him for what had happened in the past. Med school was volatile, stressful, and exhausting, so it wasn't entirely surprising Chad and I had hit some rough patches along the way. I also recognized Chad and I had matured since med school began. We had a clearer sense of who we were and what we wanted in life. For all those reasons, I was convinced our relationship would finally succeed.

It wasn't long, however, before Chad and I hit the first hiccup in our new-and-supposedly-improved relationship, and it was a doozy: Chad didn't want to enroll in the residency couples match—the version of the match process where two people designate themselves as a couple and apply for residency together. In a couples match, you're committing as a team, so the hospital either accepts both applicants or neither of them. In our case, I would have applied to emergency medicine residency programs, and

Chad would have applied to radiology residency programs at the same hospitals.

When Chad told me he didn't want to do the couples match, it felt like he pulled the rug out from under me again. I had simply assumed a couples match would be part of the plan for us. Chad, however, insisted we would make our relationship work even if we matched at separate places and lived far apart during residency. He deemed it more important for both of us to apply to residency programs where we would get the best training, rather than limiting ourselves only to hospitals where we might both match so we could go as a couple.

Part of me was immensely injured by Chad's decision. Once again, though, I also couldn't entirely disagree with his logic. I knew Lakewood was probably going to be my number-one choice for residency training, and I knew Chad's top choice for residency was elsewhere. So did it make sense for one of us to give up our dream program to accommodate the other? If so, whose preference would get priority? Or would we both walk away from the programs where we most wanted to train and instead go together to a place neither one of us was excited about? It seemed there was no clear answer.

What was clear was that everything else about our relationship seemed to be going well. So although Chad didn't want to match as a couple, I wasn't worried.

And then he pitched strike three.

The night before I drove out here for the month, Chad took me out to dinner. And he broke up with me. Again. He acknowledged his decision probably caught me by surprise (major understatement), but he went on to say he was certain it was the right thing to do. He felt a long-distance relationship wasn't "fair" to either of us.

Since that night, I've spent an immense amount of time searching my heart. One would think that after hours of driving across the country, with nothing to see but flatlands and antelope, and nothing to listen to but radio static, I would have come to a clear conclusion about how I felt. But I didn't, and I still haven't. The situation is immensely complex and confusing, and it seems the more I try to sort it out, the more unsure I become.

I realize Chad's ringtone is nearly finished. At the last possible moment, I lunge for the nightstand, grab my phone, and answer the call.

"Hello?" I say, putting the phone to my ear.

"Hey. I'm calling to see if you got settled into your new place all right."

The sound of his voice causes more emotions to tangle within me. Taking a moment to collect myself, I wander out of the bedroom, go into the kitchen, and take a seat on the least wobbly chair at the table.

"Yes, I got settled in all right." I glance down at the linoleum floor and its numerous stains of unclear etiology, and I wrinkle my nose. "Granted, the apartment isn't as nice as I expected, but it'll tide me over for three-and-a-half more weeks."

I emphasize the last point, hoping to remind him that it will only be a few weeks before I return home for the final months of med school. Perhaps if Chad thinks about the fact that we'll be seeing each other again soon, he will realize a long-distance relationship isn't necessarily an insurmountable obstacle. Frankly, if there's going to be any chance Chad and I will reconcile, he's going to have to get used to a long-distance aspect to the relationship, at least for the upcoming years of residency.

"Glad to hear the accommodations aren't too bad," Chad says evenly. "How has your rotation been treating you so far?"

I settle back in the chair, my emotions calming as the conversation starts feeling like the hundreds we've had before.

"I've only had one shift so far, but I learned a lot." I gaze out the window at the abandoned, boarded-up building on the other side of the street. "Admittedly, though, I really felt the pressure of working in such a busy, high-acuity place. On top of that, word has already started spreading that I'm one of the new EM residents starting this summer, so it's like I'm wearing a huge target." I sigh. "I'm worried people are going to start wishing someone else had matched instead."

"Quinn, you're over-thinking it. You were good enough to match at Lakewood, so don't worry. You'll be fine."

I open my mouth but close it again, unsure of how to reply. I let a second or two pass before I change the subject:

"How's your rotation going this month?"

"Well, I certainly don't plan on doing a fellowship in neuroradiology, but the rotation has been fairly interesting."

"That's great," I tell him because it's the only thing I can think of to say.

More silence settles over us. After a second or two, I intuitively sense a shift in the vibe of the conversation, and it makes my pulse tick up a few notches. Sure enough, Chad clears his throat and says in a softer tone:

"Quinn, even though you've only been gone a little over a week, I've missed you. A lot. It's lonely without you."

I draw in a ragged breath. Why does Chad do this? Why does he always pull me onto his emotional roller coaster? Why didn't he think about the loneliness factor before he broke up with me? Or before he decided we shouldn't do the couples match for residency? In the residency situation, at least, though we might not have been at our number-one choices of training programs, we would have been together.

The quiet drags on as I hesitate to reply. Finally, though, I tell myself I've known Chad far too long to play games with him or hide what I'm feeling.

"I miss you, too," I tell him honestly.

Another pause.

"Quinn." Chad's voice gets even lower. "Having you so far away has caused me to do a lot of introspection. I suppose breaking up for circumstantial reasons felt easy when we were still living close to one another." He clears his throat. "Having you far away, though, has made breaking up a lot more difficult."

I get to my feet and restlessly start pacing the kitchen. My heart is clattering. My mind feels like a shaken-up snow globe that's filled with a flurry of confused, jumbled thoughts.

"Quinn, I guess what I'm trying to say is—"

My surprised shriek drowns out the rest of Chad's words as frigidly cold water starts pouring down on top of me. With another startled, confused cry, I stagger backward out of the kitchen, wipe the water from my face, and whip up my head. And I gasp.

Water is dumping down from a gap between two of the kitchen's ceiling panels and splashing onto the floor. I think a pipe has burst.

I hear people starting to shout and run around in the apartment above mine. I also hear them turn up their music.

Wide-eyed, I recover from my shock enough to put the phone to my ear and yell over the din, "I'm sorry, Chad! I have to go!"

"Is everything okay?"

"My apartment is flooding! I have to call the landlord! I'm so sorry to end our conversation, but I'll be in touch soon!"

I hang up, run into the bedroom, toss the phone onto the bed, and frantically start hunting for the scrap of paper Mr. Utteley gave me with his number on it. Yet even amidst the chaos, my conversation with Chad is replaying in my mind. Chad wants to get back together, I'm sure of it.

What am I going to do?

Six

A Van Halen tune has begun accompanying the sound of water pouring down from the kitchen ceiling while I scour the bedroom. At last, I find the paper with Mr. Utteley's number on it. I grab my phone from off the sweatshirt-covered bed and call the number.

The phone rings . . . and rings.

Cradling the phone against my ear, I race out of the bedroom and head for the kitchen. When I reach the edge of the linoleum, I halt in dismay. Water has already spread across the kitchen floor, and the amount of water falling down from the ceiling is increasing by the second.

There's a loud beep in my ear, followed by an automated message that informs me my landlord's voicemail box is full and cannot receive any more messages.

With a groan, I shove my phone into the back pocket of my jeans and run through the waterfall to enter the kitchen. I'm hit by the spray as I scoop up the groceries I have out on the counter, saving them from the deluge. Arms full, I sprint from the kitchen into the main room and dump the groceries onto the dingy couch. After shaking the water from my drenched-and-now-excessively-curly hair, I tug my phone from my pocket and text my landlord. As soon as I hit the *send* button, my phone pings with an alert message. The text I tried to send my landlord didn't go through because his number has been disconnected.

Of course it has.

Jamming the phone into my pocket once more, I spin around to face the kitchen. For a second or two, I stare helplessly at the water tumbling out of the broken ceiling pipe. Then an idea strikes me:

Plumber. I need a plumber.

I reach for my phone yet again, about to instigate an Internet search for an after-hours plumber, but I pause when I notice the time. It's seven pm. I'm supposed to be at Danielle and Savannah's place, partaking of the undoubtedly delicious dinner they prepared. Instead, the dinner is probably getting cold while they're wondering where I am.

I wipe my phone against my pant leg to dry off the water droplets, and I call Danielle.

"Hi, Quinn!" she answers cheerily.

I have to press my free hand against my other ear to block out the music from upstairs. "Danielle, I'm so sorry, but I'm not going to be able to make it tonight. My apartment is . . . well, it's flooding at the moment." I cast a nervous glance at the water, which has begun creeping across the floor toward the main room.

"Unfortunately, I can't get through to my landlord. You don't happen to know an after-hours plumber in the area, do you?"

Long pause.

"Your apartment is flooding?" Danielle's voice rises about two octaves. "Are you serious?"

"Yeah." I wince when I hear a clank in the ceiling and water starts dumping down harder. "So I was wondering if either you or Sav happen to—"

"Text me your address! We're coming to rescue you!"

The folks upstairs raise the volume of their music. Keeping the phone smashed against one ear and my free hand pressed against the other, I practically have to shout for Danielle to hear me:

"Thanks, but I don't want to make you come all the way out here. If I can get in touch with a plumber, I think—"

"Text me your address!" Danielle repeats, and she sounds as though she's running. "We're already getting in the car!"

Danielle ends the call. Dropping my arms to my sides, I look over at the kitchen again. My eyes get wide.

There's a lake in the apartment. A lake.

Retreating farther into the main room, I text Danielle my apartment info. I next make another desperate attempt to call the landlord. This time, to my relief, at least I hear an automated recording that tells me I can leave a message.

"Mr. Utteley, this is Quinn Meyers," I say as soon as I hear the beep. "Another pipe has burst in the ceiling, and water is spilling all over the place." I bend at the waist and snatch up my jacket from the floor, saving it from the advancing flood. "I'll try to rescue whatever I can and contact a plumber, but some help would be appreciated. Please call me as soon as you get this."

While water keeps spraying from the ceiling and Lake Kitchen continues to expand, I put away my phone and commence a frenzied race around the main room and foyer, gathering my belongings and transferring them to the relative safety of the couch. When I'm done, I yank off my ankle boots and socks, and I return to the kitchen to rescue the items my landlord uses to outfit the place. I carry out a broken spice rack, a cracked cutting board, the ancient coffee maker, an even more ancient microwave, and a set of extremely dull knives. I even take down from the wall the faded and cheaply framed watercolor print so it won't sustain further damage . . . though, to be honest, I don't think anyone would notice the difference.

I check my phone. There's no word from Mr. Utteley. So I spend the next several minutes searching online for an after-hours plumber, but about half the listed phone numbers are no longer in service, and the other half ring without anyone answering. Abandoning my efforts, I put aside my phone and push up my sleeves, and I'm about to start moving the kitchen table and chairs out from underneath the waterfall, when there's a brisk knock on the front door. I almost let out a cheer. The landlord is here, and hopefully he's either a skilled handyman or he brought one with him.

I slosh out of the kitchen, being careful not to slip as I go, and I charge to the foyer. After wiping the water from my eyes, I unlock the deadbolt and open the door.

"We're here!" Danielle bursts into the apartment, her red hair bouncing on the shoulders of her pea coat. She reaches out to give me a hug, but she stops with her arms partly outstretched, her eyes getting big as she takes in the sight of me. "Oh my gosh. You're drenched."

"Tell me about it." I actually laugh as I push my soaked hair from my face. "I'm sorry I didn't let you know I finally managed to leave a message for my landlord." I grab the hem of my sweater and squeeze water out of it. "It would have spared you the drive out here."

"Landlord, shmandlord. We wanted to come." Danielle's eyes scan the entryway, and she shudders. "Ugh. This place is even worse than I expected. That's why we're moving you out of here. Immediately."

My mouth drops open. "What?"

Danielle pulls out her phone from the pocket of her coat. "As soon as I saw your address and realized where you were living, I knew we had to save you. So gather your things. You're not staying here another minute. You're moving in with Savannah and me."

"I'm . . . what?" I keep gaping at her.

Danielle doesn't answer. Instead, she calls out the open door into the hallway:

"Sav! We're in here!"

I hear approaching footsteps, and then a gal who looks to be around my age appears in the doorway. She's dressed in a sapphire-colored puffy jacket and dark jeans. Her brown hair is pulled into a braided ponytail, and as she shifts her blue eyes between Danielle and me, a smile appears on her face.

"Sorry it took me so long to get up here. We couldn't find a decent place to park, so the guys finally dropped me off at the front door while they continued the search. I then discovered the elevator wasn't working, so I had to locate the stairwell." She laughs and faces me. "You must be Quinn. I'm Savannah Drake. I've really been looking forward to meeting you . . . though I'm sorry it's under these, um, slightly weird circumstances."

I grin. "It's great to meet you, too."

Still smiling, Savannah steps farther inside. "Danielle told me the exciting news that you're rotating in Lakewood's ED this month. Even better, I heard you're part of the incoming emergency medicine . . ." she trails off. Her smile disappears. "What's that noise?"

"Uh, I think it's Van Halen." Danielle's eyes drift up to the ceiling. She tips her head slightly to one side. "And maybe the people up there are jumping rope?"

"No, not that noise." Savannah pointedly looks down the entryway. "*That* noise."

The three of us fall silent. I gulp when the all-too-familiar sound of running water reaches my ears. The pipe. The broken pipe. For a few moments, I had forgotten all about the water that's flowing out of the kitchen ceiling.

With a gasp of alarm, I spin around and race for the kitchen. I hear Danielle and Savannah following on my heels. When I reach the end of the foyer, I stop fast, nearly causing the others to crash into me from behind.

"Holy smokes," Savannah utters, taking in the scene.

Danielle partially stifles a giggle. "Sorry. I know I shouldn't laugh, but this is . . . wild."

The three of us continue staring. Water is plummeting down faster from the ceiling, the kitchen is officially flooded, and the lights are flickering as if they're about to short out.

Danielle's phone chimes. Pulling her eyes from the mess, she checks a new text. "Good news: the guys finally found a place to park, and they're on their way up to help."

"Great," Savannah says. She then motions to the couch on the far side of the main room that's piled high with everything I rescued from the flood, and she fixes an inquiring look on me. "Are those your things?"

I can't help cracking another grin. "Well, the books, food, jacket, and exercise bands are mine. But as much as I would love to claim ownership of the, um, beautiful painting and the ancient kitchen appliances, I can't say any of the rest belongs to me."

Savannah snorts. "Good to know. I was definitely wondering about the microwave. It certainly looks . . . old."

"No kidding. I'm guessing it emits more radiation than a CT scanner." I begin snickering along with Savannah. "The one time I used it, in fact, I was so nervous that I waited in the bedroom until my food finished heating up."

"I don't blame you." Savannah breaks into more laughter as she begins tucking her jeans into the rubber boots she's wearing. Standing up straight again, she says to Danielle and me, "Okay, Operation Lifeboat can commence. I'll take what's on the couch down to the lobby while the two of you gather what's in the bedroom and bathroom."

"You got it." Danielle salutes. "The guys will soon be up here to help, so between the five of us, it shouldn't take long to haul Quinn's things downstairs."

Savannah shows a thumbs-up and begins wading toward the couch.

"All right, Quinn, let's get you out of this dump." Danielle tucks the hems of her pant legs into her rain boots. "Lead the way."

I crouch down and roll up my jeans to my calves, though it's kind of pointless, since my pants are already soaked to the knees. "Are you really sure about this? I mean, are you sure about letting me move in with you?"

Danielle glances across the room at Savannah, and they share one of those best-friends-who-can-read-each-other's-minds moments of silent communication. Savannah then resumes gathering my things while Danielle looks my way once more.

"We're definitely sure," Danielle tells me. "There's no way we're letting you stay here another night." She peers around the room again with a grimace before she goes on. "We have an extra bedroom we use as an office—not that we actually study in there, but you get the idea— and it has a comfy futon, a closet, and a bathroom right across the hall. It'll be perfect for you to use." She tucks her hair behind her ears. "And even if we didn't have the extra bedroom, we would never let you remain here. Heck, we would get bunk beds if we needed to."

I sigh with relief. "I can't tell you how much I appreciate this."

"It's our pleasure." Danielle points toward the bedroom. "Now let's get you out of this hole before the place falls apart completely."

While Savannah heads out the front door carrying a bunch of my belongings, Danielle and I splash our way across the main room. I step ahead of Danielle and enter the bedroom first. She watches as I tug open the mirrored closet door, which requires a certain finesse to make it move because it has partly fallen off its broken track.

"I've got two suitcases, and they should hold almost everything else of mine," I explain while pulling the first suitcase from the closet.

Danielle's mouth drops open. "Whoa. That's the biggest suitcase I've ever seen in my life."

I grunt as I heave the suitcase up onto the bed. It's absurdly heavy even when it's empty. "Wait until you see the other one," I pant. "Believe it or not, it's bigger than this one."

Reaching into the closet again, I roll out the second bag. Danielle helps me hoist it onto the bed next to the first. She then points to the luggage and shoots me a sideways glance.

"Permission to jam everything I can inside those things?"

I laugh. "Permission granted."

"Perfect. I'll pack up the bathroom while you tackle what's in here." Danielle heads into the adjoining bathroom. She lets out a strange choking noise. "It looks like this bathroom has been abandoned since the seventies! I can't believe you were going to have to live in this place for another—"

"Hon?" A guy's call from the entryway is barely audible above the combined noise of the pounding music and the waterfall in the kitchen. "Are you in here?"

Danielle returns to the bedroom, smiling with obvious delight. "Hi, Joel!" she yells. "Yes, Quinn and I are in the sad excuse for a bedroom!"

I hear the sloshing noise of someone approaching, and a moment later, a guy pokes his head into the bedroom. The guy is dressed in a t-shirt and jeans. He's fairly tall, and he's lean in a fit, athletic way. He has sandy blond hair and round glasses.

"Geez, you weren't kidding when you told Danielle this place was flooded," the guy says to me in an amused tone, grinning like we've been friends for a long time.

I snicker. "Nope, I wasn't kidding."

"You see? I knew you should've brought your rain boots," Danielle tells him. She motions between the guy and me. "Quinn, I would like you to meet my boyfriend, Joel Lambert. Joel, this is Quinn Meyers. She's gonna live with Savannah and me for the rest of the month, and she'll be returning in July because she's part of the incoming emergency medicine residency class at Lakewood. Isn't that cool?"

Joel nods. "Welcome aboard, Quinn. It's great to meet you." He leans toward me, and now there's a humorous gleam in his eye. "And I wish you luck living with Danielle and Sav. They're pretty ruthless."

I adopt a feigned expression of concern. "That was my first impression."

Danielle rolls her eyes. "You're practically a roommate, too, Joel, and you don't seem to mind us too much."

Joel chuckles and kisses Danielle on the cheek. "No, I most certainly do not."

As I watch them, I can't help smiling. Joel and Danielle are clearly one of those super lovey-dovey couples, but their interactions are genuine and sweet, and not at all annoying. They seem completely . . .

My smile falters. I'm not sure what Joel does for work, but he and Danielle have obviously figured out how to make their relationship thrive despite the stresses and challenges of her medical training.

Why haven't Chad and I been able to make things work?

There's another loud clank in the kitchen ceiling. In response, Danielle looks past Joel and peers out of the bedroom at the flood. Her eyes get huge.

"Hey, I'd love for us to continue getting acquainted, but considering this place is going down like the *Titanic*, we should probably save chit-chat for later," Danielle states, actually sounding a little nervous.

Joel starts moving for the door. "While you ladies get those suitcases packed, I'll help Savannah haul out what's left in the main room."

"Thanks, Joel," I call after him.

"No problem." Joel darts off.

As Danielle watches him depart, she lets out a whimsical-sounding sigh. "I adore that man."

"I can tell." I'm grinning again as I start tugging my clothes off the misshapen hangers in the puny closet. I toss each article onto the bed. "How long have you two been together?"

"We met and began dating when we were seniors in college. It was love at first sight." Danielle still has a dreamy look in her eyes as she returns to the bathroom. "He's the most incredible man in the world. I feel so lucky to be with him."

Something pricks at my heart. I duck my head deeper into the closet and continue pulling clothes off the hangers. "That's awesome, Danielle."

Danielle reemerges from the bathroom, somehow managing to carry my shampoo and conditioner bottles, loofa, shaving razors, makeup, hairbrush, towels, deodorant, toothbrush, toothpaste, dental floss, and hygiene products. She dumps everything into one of the suitcases and turns to me. Her expression grows serious.

"Speaking of relationships, what about you? The other day, you mentioned something about a recent breakup? Are you doing okay?"

I slowly back out of the closet. "Yeah, I'm okay, all things considered."

Danielle starts stuffing my clothes into the suitcases. "May I ask what happened?"

I take a second to figure out where to begin. "Well, Chad broke up with me—for the third time in the three-plus years we've been together—the night before I moved out here."

Danielle does a double take. "*He broke up with you the night before you moved out here?*"

"Yep." I make myself busy packing. "I was completely blindsided."

Danielle clamps a hand over her mouth. "I'm so sorry."

"Thanks." I jam another shirt into the suitcase with extra gusto. "To make matters more confusing, Chad actually called me tonight. We weren't able to finish our conversation before the pipe broke, but I'm certain he was calling because he wants to reconcile." I stop what I'm doing and look over at Danielle. "As you can imagine, I'm not sure how I feel about it."

Before Danielle can reply, there's a knock on the front door.

Danielle scrunches her face with a look of confusion. "Why would Sav or Joel knock? They know they can come inside."

"Maybe it's the landlord." I hurry to leave the room. "Or it's possible Sav and Joel got locked out. The front door sometimes swings shut and gets stuck, and you have to hit it a certain way to get it to reopen."

Danielle shakes her head and resumes packing. "I'm so glad we're getting you out of this joint."

I leave the bedroom and cross the main room, wading through water that's at least a couple inches deep. I pass the kitchen, getting freshly drenched by the spray coming from ceiling pipe, and then I finally make it to the foyer.

There's another knock on the door.

"I'm coming!" I call out, hoping I can be heard above the music playing upstairs.

I get to the front door and go through the necessary steps to make it unstick: a kick to the door's base, a jiggle of the doorknob, a slap to the center panel with the palm of my hand, and then another rattle of the doorknob. At last, with water rolling down my face, I'm able to yank open the door.

"Sorry about that," I say. "It jams sometimes, and . . ."

The rest of my words get stuck in my throat.

Hot Park Ranger is standing outside my door.

Seven

Hot Park Ranger does a double take when his green eyes land on mine. For a few seconds, we stare at each other in the silent, stunned communication of recognition.

And I can't help admiring the view.

Ranger Gillespie is dressed casually in a navy blue, long-sleeved shirt and jeans, which happen to perfectly emphasize his tall, muscular build. This is the first time I've seen him without a hat, so I have a full view of his hair, which is thick, brown, and slightly tousled. Unlike when he was cleanly shaven in the park, he's currently sporting some facial scruff, which gives him a rather ruggedly handsome appearance. He also—

I snap out of my daze. Hang on. How . . . why . . . is Ranger Gillespie standing in my doorway?

Did I forget to pay a Yellowstone Park fine or something?

"Dylan? Is that you?" Danielle unexpectedly shouts from the bedroom.

I tear my bewildered gaze from Hot Park Ranger, retreat from the doorway, and turn to look across the apartment at the bedroom.

Through the open door, I see Danielle standing beside the bed, craning her neck in an attempt to view the entryway.

"Is that Dylan?" she asks me.

"I'm, um, not sure," I awkwardly call back to her. I peer again at Hot Park Ranger. "Is it?"

Hot Park Ranger watches me a moment longer, and then he shifts his gaze toward the bedroom and says loudly enough for Danielle to hear him over the music of Skid Row:

"Yes, it's me. Sorry it took so long to find a place to park."

My eyes have begun leaping between Danielle and Hot Park Ranger like I'm watching a table tennis match. Hot Park Ranger—Ranger Gillespie—is also referred to as Dylan. And somehow he knows Danielle.

What is going on?

"Glad you're finally here! We need your help!" Danielle shouts to him. "We're rescuing Quinn from this disgusting place and moving her in with us! We need your humungous muscles to help carry her suitcases, so get in here!"

My cheeks ignite. No. Not the suitcases. Hot Park Ranger does *not* need to be reminded about the suitcases.

I shoot Danielle a slightly horrified, wide-eyed look before turning back to Hot Park Ranger . . . I mean, Ranger Gillespie . . . I mean, Dylan. He meets my gaze, and I swear he's trying not to grin. My cheeks get even hotter.

"May I come in?" he inquires in his deep voice.

"Wh-what?" I sputter. "I mean, yes. I mean, of course. Thank you."

I open the door the rest of the way. Hot Park Ranger enters the apartment, his commanding presence seeming to fill the entire space. I get a subtle whiff of his woodsy-smelling cologne. There's a flutter inside my chest.

"Dyl, everything's almost packed and ready to go!" Danielle yells.

I face the bedroom once more, and I see Danielle tossing the last few articles of my clothing inside one of the suitcases. I can also see she has both bags so haphazardly packed that they're never going to shut. Yet Danielle seems totally undeterred. She lifts one side of the first suitcase and drops it over the other side, and then she proceeds to hurl herself on top of the bag to smash it down. Gritting her teeth, she starts pulling on the zipper. I cringe as I watch. Either Danielle is going to tear off the zipper completely, or that suitcase is going to explode open and jettison her across the room.

"I should, um, probably go help her with that," I mumble to Hot Park Ranger without quite looking at him.

Leaving Ranger Gillespie behind, I charge away from the foyer and begin sloshing through the water that covers the main room. Heat is coursing through me, and my breathing remains stilted. Hot Park Ranger is inside this apartment. Why is Hot Park Ranger inside this apartment?

Danielle looks up when I enter the bedroom. She's breathing hard from exertion as she continues doing battle with the zipper. "I've . . . almost got this one . . . shut. You do . . . the other one."

My eyes shift to the second suitcase—the one that's even larger than the bag Danielle is grappling with. It's completely buried under the gigantic pile of everything Danielle threw at it; there's no way it will close. I step up to the bed, ready to repack the suitcase in a more organized manner, when I note my bras, panties, pajamas, and hygiene products happen to be at the top of the massive pile for everyone—including Hot Park Ranger—to see.

Why? Why this again? Why?

Abruptly deciding to forgo the repacking, I instead choose to adopt Danielle's less-conventional technique. I drop one immensely heavy, overstuffed side of the suitcase on top of the other. I then climb onto the bed, lie on top of the suitcase, and begin attempting to zip it shut. I glance over at Danielle, who's still fighting the other bag.

"I take it you've . . . done this before?" I'm actually growing winded.

"Lots of . . . times," Danielle exhales in response. "My motto is . . . you can always . . . make everything . . . fit in a . . . suitcase."

Danielle and I continue wrestling the suitcases like they're a couple of wild boars. Meanwhile, water keeps filling the apartment and eighties music is shaking the furniture. I can't stop a laugh from escaping my lips. This evening is getting more and more absurd by the moment.

Danielle finally stands up straight and brushes off her hands. I look her way. In what is nothing short of a small miracle, she managed to shut her bag.

"You see?" She tips up her chin victoriously. "You can always make everything fit."

I laugh again while giving the zipper of my suitcase another futile yank. "Apparently, I don't have . . . your knack for packing. I'm not sure this one . . . is going to . . . close."

"May I be of help?" someone asks from behind me.

I freeze. Dylan must be standing in the bedroom doorway.

How long has he been standing in the doorway?

I clumsily slide off the suitcase, and once my feet touch the floor, I turn his way.

Dylan is leaning casually against the door frame, his arms crossed over his broad chest. He's observing Danielle and me with a deadpan expression, yet there's an unmistakable glimmer of amusement in his eyes.

"Yeah, come over here and make yourself useful," Danielle orders him in a jokingly chastising tone.

Dylan pushes off from the doorway and enters the room. Only then do I notice that he, too, is wearing a pair of waterproof boots. In stark contrast to Danielle's polka-dot-patterned footwear, however, Dylan's boots are thick, tall, and sturdy enough that I would bet you could kick down a door with them. Too bad I didn't have a pair to use on this apartment's front door.

Dylan steps between Danielle and me to reach the bed. He presses down one hand on the top of the suitcase I was working on, and with his other hand, he zips the luggage shut with ease. My eyebrows shoot up. Dylan is either The Suitcase Whisperer or he's just that impressively strong. Perhaps both.

Still without a word, Dylan takes hold of the larger suitcase with his right hand and grabs the other one with his left. He then proceeds to lift them both off the bed as though they weigh nothing more than a credit card. My pulse rises even higher as I watch him.

"Thanks, Dyl. This is why we continue bribing you for favors by inviting you over for dinner." Danielle gives him a playful slap on the shoulder. She then motions my way. "Dylan, I'd like you to meet my new friend and roommate, Quinn Meyers. She's doing a month-long rotation in Lakewood's ED, and she's moving back here in July to start her emergency medicine residency." She pauses, focuses on me, and gestures to Dylan. "Quinn, this is my big brother, Dylan Gillespie. He's a second-year emergency medicine resident at Lakewood, so you'll probably see him around the ED this month, and you'll definitely see him a lot once you start residency."

Everything seems to become totally still as I process what Danielle said. Hot Park Ranger is Danielle's brother. He's an emergency medicine resident at Lakewood. He really must have been the guy in the dark green scrubs I saw the other day in the ED.

But how can Dylan work as a park ranger at Yellowstone and be an emergency medicine resident at Lakewood? More importantly, why does he always seem to show up whenever my underwear is scattered all over the place?

Mind reeling, I resume shifting my gaze between the siblings. Now I see the family resemblance, especially in their vibrant green eyes. I peer at Dylan more closely, and as I do, our gazes suddenly seem to lock in an intense way. A rush of heat rises up inside me, and my breathing hitches again.

Danielle clears her throat, and I realize she's waiting for one of us to say something.

"Um, hi, Dylan," I finally manage to articulate. "It's nice to see you . . . again."

Dylan's eyes remain on mine. "It's nice to see you—and your luggage—again, too, Quinn."

My face flames.

"Wait a sec." Danielle is slack-jawed. "The two of you have met before?"

"We have." Dylan turns to his sister, his expression giving away nothing. "I'll take these bags downstairs, and I'll help Savannah and Joel load the cars."

Saying no more, Dylan carries the huge, heavy bags out of the room, keeping them held above the water without a hint of difficulty.

Once he's gone, Danielle faces me with eyes that are wide. "When did the two of you meet?"

I resist the urge to use my hand to fan air past my flushed face. "I ran into your brother a couple times while I was visiting Yellowstone last week," I explain, conveniently leaving out any mention of how I humiliated myself in front of him on more than one occasion.

Danielle's eyes are practically falling out of their sockets. "Are you serious?"

"I'm serious."

Danielle looks in the direction Dylan went. "So that explains . . . I mean, I haven't seen him . . ." she trails off. There's a pause before she peers at me again. "Well, what do you say? Ready to get out of this joint?"

I glance down at the water, which is persistently inching farther into the room. "Yep. I don't think there's anything more we can do here. In the meantime, I'll keep trying to locate a plumber and get through to Mr. Utteley."

Danielle and I exit the bedroom and begin wading through the standing water toward the entryway. We're about midway across the main room when the apartment's front door is unexpectedly flung open and someone stomps inside. Danielle and I both come to a startled halt.

The landlord is here.

Mr. Utteley, who's again dressed in a sweater vest over a button-up shirt paired with wrinkled khaki slacks, reaches the edge of the main room and stops before his loafers get wet. As he takes in the scene, his face gets blotchy, and his eyes become big and angry behind his glasses.

"Miss Meyers, what have you done?" he bellows with more fierceness than I would expect from such a mousey fellow.

My eyebrows shoot up. "What do you mean, what have *I* done?"

He uses an arm to gesture around the apartment. "Do you see all this water damage? This is going to cost thousands to fix. Not to mention, I'll lose weeks of income because I won't be able to rent the apartment while repairs are taking place." He fixes a glare on me. "I certainly hope you're prepared to reimburse me for the damage."

"I . . . what?" I shiver as the cold water covers my feet. "Of course I don't have money to—"

"Well, I suggest you get your hands on some funds *promptly*." Mr. Utteley's mouth slowly curls up into an unnerving smile. "It will certainly be easier and less expensive for you to settle with me out of court."

Beside me, Danielle sputters something incoherent. I stare at Mr. Utteley while nauseating thoughts of bankruptcy, destroyed credit ratings, attorneys, and courtrooms start swirling in my head. I'm a dirt-poor medical student who's racking up educational debt by the second. I'll be working on a pathetically meager resident's salary for the next three years and paying off student loans for decades afterward. There's no way I'll be able to pay Mr. Utteley what he's demanding.

The landlord adopts a more patronizing tone. "I realize this is hard for you to understand, Miss Meyers, so I'm willing to cut you a deal. If you transfer twelve thousand dollars into my bank account by the end of this week, we'll consider the matter resolved."

Danielle lets out a squeak, and her lips start moving as though she's trying to say something more but can't eke out another sound

"*Twelve thousand dollars*?" I feel as though the air has been sucked from my lungs.

Mr. Utteley doesn't reply. Instead, he peers around the apartment and lets out another dramatic groan. He then removes his phone from the pocket of his slacks and start recording a video of the water pouring out from the ceiling.

"I can't believe this!" Mr. Utteley emphasizes each word while he records. "I've had some bad tenants in the past, Miss Meyers, but no one has ever caused this type of damage!"

Danielle and I exchange a glance.

"*Bully*," Danielle mouths, flicking her narrowed eyes in Mr. Utteley's direction.

I nod in reply. Danielle is absolutely right.

"Mr. Utteley." I take a step toward him, causing the water to slosh around my ankles. "You know as well as I do that I didn't cause this. Obviously, a ceiling pipe burst. I'm in no way responsible for what happened."

"Actually, you are responsible." Mr. Utteley stops recording. "It's spelled out quite clearly in the rental agreement you so eagerly signed."

My stomach lurches. "What?"

Mr. Utteley chuckles. "Upon signing, as the document states, you accepted sole responsibility—financial and otherwise—for any and all damages to the premises that occur during your lease period." He has the nerve to bow slightly. "I do thank you, Miss Meyers. I've needed to do some repairs for quite a while, and I appreciate you making it financially possible."

"So this was a set up!" Danielle fumes. "You let Quinn sign that agreement when you were fully aware things were in such disrepair that something would undoubtedly go awry while she was here!"

"Now, now." Mr. Utteley makes a tsking noise. "Let's not make accusations, young lady. Slander will only get you into even more trouble."

I begin to shake my head. "I'm not paying for this, Mr. Utteley."

"Suit yourself." Mr. Utteley shrugs. "Either you pay, or I'll see you in court. It's your choice." He smiles again. "As I said, though, per the contract you willingly signed, you did accept full and complete responsibility for damages that occur during your lease—"

"Unless you, as the landlord, haven't been adhering to your responsibilities, which are mandated by law," someone with a recognizable voice states from the entryway.

Mr. Utteley, Danielle, and I all spin toward the sound. Dylan is standing in the foyer. His posture is relaxed, yet his presence commands complete control as he fixes a firm gaze on Mr. Utteley.

Mr. Utteley's eyebrows rise. He jams his phone into the pocket of his slacks. "Who are you?"

"Someone who understands implied warranty of habitability enough to know landlords must meet basic requirements before legally renting a property." Dylan's eyes never leave Mr. Utteley's face. "This includes, of course, ensuring the property complies with all safety codes, such as having working smoke detectors, guards on the windows, and proper electrical wiring."

Dylan shifts his attention to one of the light switches on the wall beside him. It's hanging crookedly and exposing the wires behind it. Dylan flips the switch. There's a spark and a loud pop in the light fixture above his head. Danielle lets out a startled gasp. I flinch, hoping we won't get electrocuted while we're standing up to our ankles in water.

"That light . . . I h-had nothing to do with that light," Mr. Utteley sputters. "I'm sure Miss Meyers broke that, too."

Dylan doesn't humor him with a reply. Instead, he removes his own phone from the pocket of his jeans and starts taking photos of some of the most obvious code violations within view. As Mr. Utteley watches, his face takes on such an impressively dark shade of red that his whole head appears almost purple.

"Of course, your legal obligations also include having appropriately maintained plumbing on the premises," Dylan eventually remarks, his steady voice cutting through the tension. He snaps a photo of the water coming down from the ceiling. "And as Miss Meyers has suffered from your failure to adhere to your legal obligations, she would obviously be justified in pursuing legal action against you, especially if the apartment was falsely advertised as being up-to-code before she signed the lease agreement."

Mr. Utteley's nostrils flare. Dylan calmly, but unflinchingly, watches him in return. The apartment would be pin-drop silent, were it not for the fact that water is falling from the ceiling and a song by Poison is playing upstairs. Deciding to use the segue Dylan created, I let out a melodramatic sigh that could rival my landlord's, and I say to Mr. Utteley:

"And given the dangerous, illegal, and otherwise uninhabitable living circumstances here, I have no choice but to vacate the premises. I'll expect to see my damage deposit transferred into my account by Monday." I smile innocently at him. "That is, unless you would still like to take this to court. In that case, I'll request a building inspector come assess this apartment immediately."

Mr. Utteley's face goes from purple to pasty white. "No. That won't be necessary. You . . . you can expect to see the damage deposit and your down payment refunded on Monday."

Suppressing a smile, I glance at Dylan and Danielle, and then I stroll out of the apartment. The siblings follow, and the three of us make our way to the end of the hall, exchanging glances without saying a word. When we reach the stairwell, Dylan opens the door. Danielle and I enter the stairwell first, and Dylan steps in next. As the door swings shut behind us, the last thing I hear is another Bon Jovi tune playing in the apartment upstairs.

Eight

"Good afternoon, sir. My name is Quinn Meyers. I'm a fourth-year medical student, and I'll be helping to care for you today. Please tell me what brings you into the emergency department."

Sean Tedest, the twenty-five-year-old man with dark blond hair who's seated on the hallway stretcher, winces with obvious discomfort. "My left arm hurts bad, man."

I glance down at his arm, but it's concealed by the sleeve of his sweatshirt. At this point, the only objective information I have is the set of vital signs that was obtained when Sean arrived at front triage a few minutes ago. At that time, he was found to be tachycardic with a low-grade fever.

I focus again on Sean's face, noting he appears pale. "Please tell me more about your pain."

Sean seems to hesitate, and then he leans closer toward me and lowers his voice. "Okay, I'm gonna be straight up with you, all right? I shoot heroin."

"I appreciate you telling me." I keep my expression and tone steady. If Sean has things to disclose that will help me give him the medical care he needs, I want him feel comfortable sharing that information. "Please go on."

Sean flinches again, as if he's experiencing another wave of pain. "This morning, I noticed a big sore where I recently shot up." He uses his right hand to motion to his left forearm. "The pain got so bad, I couldn't take it anymore."

I maintain my calm demeanor, but a sense of apprehension is beginning to course through me. "Before we do anything else, Sean, I need to get a good look at your arm. So let's have you change into a gown." I pick up the folded hospital gown from the foot of his stretcher. I glance up and down the crowded hallway. "I'm sorry there's not much privacy out here. You're welcome to change in the bathroom at the end of the hall."

"It's okay, I don't care about privacy." Sweat is forming on Sean's brow. He takes the gown from my hands. "I'll do whatever you need. I just want my arm to feel better."

Sean pushes himself to his feet and reaches with his good arm to start pulling off his sweatshirt. But he sways, and I see the little color that's left in his complexion drain away.

"Why don't you sit back down." I wrap a hand around his upper right arm, and I keep it there until he sits on the stretcher once more. "Instead of doing this out here, we're going to move you into an exam room. Hang tight."

I look to my left and peer through the fray, trying to locate someone who can assist me, and I spot one of the ED nurses standing in front of a computer. The nurse appears to be in her early fifties, she has flawless ebony skin, and her dark hair is in a bun. Seeming to sense me watching her, the nurse looks up from what she's doing and checks down the hallway. As soon as her eyes meet mine, she leaves her computer and comes my way.

"Hi there," she says. "I'm Kathy. It looks like you need some help?"

"Yes, thank you, Kathy. My name is Quinn, and I'm a visiting med student." I motion to Sean, who's lying on the stretcher and occasionally letting out a moan. "This gentleman has pain in his left forearm, and I'm concerned about an infection. I'd like to get him into an exam room as quickly as possible, since I suspect he'll need IV antibiotics, pain medication, and fluid." I flick my eyes around the department once more. To my dismay, I don't see an empty exam room anywhere.

Kathy checks over her shoulder and also surveys the scene. "Give me two minutes. I'll move one of my admitted patients into the hallway, which will free up an exam room. We can put this gentleman in there."

Kathy hurries off while waving an arm to catch the attention of one of the ED techs, and I overhear her ask the tech to help her with a patient swap. While Kathy and the tech get to work, I turn back to Sean, and I'm hit with a punch of alarm. Sean is staring blankly at the ceiling, and he already looks pastier than he did only minutes ago.

I lower the head of the stretcher so Sean is lying flat. "We're going to get you into a room, Sean. We'll place an IV, and we'll give you some fluid and medication to help you feel better."

Sean mumbles something I can't quite understand. He continues staring up at the ceiling in a frighteningly distant way.

"Okay, Quinn, we're ready."

I raise my head and see Kathy gesturing for me to bring Sean's stretcher to the newly vacated exam room, which is around the corner.

Moving fast, I go to the head of Sean's stretcher, release the brake, and begin driving it as quickly as I can without crashing into the other patient-occupied chairs and stretchers that line the narrow hallway. Reaching the end of the corridor, I guide the stretcher around the corner. Kathy holds open the curtain of the exam room, and I steer Sean's stretcher inside.

The odor of cleaning solution is strong in the air as the ED tech, whose ID badge reveals his name is Finn, finishes wiping down the equipment. Finn then slides aside so I can park Sean's stretcher where it belongs. Kathy enters the room and lets the curtain swing shut behind her. Working together with a silent, understood sense of urgency, Kathy turns on the monitor and logs into the computer, and Finn and I assist Sean with carefully removing his sweatshirt. Even a light brush of the fabric against his left forearm causes Sean to let out an involuntary cry of pain.

Finn assists Sean into a hospital gown and helps him lie flat on the stretcher. Kathy clips the pulse oximeter to one of Sean's fingertips and wraps the blood pressure cuff around his upper right arm. While Kathy gets a fresh set of vitals cycling, I turn on the light directly above the stretcher and put my full attention Sean's left arm, which is now on full display. My stomach sinks with dread. From just below the elbow joint all the way down to his fingertips, Sean's arm is circumferentially swollen and strangely taut. The skin is an ominous shade of purple-red.

I exchange a glance with Kathy, and from her creased brow, I can tell she understands what's going through my mind. As I feared, Sean appears to have necrotizing fasciitis, otherwise known as "nec fasc" or "flesh-eating bacteria." It's a frighteningly fast-moving infection that's destructively invading all the layers of tissue in Sean's arm to swiftly advance farther into his body. Nec fasc is a diagnosis medical providers truly fear. It spreads so rapidly that every minute—every second—counts, and even the promptest of care may not be enough to beat it.

In other words, we're in a race against time to save Sean's arm—and his life. And his infection has already had a several-hour head start on us.

I take only a few more seconds to perform a preliminary exam. There's a large abscess on Sean's forearm, no doubt the site of a recent heroin injection and the source of his life-threatening infection. When I rest my fingertips on a particularly red part of his arm, Sean moans again with pain, and I feel the eerie sensation of air crackling underneath his skin. It's a classic sign of nec fasc.

"Sean, we need to get an IV in you." I peer into his eyes. "Do you have any good veins left?"

Sean swallows as though his mouth and throat are parched. "I never shoot up in my right arm. I leave it alone, in case I need something like this."

I look at Kathy. "Please get an IV placed—two, if you can—and start some fluid. I'll call surgery and enter orders for IV antibiotics. I'll also get labs, an x-ray, and pain meds put in the computer."

"You got it." Kathy opens the drawers of the supply cart to gather what she needs.

"Whoa. Hang on." Sean raises his head. "Did you say surgery?"

I meet his gaze once more. "Yes. I believe you have an extremely serious and rapidly spreading infection in your arm. We have to move quickly if we're going to have any chance of getting ahead of it."

Sean's eyes become wide. "What do you mean? Exactly how serious is it?"

"To be blunt, this type of infection is so serious that it could cause to you lose your arm. It could even kill you." I put my hand on his shoulder, and I make sure to speak clearly and calmly. "I'm extremely sorry we don't have the time to talk as thoroughly as I would like, but as

I said, every moment matters. I need to call the surgeon so he or she can come assess you. I suspect they'll want to take you to the OR right away. In the OR, they'll probably make some incisions to relieve the pressure that's building up in your arm, and they'll clean out the infection."

Sean drops his head onto the pillow. "Do whatever you have to do, man. Don't let me die."

I keep my hand on Sean's shoulder a moment longer before I whip around, open the curtain, and charge out of the room. Without slowing my pace, I go to my workstation. Dropping down onto the chair, I pick up the phone receiver and ask the hospital operator to send a STAT page to the on-call resident for the surgical service. I then log into the computer, open Sean's chart, and place orders for IV antibiotics, labs and blood cultures, and pain medication. I also order x-rays of Sean's forearm and hand, which can be used to look for visual evidence of the air under his skin that I felt on exam.

I sign the orders and restlessly check the clock. Even in my relatively short time working in a medical setting, I've already known of young, otherwise-healthy people who, like Sean, arrived to the ED appearing reasonably well but died from nec fasc only hours later.

The phone rings. I snatch up the receiver and put it to my ear.

"This is Quinn Meyers, fourth-year med student in the emergency department."

"Hi, Quinn," a guy with a southern drawl greets me. "This is Jay Moen, third-year resident on surgery. How can I help?"

"I've got a twenty-five-year-old male who I suspect has left upper extremity nec fasc," I report.

There's a microsecond pause.

"I'll tell the OR to get a room going, and I'll be right down."

Dr. Moen ends the call. I hang up, push back from my desk, and get to my feet. As I spin around, I see Dr. Santiago coming my way. His expression is calm, yet his gaze is focused as though he can sense something bad is going on.

"Talk to me about your patient, Quinn," he says, getting to my side.

"Twenty-five-year-old male. IVDA. Left upper extremity pain. Based on his history and exam, I suspect nec fasc. Doctor Moen from surgery is on his way down, antibiotics are being hung, and orders for labs, blood cultures, and x-rays have also been placed."

Dr. Santiago starts moving away. "I'll notify the charge nurse. She'll start making the arrangements for the patient to transfer to the OR."

Dr. Santiago strides off. I stare after him. Should I have spoken first with the charge nurse? Did I mess up Sean's care? Considering how time-sensitive his infection is, will Sean suffer because I did things in the wrong order? Is Dr. Santiago wishing someone more capable of managing critically ill patients had matched with

Lakewood's incoming emergency medicine residency class?

I break out of my worried, racing thoughts when I notice a guy walking quickly toward Sean's exam room. The guy is dressed in scrubs and a long white coat, and his brown hair is cut short, military-style. I'm guessing he's Jay Moen, the on-call resident for the surgical service. Leaving my workstation, I head toward him.

"Hi, I'm Quinn," I say as we meet outside Sean's room.

"Hi. Jay Moen from surgery." He pulls aside the curtain and waits for me to enter.

I step into the exam room, and Dr. Moen follows. Kathy is at the bedside running antibiotics and fluid through the patient's IVs. I immediately focus on Sean. His eyes are closed, and he remains pale and sweaty. Even more alarming is that Sean's left arm is already more red and swollen than it was before, and the monitor shows the patient's pulse is trending higher while his blood pressure is drifting down.

What happens next passes in a fast, intense blur. Dr. Moen goes to Sean's bedside, introduces himself, and performs a focused exam while explaining his recommendation that Sean go to the OR immediately. There's a rumbling sound on the other side of the curtain as the radiology tech arrives with the portable x-ray machine. Dr. Moen makes a call from his phone to confirm the OR is ready. The x-ray tech obtains the images of Sean's arm and then departs. Kathy pokes her head out past the curtain and calls for Finn to come assist with transport. Finn hurries in, hooks Sean to the portable monitor, goes to the head of the stretcher, and drives the patient out of the room. Dr. Moen follows while still talking on the phone. Kathy hurries after them, carrying another bag of IV fluid and a repeat dose of pain medication, in case Sean needs them en route.

An instant later, I find myself alone in the room. Everything feels strangely quiet while I take a few seconds to mentally recap what occurred. As the adrenaline coursing through me gradually subsides, I emerge from my laser-locked state to become aware of my surroundings once again. I hear phones ringing and patients shouting. I can smell the potent disinfectant someone from environmental services is using to mop the hallway where a patient vomited. I catch glimpses around the edge of the curtain of people who are rushing by the room.

I look again at the spot where Sean's stretcher was only moments ago. I can only hope Sean presented early enough in the course of his infection that surgery will be successful. Perhaps even something good will come of this. Perhaps Sean will find the motivation he needs to seek help for his drug addiction. He's young and has so much life left to live. I certainly hope he gets that chance.

Lost in thought, I open the curtain and step out of the room. And I nearly crash into someone.

"Sorry!" I snap to awareness. "I . . ."

I trail off when I realize I nearly crashed into Hot Park Ranger. Ranger Gillespie. Dylan. Danielle's older brother. Dr. Gillespie.

Whoever the heck he is.

The truth is, I still don't know much about him. Last evening, after we escaped Mr. Utteley's deathtrap-of-an-apartment, Dylan, Danielle, Joel, Savannah, and I made fast work of loading my things into the guys' vehicles. Once we were done, Dylan got into his pickup truck, Danielle hopped in Joel's car, and Savannah rode in my car with me. We caravanned across town to Heritage Meadow Apartments, the sprawling complex where Danielle and Savannah live. I didn't even need to finish pulling into the parking lot before I was convinced my new living quarters would be infinitely nicer than the hole I had fled from.

Thanks to the group effort (and a functional elevator), it didn't take long to move me into Danielle and Savannah's spacious, dry, and hazard-free apartment. Afterward, Danielle declared it was time to reheat and enjoy the dinner she and Savannah had prepared. However, Dylan politely declined, said a quick goodbye to all of us, and left. Dylan . . .

Dylan.

I suddenly remember that I'm standing in the middle of the ED walkway only inches away from him.

I meet Dylan's gaze, and there's an immediate whoosh inside my chest. I can't help it. Every time I'm sure Dylan can't get any more handsome, he manages to prove me wrong. He's wearing blue scrubs with a white t-shirt underneath, and he has his stethoscope around his neck and his ID badge clipped to the waistband of his scrubs. While for ninety-nine percent of the human population, hospital-issue scrubs are probably the most unflattering clothing in existence, Dylan makes them look good. Extremely good.

"Hi, Quinn," he says.

"Hi." I sweep a loose strand of curls from my face. "How are you?"

"I'm fine, thanks." Dylan watches me adjust my hair and then returns his gaze to mine. "Did you finish getting settled in last night?"

"Yes, thanks in large part to you." I venture a smile. "Between managing another run-in with my suitcases and dealing with my bully-of-a-landlord, you saved the day. Your help was appreciated more than I can say. Thank you."

"I was happy to help." Dylan is peering into my eyes. "Though I must admit: I can't help wondering if your ex-landlord was actually in the right."

My smile vanishes. "What? But there's no way I caused . . . I mean, you saw the condition of that place . . . it was—"

"Totally uninhabitable, I know." Dylan unexpectedly cracks a grin. "However, it has also become clear to me that disaster strikes wherever you and your suitcases go, so maybe your landlord wasn't entirely to blame after all."

I stare at him for a second or two, and then it dawns on me: Dylan is joking. Dylan Gillespie is actually being funny. And now that I think about it, this might be the first time I've even seen him really smile. The change in his countenance is so pronounced that it seems to reveal a completely different side of him. His aura is warm and inviting, and it's made even more so by the unabashedly amused gleam in his eyes. As I keep observing him, I sense my own smile return. The next thing I know, I've started to laugh.

"Fair enough," I tell him. "I can't blame you for thinking those suitcases are cursed."

Dylan laughs along with me, and for a few seconds, the sound of our mingling laughter is the only thing I hear. When our eyes meet again, Dylan and I both let our laughter fade away. There's a pause, and then, unexplainably, the gleam in Dylan's eyes disappears as though a torch has been extinguished. He clears his throat and says:

"I should go check on one of my patients. Glad you got settled in."

Dylan steps by me and heads down the corridor. I spin around, watching after him while our conversation replays in my head. Though I try, I can't make sense of it at all.

"Quinn, I heard your patient got off to the OR all right?"

I check over my shoulder and see Dr. Santiago coming my way. I face my attending, trying to refocus.

"Yes. Sean was taken to the OR a few minutes ago." My brow furrows. "I hope he'll be okay."

"I do, too." Dr. Santiago shakes his head. "Nec fasc is a terrible thing."

"Hey, Jesse?" calls a nurse—a guy who appears to be in his late forties—who's coming toward us.

"Hey, Pete. What's up?" Dr. Santiago faces him.

"Would you mind checking on Room Six?" Pete tips his head in the direction of the room. "She has been awaiting an inpatient bed for a tiny bowel perf, and the plan was for her to be medically managed. However, I did a new set of vitals on her, and she has developed a temp and become tachycardic."

"You got it."

Dr. Santiago heads off with Pete. After they're gone, my gaze drifts again to what had been Sean's exam room. Did I do everything I possibly could for Sean? Did I manage his care correctly? Am I capable of caring for the types of high-acuity patients who, like Sean, seek help at Lakewood every day? Maybe Dr. Santiago is wondering the same thing. Maybe that's why he didn't ask me to come see the patient in Room Six with him.

I shake my head, as if it will somehow clear the uncertainty from my mind, and I draw in a determined breath. I have to redeem myself. I have to prove I deserve to be part of the incoming residency class. I can't let Dr. Santiago down. I can't let myself down.

Wasting no time, I hurry to my workstation, take a seat, and shake the mouse to wake the computer. I scan the tracking board in the hopes there will be a new patient I can go see, and I discover I'm in luck: a forty-four-year-old man was recently put in Room Twelve, and no one has signed up to be his caregiver yet. The patient's name is Joe Guldstren, and his chief complaint is listed as, "*Flank Pain.*"

I hastily click on the patient's name to assign myself to him, and I get back to my feet with renewed resolve. I may not have impressed anyone yet, but I fortunately have another chance to show I'll be a great asset to Lakewood's residency program. I'm not going to mess this up.

I head for Room Twelve. Before I've even reached the closed curtain that leads into the exam room, I hear loud moans coming from the patient who's waiting on the other side. At the sound, I pick up my pace. Severe flank pain is often caused by a passing kidney stone—pain so horrible that more than one female has told me she would choose to go through unmedicated childbirth again over passing another stone—so if that's what my patient is suffering from, I certainly want to help him as fast as possible.

I reach Room Twelve and knock briskly on the door frame. "May I come in?"

The man promptly stops moaning. "Yes. Of course."

I pause, taken aback by his calm reply. Perhaps this man isn't suffering as badly as I thought.

I move aside the curtain just enough to slide into the room, and then I let the curtain shut behind me to block the view of those who are in the hallway. Curtains certainly don't provide as much privacy as a solid door, but at least they're better than nothing.

As always, in the first second I enter the room, I do a rapid assessment of everything I see, hear, and smell, trying to get a sense of what's going on with the patient and how sick he might be.

The first thing I notice is that the man who's lounging on the stretcher doesn't appear to be in any sort of distress. I also can't help noting that he's extremely burly; he looks like he could participate in one of those competitions where contestants flip giant tires, dead-lift a thousand pounds, and pull a train car by a rope with their bare hands. The patient has thinning, light-colored hair, and he has a pronounced tan, which I'm guessing isn't natural, considering it's only April. Most noticeable of all is the fact that this man is staring at me in a way that instantly makes me uncomfortable.

Breaking eye contact, I glance at the monitor and see the patient's vitals are within normal limits. I look again at the man, trying not to get unnerved by the way he's watching me. I see he has already changed into a hospital gown, which he didn't bother to tie in the back. The gown is slipping off his shoulders, giving me enough of a view to confirm he's not wearing anything underneath it. At all. Other than the gown, the only things he has on are the hospital-issued, anti-slip socks on his feet.

I meet his undeviating stare once more. Despite my immense unease, I maintain my professional demeanor and display a smile.

"Good afternoon, sir. My name is Quinn Meyers. I'm a fourth-year medical student, and I'll be helping you today. The triage note indicated you were experiencing flank pain. Please tell me more about what's going on."

Mr. Guldstren shows a thin-lipped smile in return that catches me by surprise. I've never seen anyone who's passing kidney stone (or anyone who's in severe pain for any reason, for that matter) smile easily before. That alone causes my suspicion of a passing kidney stone to drop down even lower on my suspect list.

Letting the silence drag on longer than what feels normal, Mr. Guldstren adopts a reclining pose on the stretcher as though he's lounging on a beach chair. As he does so, his gown falls off even more, and he makes no effort to fix it. Alarm bells are going off in my head, but I keep my expression impassive as I wait for him to answer me.

"What did you say your name was?" he asks, finally ending the uncomfortable quiet.

"Quinn Meyers."

His stare never leaves my face. "Hello, Quinn."

"Hello, Mr. Guldstren." I resist the instinct to put more space between us. "Please tell me about the discomfort you've been having."

"Certainly." Mr. Guldstren's smile widens. "A few hours ago, I developed flank pain. It started out-of-the-blue. I've never had anything like it before, Quinn, and when the pain kept getting worse, I realized I needed to get checked out."

"Where is your pain located?"

"Right here." Without any suggestion of difficulty, Mr. Guldstren sits up again, turns, and swings his legs off the side of the stretcher so he's sitting on the stretcher's edge. He lifts an arm, as if to point to somewhere on his body, but he unexpectedly lets out a loud moan.

"Mr. Guldstren?" I take a step toward him.

He stops moaning, and his smile returns. "I'm sorry, Quinn. I'm just so uncomfortable that it's hard for me to point to where I'm hurting. Would you please come closer, so I can use you to demonstrate?"

I hesitate. Every ounce of me is telling me something is really wrong here, and every instinct is screaming I shouldn't do what he asks. But what will happen if I don't comply? What if I upset or offend him? What if Mr. Guldstren gets called by a patient satisfaction surveyor, and he reports negative things about the care I provided him? In one phone call, my reputation at Lakewood could be destroyed.

I've already learned enough about patient satisfaction surveys to know their role in healthcare is complicated. Extremely complicated. Typically obtained by third-party companies that are hired by the hospitals themselves, surveys are being used with increasing frequency across the country. Hospitals that receive the highest patient satisfaction scores are often given awards and even monetary reimbursements in return. So there's an immense amount of pressure on healthcare providers to keep patients "happy" and "satisfied" on top of making sure patients actually survive, do well, and receive appropriate medical care.

I used to think obtaining a high patient satisfaction score in the emergency department would be straight-forward—that patients would be "happy" to have their lives saved and receive proper treatment. However, I've learned that's not necessarily the case. I've heard patients complain about the limited number of channels on the flat-screen televisions in their private exam rooms. Other patients have gotten upset— even violent—when they weren't prescribed narcotics, even though opiates were inappropriate and even dangerous for their condition. I've seen a patient become furious because a plastic surgeon wasn't brought in to suture his tiny, shallow leg laceration. I've even listened to patients express dissatisfaction about having to wait to be seen for an ankle sprain because the doctor was running a code in another room.

In other words, patients who get randomly selected for satisfaction surveys might be the same patients who were lying, experiencing a psychiatric crisis, under the influence of substances, making unreasonable demands, or violent or otherwise threatening. It doesn't matter, though. Their survey results are usually still counted.

Mr. Guldstren clears his throat, yanking me to attention. My gut is telling me not to move any closer to this guy, yet my head is reminding me that if he gives me a scathing review, it will get seen by the emergency department leadership. If the emergency department leadership sees a bad review about me, my reputation will tank. I can't let that happen.

With a silent sigh, I step up to the stretcher. "Please go on with what you were saying about your pain."

Mr. Guldstren suddenly reaches out and grabs me by the hips. I gasp in alarm, but before I can pull away, he spins me around and begins rubbing a hand along my lower back.

"It hurts right here," he murmurs, still rubbing me.

"Sir, please get your hands off me," I say while stepping forward to escape his hold.

He doesn't let go.

I freeze for one terrifying, stunned moment, and then my heart begins thundering inside my chest. I make another panicked attempt to get away, but Mr. Guldstren leaps to his feet and tightens his hold on me. I cry out again, flailing to free myself, but I'm no match for this man's strength. Tugging me backward so

I'm pressed against the front of his body, I hear him hiss in my ear:

"Unless you want to be accused of making inappropriate comments to your patient, you'll stay quiet and do exactly what—"

There's a sharp knock on the doorframe.

"Quinn?" someone with a deep voice barks through the curtain.

I inhale a stuttering breath. Dylan is standing right outside the room.

Mr. Guldstren's fingers dig painfully into my hips. "Tell whoever is outside that you're fine," he orders in a harsh whisper. "Make him go away, or I'll hurt you faster than anyone can come to your aid." He exhales, and I feel the nauseating sensation of his hot breath on my neck. "Do you understand?"

I open my mouth, but my throat has seized up too tightly for me to utter a sound. My head is growing light, and my legs are shaking so badly that I don't think I can stand much longer.

Mr. Guldstren puts his lips against my ear. "You have three seconds before I—"

The room's curtain is thrown aside so fast that it's nearly torn down from its hooks. Mr. Guldstren spins toward the doorway while keeping me trapped in his arms. Fighting to catch my breath, I look with tear-filled eyes across the room at Dylan. He meets my gaze for only a moment before locking an enraged stare on Mr. Guldstren.

"Walk away and shut the curtain," Mr. Guldstren growls.

Dylan's jaw clenches. His eyes narrow. "Code Silver, Room Twelve!"

Dylan's shout is still carrying through the air as he charges into the room, lowers a shoulder, and rams into Mr. Guldstren with full force. Mr. Guldstren lets out an enraged yell as he stumbles. His hold on me loosens. I dive forward to get away, but my foot catches on the wheel of the stretcher, and I trip, landing hard on the ground. My head spins as the air is knocked from my lungs.

A Code Silver announcement is blasting over the PA system. I grab the edge of the stretcher and pull myself to my feet. Raising my head, I see Mr. Guldstren panting as he scrambles over to a corner of the room. Dylan positions himself between Mr. Guldstren and me, his eyes never leaving Mr. Guldstren's face.

"Quinn, get out of here," Dylan says over his shoulder.

I tremblingly move to obey, but Mr. Guldstren darts forward and puts himself in front of the doorway, blocking my escape. Perspiration is streaming down his forehead. His eyes are wild and crazed as they leap between Dylan and me.

"Just leave," Dylan tells Mr. Guldstren in a low voice, tracking his every movement and staying protectively in front of me. "We don't want trouble."

Mr. Guldstren wipes the heavy sweat from his brow. With a grunt, he suddenly balls his hands into fists and charges directly at Dylan. I scream as the two men collide.

More shouts echo through the air as security personnel, Dr. Santiago, Finn, Pete, and others race into the room. Mr. Guldstren screeches. The stretcher rocks. An IV pole crashes to the floor. The supply cart is tipped onto its side, its contents spilling across the floor.

A secretary appears in the doorway and begins pointing frantically into the room. Three police officers rush in, and then things get quiet. The crowd parts as Mr. Guldstren is led out of the room by two of the officers. The patient's hospital gown, which is hanging from one arm, drags over the ground as he's taken away.

There's another beat of stillness, and then everyone starts to regroup. Pete and Finn begin cleaning up the mess. Other staff members disperse to return to their regular duties. Dylan and Dr. Santiago are in the hallway speaking with the third police officer. The security guards are making calls. Someone from environmental services arrives and commences sweeping up the supplies that were scattered across the floor and destroyed in the melee.

As I hover in the corner of the room, my mind suddenly becomes plagued by terrifying flashbacks of what happened. I can't get that man's eerie stare out of my head. He had me trapped in here. He could have . . . he was going to . . . what would have happened if . . .

I sense the color drain from my face. My legs get weak. Swallowing down nausea, I reach out to the wall to support myself.

"Quinn."

I turn toward the sound of my name, the motion causing my head to swim. Through blurring vision, I see Dylan striding toward me fast.

"Are you hurt?"

I don't reply. I know Dylan said something, but my head is getting so foggy that I can't process his words.

Dylan's brows snap together as he watches me. "Let's get you over to the residents' lounge. You should lie down before you give your statement to the police." He puts an arm around my waist, bracing me against him. "Come on."

I shuffle alongside Dylan as he leads me out of the room. I think I hear Dylan say something to Dr. Santiago, who replies, but I'm in too much of a haze to be sure. Staring at nothing, I let Dylan guide me out the back exit of the emergency department and down an empty corridor. We step into an elevator, which ascends for a short time before it comes to a stop. When its doors open, Dylan guides me out into a quiet, carpeted, door-lined hallway.

Without warning, another sickening flashback of Mr. Guldstren fills my mind. I halt with an involuntary whimper, and I stagger as my legs threaten to buckle.

"Quinn?" Dylan keeps his arm securely around me. "Are you all right?"

Tears are drifting down my cheeks as I look up at him. Only then do I realize Dylan has a cut near his lower lip and a bruise adjacent to his left eye.

"You . . . got hurt." I lift my trembling hand and touch the side of his face.

Dylan draws in a breath, and he keeps peering into my eyes. "Come on. You need to lie down."

I attempt to take another step. There's an ominous whooshing sound in my ears, and a sensation of freefall rises up inside me. My vision tunnels. The last thing I'm aware of is Dylan scooping me up in his arms.

Nine

I hear a man talking, but sounds are so weirdly garbled in my ears that I can't make out what he's saying. I then realize I'm lying down with my eyes closed. My heart lurches with alarm. What's going on? Why—

A moment later, the fog clears from my head, and as it does, every horrible thing that happened in Room Twelve returns to my mind in a sickening rush. I force open my eyes, hoping that doing so will drive away the awful memories. I blink under the glare of bright ceiling lights that are high above me.

"She's coming to," I hear the man say, and now I recognize his distinctly deep voice. "I'll call you back."

I push myself up to a sitting position and peer around. I'm on a couch in a large, square-shaped room, which I deduce must be the lounge for Lakewood's emergency medicine residents. Dusty bookshelves crammed with fat medical textbooks—books that probably haven't been opened in years—span the entire length of the walls to my left and right. A tall arched window takes up most of the wall directly across the room from me, and there are two recliner chairs situated in front of it. Near the bookcases on the right is a long desk with three computer workstations. To the left of the couch is the door, which is propped open a crack.

And there's Dylan. He's down on one knee in front of the couch, and he's studying me closely.

"How are you feeling?" He puts his phone into the pocket of his scrubs top and wraps his fingers around my wrist to monitor my pulse.

"I'm okay. I . . ."

I trail off, rendered speechless by Dylan's touch. The contact is causing a tingling sensation to zip up my arm and fill me entirely. I look down at his hand as it remains around my wrist. His hold is strong and secure, and yet it's somehow also gentle and comforting.

I realize the room has become very quiet. I raise my head and look at Dylan again. The bruise adjacent to his eye has become a dark shade of purple. Thankfully, at least, the cut near his lip is small and shallow, and it has already stopped bleeding.

"Dylan." I swallow, trying to fight down my rising emotion and steady my words. "Thank you for what you did. I don't know what would have happened, if you hadn't . . ."

When I fall silent again, Dylan slides his hand from my wrist, gets up off his knee, and sits on the couch beside me.

"I'm sorry about what happened," he tells me quietly.

I meet his gaze. There's a flicker of movement in his arm, like he's going to reach out to me again, but instead, Dylan quickly gets to his feet and strides to the opposite side of the room. He stops in front of the window and stares out at the waning daylight.

"I noticed Mr. Guldstren's name on the patient tracking board, and it caught my attention because I cared for him in the ED only two days ago," Dylan states with restraint. "When I treated Mr. Guldstren, he claimed to be having lower abdominal pain, but his exam and workup were completely normal." His eyes narrow. "During his workup, it also didn't escape my notice that Mr. Guldstren was behaving very inappropriately toward the female staff members."

I shudder, draw my knees to my chest, and wrap my arms around them.

"When I realized what was going on, I made sure that only male providers went into his room," Dylan continues. "I also reviewed his chart in depth, and I discovered Mr. Guldstren has a lengthy history of going to EDs throughout the region, sometimes multiple times a week, with complaints in his abdominal or genital areas. Not surprisingly, his workups are always normal, or he signs out against medical advice before his testing is complete." He continues staring out the window while he shakes his head. "Mr. Guldstren eventually signed out AMA when I was caring for him, too. After he left the ED, I submitted a request for an alert to be added to his chart. I'm guessing the alert hasn't been reviewed and put on his medical record yet, otherwise you would have noticed the alert when you signed up as his provider today." He turns to face me. The muscles of his jaw are working. "As soon as I realized you were seeing him, I went to the room to check on you. I'm only sorry I didn't intervene sooner."

I draw in my legs even closer. "And I'm only sorry I didn't trust my gut and have a nurse join me in the room the moment I sensed something was off."

"Don't apologize for anything that happened." Dylan's gaze is unrelenting. "It was not your fault. You were assaulted, Quinn."

I know it's true, yet hearing Dylan say the words still strikes me hard. I look away. Out of the corner of my eye, I see Dylan resume peering out the window. Silence settles over us. As seconds tick by, I find myself growing increasingly intrigued by the man who's standing on the other side of the room. I keep glancing Dylan's way, studying his profile and trying to catch a glimpse of the person I saw earlier today—the Dylan that lies beneath his stoical surface. Finally, I break the quiet:

"So who are you, anyway, Dylan Gillespie?"

Dylan shoots me a sideways look. "What?"

"Who are you?" I repeat, daring to smile a little bit. "I can't quite figure you out. So far, I've learned you're Danielle's older brother, a park ranger, and an emergency medicine resident at one of the highest-acuity emergency departments in the country." I let my smile widen. "Not to mention, based on the tackling skills you demonstrated in Room Twelve, you should probably be playing in the NFL."

Dylan's posture slowly relaxes. He leans against the window frame and crosses his arms over his chest. The waning sunlight starts casting sideways shadows upon his face, accentuating his handsome features.

"It's funny you should say that, because I actually played football while I attended college in Wyoming," Dylan tells me.

"Really?" I'm still smiling at him. "You played in college?"

"Yes. And after college, I got a job as a park ranger at Yellowstone to support myself as I was prepping for the MCAT, shadowing physicians, and volunteering at local clinics and hospitals."

I scoot myself back on the couch. "Then it sounds like you're quite the Renaissance man."

Dylan chuckles. "No, but I was fortunate to be able to pursue several areas of interest during those years."

I tip my head slightly to one side. "Do you still pursue those interests?"

"I try." Dylan shrugs nonchalantly. "I stayed in Wyoming for med school partly so I could continue working at Yellowstone whenever my schedule permitted."

"But you returned here for residency," I note.

His smile falters. "Yes. About two years ago, after graduating from med school, I moved back home for residency."

Dylan resumes watching out the window. I have the strong sense there's much more to his story, but I'm certainly not going to push him for details . . . except one.

"If you've been living here for the past two years, how come were you working at Yellowstone only a couple weeks ago?"

Dylan faces me again, and I notice a flicker of levity in his eyes. I blush, realizing I just reminded him of my underwear-filled suitcase that exploded open at the park entrance . . . and that I locked myself out of my car . . . and that I failed to notice several signs warning park visitors not to venture into the woods at the upper falls. Mercifully, Dylan doesn't refer to any of those cringe-worthy moments, though I'm pretty sure he's working to contain a smile as he replies:

"I spent all last month working at Yellowstone. During second year of residency, everyone has the opportunity to do a four-week elective rotation. I chose to spend my elective doing wilderness medicine, and I got approved to return to Yellowstone to work shifts and teach classes at my alma mater."

I skewer him with a playfully stern look. "Speaking of that, when I jumped in to help the elderly man who was having chest pain at the upper falls, you could have mentioned you were an *emergency medicine physician*."

Dylan lets his grin show. "There was no need for me to take over. In fact, it was helpful having you there. As you were assisting the patient, I was able to coordinate with the EMS crew to arrange transport."

I have to laugh. "Meanwhile, I was wondering why a park ranger was so well-versed in medicine. Little did I know the hot park ranger also happened to be an emergency . . ." I nearly choke when I realize what I said. I look away and clear my throat, taking a moment before adding, "Anyway, you were probably thinking I was screwing up everything."

There's a pause.

"No, that's not what I was thinking," I hear Dylan say.

Heat fills my chest, and I look Dylan's way once more. Our eyes meet, and the silence in the room intensifies.

A phone starts ringing. Dylan coughs, retrieves his phone from his pocket, and puts it to his ear.

"Hi." He turns away from me while using his free hand to ruffle his hair. "Yes, she's doing better . . . yes . . . I'll accompany her down there . . . I'm planning to finish my shift and stay late to help with the backlog . . . okay, we'll be down."

I watch Dylan end the call, and I'm hit with guilt as realization strikes me. "Because you've been helping me, the ED has been without one of its core providers for the shift. The other docs must be drowning in patients. I'm so sorry for the trouble."

"As I said before, don't be sorry. Don't ever be sorry for what happened." Dylan puts away his phone. "And don't worry about the ED staffing, either. Jesse took over caring for my patients, and he has been covering for me ever since. Yes, the department is busy, but they've managed to stay afloat down there, and I'm heading back to resume seeing patients. It will be all right." He takes a step away from the window. "Jesse mentioned an officer is waiting in one of the consultation rooms, so if you're feeling up to it, before I return to work, I'll take you there so you can give your statement."

I nod. "All right."

Dylan starts crossing the room. I get to my feet right as Dylan reaches the couch, and we both freeze when we suddenly find ourselves standing face-to-face with only a couple inches of space between us. My pulse rises. Dylan peers into my eyes.

This time, my phone shatters the stillness. I jump, nearly falling onto the couch behind me, and then I become totally still when I realize it's Chad's ringtone that's playing. At the sound, a wave of emotion crashes down upon me.

Dylan retreats, putting more distance between us. "Feel free to answer that. I'll wait outside, and we can head to the ED after your call."

"No, it's okay." My mind is whirling as I yank my phone from my back pocket and hit the *mute* button. "It's my boyfriend. I can call him back later." I stop and blink a couple times. "That is, Chad used to be my boyfriend, but we're . . . well, we've dated on-and-off for years, but . . ." I flounder to gather my thoughts. "What I mean is Chad dumped me—again—the night before I moved out here, but I think he wants to reconcile. So now I have to decide if . . ." I realize how badly I'm rambling, and I let the rest of my words die on my tongue.

Dylan peers at me, his expression giving away nothing. At last he says, "If you're ready, Quinn, we can head out."

"I'm ready."

"You're sure?"

"I'm sure."

Dylan opens the door. I step past him to exit the lounge, and he follows. We make our way along the hallway, and this time we enter a stairwell to go down to the ground floor. Still without a word, Dylan takes us along a route through what proves to be a labyrinth of corridors to head back to the ED.

Though I remain silent, my mind is anything but still. There's an unsettling feeling gnawing at me that I can't quite identify. It's a feeling that makes me think I've given Dylan the wrong impression and I need to fix things somehow. But what is there to fix? How am I supposed to fix anything when I don't even know how I feel or what I want?

Dylan and I reach the ED's overcrowded waiting room and venture down another corridor. Up ahead, the door for one of the consultation rooms is ajar. I can see a police officer and a nurse waiting inside. When we reach the doorway, Dylan stops and faces me.

"I hope you don't mind, but I called Danielle earlier and told her what happened. After you're done here, Danielle will pick you up in Joel's car and take you home."

"But what about the ED?" My brow furrows. "It's so busy in there, and they've been down a provider for a long time, so I assumed I was—"

"You're not expected to return to work today," Dylan interrupts. "What happened was no small thing. You should go home after this."

"But—"

"Jesse also wants you to go home to recover. So once you're done speaking to the officer, call Danielle and let her take you home. We want to make sure you're okay and that you're with someone who will watch out for you tonight."

"What about you?" I focus on the bruises on Dylan's face, not hiding my worry. "You were also in—"

"I'm fine."

Dylan doesn't give me a chance to say anything else before he looks through the open door and gives the officer and the nurse a nod. Casting me a last glance, Dylan strides away, headed in the direction of the double doors that lead to the treatment area of the ED.

I watch Dylan until he disappears from view. I then step into the consultation room and shut the door behind me. The discussion with the officer doesn't take long, and after he's finished getting my statement, he shakes my hand, gives me a card with his phone number and the case number on it, and departs. The nurse makes sure there's nothing else I need, and then she leaves to return to the ED.

Once I'm alone, I call Danielle. She answers immediately. Speaking fast, she explains that right after Dylan called her, she drove to the hospital. She has been waiting in the visitors' parking lot ever since.

I leave the consultation room, pass through the jam-packed waiting area, and exit the building. Glancing around, I soon spot Danielle maneuvering Joel's car into the circular drop-off in front of the ED. Danielle leaves the car idling at the curb, leaps out, and tugs me into a huge hug. She doesn't ask questions or press for information. She simply helps me into the car and keeps mellow music playing during the drive to the apartment.

After we get home, I give Danielle another hug and thank her for the ride. I then retreat to my room. Only then do I realize how exhausted I am, both physically and emotionally. I kick off my shoes, flop down on the futon, and stare at the ceiling. Sometimes, I feel numb. Other times, my emotions and thoughts spin as I grapple to understand everything that happened today . . . and what didn't happen.

While the jumbled mess of thoughts crashes around in my mind, I suddenly remember Chad tried to call when I was in the residents' lounge earlier. Though I know I'm in no state to tackle a conversation about our relationship status, I'm also desperate for something—someone—familiar to help me settle my angst.

Pushing myself up to a seated position, I reach for my phone and call Chad.

"Hey," he answers.

"Hey. Sorry I missed your call earlier. I was . . . in the ED."

"No worries. I was just getting back to you about the text you sent this morning. Your new apartment looks cool."

It takes me a couple seconds to figure out what he's referring to, and then I remember: this morning, I texted Chad a picture of my new apartment building and included its address, telling him to look it up online to see how great it was. Though it was a small thing, I felt a text would help ensure the lines of communication between us remained open, especially since I had been forced to end our last call right when he was trying to broach an extremely important subject.

"How did your shift go?" Chad inquires.

"It was . . . terrible." More memories of today replay in my mind. My emotions swell, and as I reach my breaking point, words begin tumbling out of my mouth. "A patient assaulted me, Chad. He tried to . . . they called a Code Silver . . . he was arrested . . . I syncopized . . . and . . . it was awful."

There's a pause.

"Yikes, I'm really sorry. I'm relieved to hear you're okay." Chad sighs, and I can almost hear him shaking his head. "I guess those types of crazy things come with working in the ED, huh?"

I become very still while holding the phone against my ear. I don't answer him.

Chad chuckles as he goes on, "I suppose you could call your experience yet another reason why I chose to go into radiology. At least I won't have to deal with wacky patients. It's a good thing there are people like you who are willing to handle those types of patients and don't get bothered by their behavior."

I look at my pale reflection in the mirror that's hanging on the wall, and I remain silent.

"Say, Quinn," Chad says after a pause, his tone more serious, "I really do want to continue our discussion from last evening. Unfortunately, I'm about to go listen in on a presentation, so this isn't a good time, but can I call you soon?"

I draw in a breath and find my voice. "Sure. Of course."

"Great. Talk to you soon."

Chad ends the call. I lower my phone to my lap while telling myself I shouldn't be bothered by the unconcerned way Chad reacted. He's on the other side of the country. He didn't see what happened in Room Twelve. He has no way of understanding how truly horrible it was.

Also, as upsetting as it is to acknowledge, I know Chad has a point. Right or wrong, the reality of having to deal with violent and threatening patients has somehow become

viewed as nothing more than a standard risk of
working in an emergency department. So I can't
let myself get upset every time something like
this happens . . . yet I grow sick at the thought of
this ever happening again.

I get to my feet and peer out the window.
Thank goodness Dylan was working today.
Thank goodness he happened to notice Mr.
Guldstren's name on the tracking board. Thank
goodness he . . .

Dylan.

Dylan's image enters my mind, but when I
glance down at my phone, I see Chad's name still
on the screen. I turn away and start pacing the
room while massaging my aching temples, trying
to clear my head. I don't know how much time
goes by before I give up attempting to make
sense of things. I peel off my scrubs, wrap a towel
around myself, and head across the hall and into
the bathroom for a much-needed, scorching-hot
shower. Returning to my room, I change into the
ultimate comfort outfit of a hooded sweatshirt
and flannel pajama pants.

There's a light knock on my bedroom
door.

"Hey, Quinn?" I hear Danielle ask gently.

"Come in," I call to her.

The door is opened, and Danielle pokes
her head inside.

"Sav and I have hot chocolate on the stove
and, like, four types of cookies baking in the
oven. Would you like anything?"

My chest warms with gratitude. Once again, I realize how fortunate I was to meet Danielle and Savannah.

I smile at her. "You know, I think that's exactly what the doctor ordered."

Ten

I nestle back in the big recliner, adjust the throw blanket I've got draped over my lap, and sigh with contentment. My stomach is stuffed with cookies and hot chocolate, and I have absolutely no qualms about considering that my dinner for the evening.

Outside, the sky has grown dark, and the main room of the apartment is now cozily illuminated by the glow from the gas fireplace and the string lights that are draped across the mantle's shelf. Deliciously sweet aromas of baked goods linger in the air. Completing the ambience is the playlist of acoustic guitar music Danielle has going on the small sound system in the corner.

"Please tell me you have room for more cookies. There are still two batches to go." Savannah is grinning as she appears from the kitchen carrying a plate piled high with chocolate-and-caramel concoctions that are fresh from the oven.

I groan jokingly as I sit up. "Well, I suppose I can force myself to eat a few more." Without hesitation, I grab two cookies from the plate and gratefully accept the paper towel Savannah hands me as a napkin. "But only because you insist."

Savannah laughs as she crosses to the other side of the room. She sits down on the couch and puts the plate at her feet. She grabs a cookie for herself, takes a bite, and swallows. "I appreciate you making the sacrifice."

"No problem." I cram the rest of my cookie into my mouth.

Danielle pokes her head out from the kitchen. "Last call for hot chocolate. Anyone interested in a refill?"

Savannah raises a hand at the same time I do.

Clearly having anticipated how we would respond, Danielle promptly steps out of the kitchen holding a tray that has three mugs upon it. The mugs are practically overflowing with hot chocolate topped with massive dollops of whipping cream.

"Good. Because there was no way I was going to drink this all by myself." Danielle is walking slowly so the drinks don't slosh. "I mean, I probably *could* drink it all, but I figured it would be wiser if I had some help."

Danielle passes the fireplace and reaches where I'm sitting. As I lift one of the mugs from the tray, the mouth-watering scents of chocolate, cream, and peppermint fill my nostrils. While I blow on my drink to cool it down, Danielle makes her way over to where Savannah is seated on the couch. In what appears to be a well-practiced sequence of events, Savannah lifts both mugs off the tray, Danielle sets the tray on the floor and takes a seat beside Savannah, and Savannah hands her back one of the mugs.

Cradling her drink, Danielle fixes her attention on me. "How are you doing? What else do you need? Do you want to watch a movie?"

"I'm doing great, thanks to both of you," I reply. "You two have done more to help me than you'll ever know. After what happened in the ED today, I have no idea what I would have done if I had had to spend tonight alone in that wreck of an apartment I used to live in."

Danielle shudders. "That would have been terrible. I'm so glad you're here."

"Me, too," Savannah concurs.

I smile appreciatively. "That definitely makes three of us."

Danielle sips her drink. "I'm also glad Dylan was in the ED today and noticed that horrible man's name on the tracking board." Her brow creases. "Dyl sounded so upset—so angry— when he called and told me what that man had done to you, Quinn."

Savannah starts nodding. "That's definitely saying something, considering Dylan rarely shows strong emotion like that."

I pause before putting down my drink. "So I'm not the only person who has noticed Dylan seems to hide his emotions?"

"Oh, gosh, no. He has always been like that." Danielle snags a cookie from Savannah's plate. "Dylan is the master of keeping his feelings close to the vest."

"Yep," Savannah agrees. "Ninety-nine percent of the time, it's impossible to tell what Dylan is thinking. It completely intimidated me when I first met him years ago. Now . . . well, actually, it's still intimidating." She laughs good-naturedly. "That being said, when I was younger, I also used to envy the way Dylan could keep his feelings concealed; I wished I could do the same."

Danielle snickers. "You mean, instead of turning bright red and losing all ability to formulate a coherent sentence any time you were in the general vicinity of a guy you were crushing on?"

"Pretty much." Sav laughs again. "That was definitely a recurring problem for me."

Danielle giggles along with her. She then looks out the window, and her smile fades. "I will say, though, that Dylan has been a lot more closed off these past two years than he used to be. I hope he'll open up again one day."

I sit taller, sensing we're getting to that elusive part of Dylan's past I've detected is there. I know it's not my place to ask about it, though, so all I can do is hope Danielle or Sav will elaborate. However, before either of them have a chance to say more, there's a knock on the front door.

"I'll get it." Sav places her mug on the floor, hops off the couch, and leaves the room.

With a silent sigh, I sit back in the chair and take another drink of hot chocolate.

I hear the front door get opened followed by the muffled sounds of two people talking.

While I listen, I grab another cookie and bite into it. As I do so, Savannah returns to the room with someone walking alongside her.

"Doctor Kent?" I sputter, causing cookie crumbs to fall from my mouth.

I spring to my feet. My pulse begins bounding with confusion and alarm. What is Dr. Kent—attending physician and director of the medical student rotation in Lakewood's emergency department—doing in Savannah and Danielle's apartment?

A split-second later, the answer hits me, and my cookie-filled stomach plummets to the floor. Dr. Kent is here to tell me he's taking me off the ED rotation because of what happened today. I guess I shouldn't be surprised. I've only worked two shifts so far, and I've already been a source of major disruption in the department.

As if that wasn't terrible enough, the fact that Dr. Kent is here also means today's incident has come to the attention of the rest of the emergency department's leadership. So it's possible I'm not only about to get removed from this month's rotation—I might be getting kicked out of Lakewood's residency program. In other words, my worst fear has come true: by doing this elective rotation, my reputation at Lakewood has been destroyed before residency even began.

Dr. Kent fixes his dark eyes on mine. I stare back at him miserably and wait for the bomb to drop.

"Quinn," he says. "I wanted to stop by to see how you were doing. I heard about what happened today, and I'm extremely sorry."

I take an extra moment to convince myself I heard him correctly, and then relief washes over me. I don't think Dr. Kent is here to kick me out after all.

"I appreciate you coming over," I recover my wits enough to tell him. "I'm doing well."

Dr. Kent is still studying me in all-seriousness. "Is there anything I can do to help?"

I shake my head. "No, but thank you for asking." I motion to Savannah and Danielle. "They've been a great support and helped me with everything I've needed."

Dr. Kent's attention shifts to Savannah and then down to the cookies and hot chocolate mugs on the floor. He unexpectedly breaks into a grin.

"Ah." Dr. Kent peers at Savannah once more, his charming grin widening. "I assume this is part of that girl-code thing you say I won't ever quite understand?"

Savannah tips back her head and laughs. "Precisely."

I arch an eyebrow while looking at the two of them. From the way Dr. Kent is smiling at Savannah, I would almost say he's being flirtatious with her. Am I missing something here?

Savannah's cheeks remain rosy as she goes on talking to Dr. Kent. "Though you may never understand, however, I have a sneaking suspicion you would still happily take some of these girl-code cookies along with you to your overnight shift tonight."

Dr. Kent chuckles. "I certainly wouldn't complain."

My jaw goes increasingly slack as I continue observing the way Dr. Kent and Savannah are bantering with one another. Yes, I am definitely missing something.

"Good," Savannah tells him. She heads toward the kitchen. "Because we made far more cookies than we could ever get through on our own, so there are plenty to share."

Savannah disappears from view. Dr. Kent turns my way. I quickly shut my mouth, pretending as though I wasn't just staring at him in total confusion.

Dr. Kent's demeanor grows serious once more. "Again, I'm immensely sorry about what occurred, Quinn. I was glad to hear from Dylan that the man was arrested. A warning will be added to the patient's chart, so if he ever returns to the ED, staff will take the appropriate precautions." He exhales. "What else can we do to support you? Would you like to modify your schedule? Take a few days off?"

"I appreciate you asking, but I should be able to handle my schedule as it is," I reply. "In fact, I think it'll be a good thing for me to get back to the ED."

Dr. Kent nods understandingly. "You have my personal cell number in your orientation packet, so don't hesitate to call me if you change your mind or think of anything else we can do for you."

"Thank you, Doctor Kent."

"You're more than welcome."

Savannah returns from the kitchen, holding a gallon-sized plastic baggie that contains so many cookies she can barely get it to close. She hands over the baggie to Dr. Kent.

"Fuel to keep you going during your overnight shift, and plenty to share with the rest of the ED staff."

"Who said anything about sharing?" Dr. Kent grins at her again before he leans in and gives Savannah a kiss. "Thanks."

My eyebrows nearly blast off the top of my head.

Dr. Kent's phone starts to ring. He steps away from Savannah, pulls the phone from his shirt pocket, and puts it to his ear.

"Doctor Kent," he answers while striding out of the room.

Savannah doesn't seem to notice the way I'm gawking at her. Humming to herself, she makes her way over to the couch and drops down beside Danielle.

Danielle moves to take another sip of her drink, but when she sees me staring, she stops with her mug halfway to her lips. "Um, Quinn? Is everything all right?"

I blink and point in the direction Dr. Kent went. "That was Doctor Kent."

Savannah and Danielle exchange a perplexed glance and then set confused stares on me.

I give up trying to be subtle and look Savannah directly in the eyes. "You kissed Doctor Kent."

Savannah goes totally still for a long moment, and then her face becomes bright red. "Oh my gosh!" She claps a hand over her mouth, and I can't tell if she's horrified or about to laugh. "I never told you!"

Danielle's eyes are wider than mine as she turns Savannah's way. "You never told Quinn?"

"No." Savannah groans, dropping her head in her hand. "I was going to tell her this evening, but with everything that happened, I forgot."

I'm looking fast between them. "Tell me what?"

Savannah lifts her head and shows an apologetic smile. "That Wes and I are dating."

I need a second to process this information. "You're dating Doctor Kent?"

"Yes. We've been dating since last August. We try to keep things pretty discreet around the hospital, of course."

Once I finish registering what Savannah said, I break into a smile of my own. "That's great. It looks like the two of you are super happy together."

"They are. They're a perfect match," Danielle chimes in. "For the record, it was obvious to me from the day they met that they were soulmates." She nudges Savannah playfully. "However, it took you guys a hot minute to acknowledge how you felt about one another." She pauses before adding, "I suppose, though, juggling the med student-attending dynamic didn't make it any easier."

"No, it definitely did not," Savannah agrees. She then tells me, "Wes was my ED attending when we first met, so you can imagine how that wound up adding a layer of complexity to it all."

"Yikes." I take a seat. "I bet that was hard."

"It was, but I definitely can't complain. We figured things out, and I couldn't be happier." Savannah glances in the direction Dr. Kent went, and her eyes sparkle with a look of delight. "I think when two people are in love, they somehow just find a way to make their relationship work, you know?"

A heavy ache suddenly presses upon my chest. I pull the blanket closer around me and don't reply.

Danielle flicks her eyes my way. Her brows pull together. "Sorry, Quinn. We didn't mean to bring up a bunch of lovey-dovey stuff after you broke up with your boyfriend."

Savannah makes a choking sound. "What? Quinn, you recently broke up with someone?"

I sigh. "Yeah."

Savannah appears horrified. "That's awful! I'm so sorry! I didn't know!"

"No worries." I restore my smile. "It's a long story, but the gist is that Chad and I have had this on-again-off-again relationship since our first year of med school. The night before I moved out here, Chad broke up with me . . . again." I blow a curl from my eyes. "However, I think he already wants to get back together . . . again."

Savannah and Danielle exchange another glance.

"Don't get me wrong, Chad is terrific," I feel compelled to add. "He's kind, considerate, funny, and super smart. We're a great match. We've just run into problems with timing and circumstances over the years."

Before either Savannah or Danielle can respond, Dr. Kent returns to the room.

"Sorry about that." He takes a seat beside Savannah. "It was a call regarding final plans for the new department. I—"

There's another knock on the front door.

"Come in, Joel!" Danielle calls out.

I hear the door get opened and shut, and soon Joel strolls into the room. He's carrying bags of Thai takeout food, and its savory smells begin wafting through the air.

"Hi, everyone," Joel greets us. "I brought dinner, in case anyone might be hungry for real food." He glances at the cookie plates and mugs on the floor, and he grins. He lifts the bags of takeout food a little higher. "I'll go put these in the kitchen."

Danielle is gazing at him adoringly. "Thanks, hon."

Joel heads into the kitchen to drop off the food. He returns to the main room, takes a place on the couch next to Danielle, and plants a kiss on her cheek.

I experience another ache in my heart. Savannah and Wes, and Danielle and Joel, are clearly making their relationships thrive despite the rigors of their medical training, work, and other challenges life undoubtedly throws in their paths. Why haven't Chad and I been able to do the same?

"Oh, hey, before I forget, I wanted to ask you all something," Joel says. "I'm planning to host a party for Danielle's birthday, and I wanted to make sure everyone will be available."

"Huh?" Danielle fixes a quizzical stare on him. "We've never hosted a party for my birthday before."

Joel shrugs. "I know, but I thought it would be cool to do something this year, since it might be the last hurrah before some of your friends move away for residency."

Danielle appears to be thinking this over. "You're right. It would be fun."

"And since folks are so busy," Joel goes on, "I figured we should start telling people now, so they can have time to save the date or free up their schedules."

Danielle displays a renewed smile. "You know, the more I think about it, the more I like the plan!" She kisses him. "Great idea, hon!"

"Thanks." Joel seems pleased as he drapes an arm across Danielle's shoulders. "So in addition to everyone here, I was thinking we could invite your med school friends, including Rachel, Austin, and Tyler. And Dylan and your parents. And your friends who live in the area. What do you think?"

"I think it's perfect. Birthday or not, it'll be really special to get everyone together before so many of us start the next phases of our lives." Danielle pauses. "What day of the week is my birthday on this year, anyway?"

"May first is on a Friday," Joel replies. "Thankfully, that means a lot of people should already have the evening off. For those who don't, I'm hoping they'll have enough advanced notice to be able to free themselves up for the night."

Savannah shows a thumbs-up. "It's a fabulous idea, Joel. Count me in, obviously."

Dr. Kent is checking his phone. "Me, too. I should be able to trade a shift to free up my schedule."

"Awesome." Joel peers my way. "What about you? Are you free?"

"Me?" I ask, not hiding my surprise.

Danielle almost appears affronted. "Of course, Quinn! You're our friend, and if we're having a party, you're absolutely invited!"

I smile gratefully. "Then, yes, I should be able to join. My ED rotation will have ended the day before, and I can certainly stay in town an extra day before starting the drive home." I look between the gals sheepishly. "That is, as long as you don't mind me staying here an extra night."

"Of course not," Danielle declares.

"You're welcome to stay as long as you want," Savannah agrees.

"Cool. It sounds settled, then." Joel turns to Danielle. "Tell me what you think about this idea: I was envisioning an outdoor dinner party at that lakefront Italian restaurant you love."

"Are you serious? That's my favorite eatery in the world!" Danielle clasps her hands to her chest. "Let's do it!"

"Consider it done." Joel gets to his feet and looks at the rest of us. "All right, all this talk about restaurants has reminded me of how hungry I am. Does anyone else want Thai food?" He glances down at the cookies again. "That is, is anyone else even hungry?"

"Hungry doesn't matter tonight, hon." Danielle stands up beside him. "We're *indulging*. It's a girl-code thing."

Joel quirks an eyebrow. "Huh?"

Dr. Kent gets off the couch and gives Joel one of those man-slaps on the shoulder. "I've found it's easier to go along with it and not ask too many questions."

Savannah snickers as she stands. "Exactly. I may have eaten countless cookies and consumed two huge hot chocolates, but I don't care tonight. I would love to have some takeout food." She turns to me with a humorous gleam in her eye. "How about you?"

I push myself up from the recliner. "In a show of solidarity for my girls, I echo your sentiment: bring on dinner."

Danielle points at me. "And that's one of the many reasons why we love you, Quinn."

We laugh and make our way into the kitchen. Soon, the sounds of clanking dishes and lively conversations are filling the air. Once my plate is piled high, I head to the table and take a seat next to Danielle. I'm enjoying my first bite when I see Danielle pull her phone from her pocket and read a new text. Unexpectedly, she then raises her eyes from her phone to peer at me intently.

"Everything all right?" I ask her, blotting the corners of my mouth with a napkin.

Danielle leans closer and lowers her voice. "Dylan just texted to ask how you're doing."

The sound of Dylan's name causes something delightfully warm to fill my chest, yet I keep my demeanor unaffected as I reply, "That's really nice of him."

Danielle wags her eyebrows. "I know," she says to me before ducking her head and texting a response with supersonic speed.

I shift my attention back to my meal, but I can no longer focus on food. I reach into the pocket of my flannel pants, pull out my own phone, and glance down at it. The warm feeling within me vanishes. Chad hasn't tried to check in on me. No voicemail, no email, and no text. Nothing.

I return my phone to my pocket and look around the table. Simply by the way they're interacting over a casual takeout dinner, it's clear Wes and Savannah are totally in tune with each other and completely in love. The same goes for Joel and Danielle; when observing them, there's no question they're absolutely crazy about one another.

What about Chad and me? We love each other, too. So why aren't we able to make our relationship work? Why doesn't it feel as though we have the *spark* these couples have?

I lower my eyes, mulling this over. I'm convinced Chad wants to talk about reconciling again. If love is about patience and forgiveness—and if Chad and I are in love—isn't it right to give him another chance?

Eleven

"No! I want to see him right now!"

A woman's scream rips through the emergency department, causing a rare split-second of total silence as everyone stops what they're doing to figure out where the yelling is coming from.

Standing up from my workstation, I follow people's stares down the patient-and-stretcher-lined hallway that leads to the double doors separating the treatment area of the ED from the waiting room on the other side. One of the doors is slightly ajar; it appears a nurse triggered it to open so she could call for the next patient from the waiting room.

The screaming continues, and it doesn't take me long to spot the source of the ruckus: a woman with bleached blonde hair who's wearing a low-cut shirt and a short skirt. She's trying to force her way through the open door to enter the treatment area of the ED. Meanwhile, the nurse who opened the door is making a noble—though futile—effort to block the screaming woman from getting through.

Ignoring the nurse's instructions to remain in the waiting room, the woman finishes bulldozing her way into the treatment area and begins advancing down the corridor, passing a long lineup of patients on hallway stretchers who are gawking at her. From the unsteadiness of the woman's gait as she draws closer, I'm guessing she has enjoyed more than a few drinks this evening.

"Where is he?" the woman demands while mascara smears down her cheeks, and her crazed, bloodshot eyes flick around the department.

The nurse, Pete, approaches the woman while speaking to her in a calm, deescalating tone. The woman, however, isn't having any of it. She spins toward Pete and clumsily begins swinging her purse out in front of her as if she's wielding nunchucks.

"Stay away!" she screeches.

Pete wisely retreats a few steps.

More commotion fills the hallway. I see security guards gathering, and other patients and visitors poking their heads out of exam rooms to see what's going on. All the while, the woman keeps stampeding toward the charge nurse's station, snorting like an enraged version of the bison I saw at Yellowstone.

"Where is he? Where's my baby? I demand to see my baby! You can't keep me from him!"

I'm hit with a sudden pang of sadness for this woman. Her baby? Has something awful happened to this poor woman's child?

Two of the security guards are moving in on the woman from behind, and the other guard is speaking into the walkie talkie on his shoulder to request reinforcements. The woman either doesn't notice or doesn't care; she continues staggering nearer while haphazardly flailing her purse, almost striking a few patients and staff members in the process.

"Where is he? Where's my baby?" The woman's speech is heavily slurred, and I'm catching potent whiffs of alcohol radiating from her direction. "I demand to see my baby! Baby? Baby, where are you?"

"I'm in here, babe!"

The shouted response—which was most definitely uttered by an adult male and not a child—came from the nearest resuscitation bay. Like everyone else in the department, I now look that way. The door leading into the resuscitation bay is wide open, providing a view of the inside. I see a male patient in a hospital gown lying flat on his back on a stretcher. The man has been placed in a cervical collar, and he's connected to a cardiac monitor. I also see one of the ED doctors seated on a stool beside the stretcher, and if the yellow protective gown, hair cover, eye protection, mask, face shield, and gloves the doctor is wearing are any indication, he or she is in the middle of performing some sort of procedure.

"Baby, I hear you!" the woman screeches, spinning frantically. "Where are you?"

"In here, babe! In here!" the man shouts again, his speech as drunkenly slurred as the woman's.

"Baby!" The woman dashes into the resuscitation bay, leaving the approaching security guards in her wake. She reaches the foot of the man's stretcher, lets out a horrified gasp, and clutches her hands to her chest. "Oh, baby, what are these terrible people doing to you? Oh, baby, I'm so sorry they're hurting you!"

I hear a rumble of conversation at the charge nurse's station, and I check that way. The same nurse who gallantly tried to stop the woman from infiltrating the treatment area is now speaking with the charge nurse, Laura.

"Per EMS, that woman is the girlfriend of the patient in the resuscitation bay," the nurse is explaining to Laura. "The patient was driving while intoxicated, and he rolled his car. The girlfriend was driving behind him when the rollover occurred, and she called nine-one-one. Per the EMS crews and police who responded to the accident, the girlfriend seemed as intoxicated as her boyfriend. She demanded a ride to the hospital in the same ambulance—literally on the same stretcher—as her boyfriend, and she actually became combative when she was told it was against EMS policy for her to do so." The nurse glances toward the resuscitation bay with a shake of her head. "The girlfriend was transported here separately, but as soon as the ambulance came to a stop outside, she jumped out of the rig and ran into the ED via the main entrance, winding up in the waiting room. When

I opened the security door to bring someone else back for treatment, the girlfriend bolted in here."

My eyes are getting wider as I return my attention to the resuscitation bay. I start maneuvering through the crowd to get a better view of what's happening inside the room. The girlfriend is still wailing and aimlessly pacing. The patient continues crying along with her, his gasping sobs interspersed with loud hiccups. Meanwhile, as I can see from my new vantage point, the doctor at the bedside is suturing a large, jagged laceration on the patient's right arm. And it's only the first of numerous lacerations that will need repair.

I cringe at the sight. Those aren't simple lacerations the doctor can just walk away from until the commotion dies down. No, that doctor is stuck trying to suture amidst the melodrama— a situation that's not only profoundly distracting but also dangerous, considering how emotionally labile the patient and his girlfriend are behaving while there are sharp instruments within reach.

"Baby, I love you! You're the best!" The girlfriend kicks over a hazardous-waste bin before running back to the patient's stretcher.

"No, you're the best!" the patient declares at the top of his lungs. "You are the very best, babe!"

I hear someone come up beside me and let out a low whistle. "What's going on in there?"

I glance to my right. Dr. Santiago is standing next to me, and he's watching what's unfolding inside the resuscitation bay with his head tipped slightly to one side.

"The patient's girlfriend arrived," I tell him, figuring that's all I need to say.

"Ah." Dr. Santiago seems to understand perfectly. He observes the spectacle a moment or two more, and then he makes eye contact with Laura. "What's the status of that guy's inpatient bed?"

"His inpatient bed is ready, but they won't accept him up on the floor until all his lacerations are repaired," Laura states, and from the look on her face, she's clearly unhappy about the situation. "The doc in there is doing a great job, but given the number of lacs the patient sustained, it's going to be quite a while before we can move the patient out of here."

"Baby, I love you so much!" the girlfriend announces, using her purse to smack an IV pole for emphasis.

"I love you, too, babe!" the patient bellows in response, his voice warbling with emotion.

The security guards are congregating outside the resuscitation bay, talking in low voices while they strategize how to proceed. As I've learned in the few years since starting my medical training, it isn't easy to deescalate someone who's behaving irrationally, under the influence, or otherwise violent or uncooperative. You can never predict who will comply and who will become even more of a danger to self or others. If you move in too fast, someone may lash out. If you wait too long to intervene, someone may have time to cause harm that could have otherwise been avoided. It's a fine line, and often there are only seconds to decide what to do.

Laura lets out an exasperated sigh and continues speaking to Dr. Santiago. "Given how slammed we are down here, you would think the admitting team would be willing to do some of the lac repairs up on the floor so we could free up the resuscitation bay for another patient. But the admitting team refused."

Dr. Santiago removes his stethoscope from around his neck and slips it into the pocket of his scrubs. "I'll go assist with suturing. Hopefully, with two of us working, it'll—"

"Jesse?" someone calls out.

Laura, Dr. Santiago, and I all look toward the sound. Another ED nurse—a guy with dark hair and dark eyes who's probably around my age—is hurrying our way.

"Hey, Hadi," Dr. Santiago greets him. "What's up?"

Hadi comes to a stop in front of Dr. Santiago. "Would you come take a look at the patient who's boarding in Room Three? She's becoming more unstable, and I think she needs to be started on pressors. She was Henry Ingram's patient, and he got her admitted to the ICU a while ago, but the intensivist is busy managing another crashing patient, and Henry is tied up with a STEMI."

"I'll be right there," Dr. Santiago replies.

"Thanks." Hadi jogs off, going back in the direction of Room Three.

Dr. Santiago glances at the resuscitation bay again and then gives Laura an apologetic look. "I'll check on Hadi's patient, and as soon as I'm done, I'll help with suturing."

"I can assist with suturing the lacs," I hear myself say.

Both Dr. Santiago and Laura stop and turn toward me.

I flinch, wishing I could retract my offer. I shouldn't insert myself into patient care when I haven't been invited. That's the type of thing a new, annoyingly over-eager med student who doesn't actually have a clue about what's going on would do. Considering how crucial it is for me to establish a good reputation around here, getting labeled as "nosy" or "annoying" definitely isn't going to help.

I clear my throat and go on, "I mean, I discharged my last patient, so I'm caught up and happy to help, but only if you would like me to assist."

Laura shoots Dr. Santiago a glance. "Some of those lacs are pretty complex," she tells him, sounding wary.

Dr. Santiago keeps his eyes on me. "Thanks, Quinn. All the supplies you need should be in there."

Saying no more, Dr. Santiago strides off toward Room Three, leaving Laura and me behind.

I cough and face her. "So I'll, um, head in there and start suturing."

"I'll send in Finn to assist you." Laura starts typing on her computer keyboard before adding in monotone, "Good luck."

Frankly, I'm not sure if Laura's words are meant to be a help or a warning. With a silent sigh, I put my attention on the resuscitation bay once more. Though the patient and his girlfriend are still wailing, the doctor is somehow remaining focused on the laceration repair. However, despite the doctor's impressive concentration, given the size and complexity of the wound—plus the many other lacerations the patient sustained that also need stitches—getting the patient ready for admission is going to be a slow, arduous process.

I mentally kick myself again for offering to help. Even from where I'm standing, it's evident that several of the lacs are more complicated than anything I've sutured before. What if I suture one of them incorrectly? What if I can't figure out how to sew some of them at all? What if I only wind up slowing down care because I have no clue what I'm doing? Not only will I leave the patient with scars or worse, I'll humiliate myself in front of the doctor who's in the room, prove Laura was right to doubt me, and shatter Dr. Santiago's confidence that I could handle these types of lacerations.

I was an idiot for offering to help, but there's nothing I can do about it now.

I tuck my curls behind my ears, weave past the throng, and enter the resuscitation bay.

"Baby!" the girlfriend is yelling. "You're so brave! I love you so much! Why . . ." she trails off when she notices me. Her eyes narrow, exaggerating the raccoon-like effect of her smeared mascara. "Who are you, and what are you doing in here?"

There's a pulse of quiet. The girlfriend continues skewering me with a glare. The patient—who can't turn his head because of the collar around his neck—snaps his buggy eyes in my direction. The doctor stops suturing, looks up at me, pauses, and then resumes working on repairing the laceration in the patient's right arm.

I shift my eyes between the patient and his girlfriend while adopting a professional smile. "My name is Quinn Meyers. I'm a fourth-year medical student, and I'm here to assist with suturing."

Before either of them respond, Finn swoops into the resuscitation bay. He pulls open the drawers of the cart that contains laceration repair supplies, and he starts rummaging through the items stuffed inside.

"What size gloves?" Finn asks me over his shoulder.

"Seven," I reply while hurriedly donning the procedure gown, hair cover, eye protection, and mask Finn tosses to me in rapid succession.

"Great." Finn lastly pulls out a packaged pair of gloves from the cart and shuts the drawer. "I'll get you set up."

Finn grabs a stool and rolls it across the floor, positioning it directly across the patient's stretcher from where the doctor is seated. Next, Finn positions a tray beside the empty stool and covers it with a sterile pad. Still moving fast, Finn proceeds to place out on the sterile field some sutures, a suture kit, sterile gauze, bottles of saline, lidocaine, syringes, needles, and anti-septic swabs.

"All right. You're good to go. The wounds have been irrigated already." Finn hands me the packaged gloves, and without waiting for my reply, he jogs out of the resuscitation bay, headed for a hallway patient who's screaming something about wanting a tuna sandwich.

"Thanks," I call after him.

Finn disappears into the madness, and I turn around to face the patient's stretcher once more. The girlfriend is still scowling, and she begins tapping her shoe in a show of impatience. The patient says nothing as he keeps tracking me with his eyes. The doctor continues placing sutures in the patient's gaping wound.

I guess this is my cue.

I wet my lips behind my mask and take a seat on the empty stool, which I slide as close as I can to the stretcher. The only sounds filling the room now are the beeping of the cardiac monitor, the girlfriend's shoe tapping the floor, and the patient's heavy breathing. Leaning farther forward, I lower my head and begin surveying the lacerations on the left side of the patient's body, trying to decide which one needs to be repaired first.

"I appreciate you coming in to help, Quinn," I hear the doctor say in a familiar, deep voice.

My heart lurches, and an electric sensation zips down my spine. Slowly, I raise my head.

The doctor seated across from me might be almost entirely concealed by the PPE he's wearing, but there's no mistaking his green eyes, which I have a clear view of now that they're fixed on mine. I haven't seen Dylan since he came to my rescue several days ago, and the sight of him now ignites within me a sensation that's simultaneously thrilling and petrifying.

"Hi, Doctor Gillespie," I squeak out, relieved to note the bruise adjacent to his eye has nearly healed. "It's no problem. I'm happy to help. I . . ."

I trail off when I realize how close Dylan and I have gotten to one another while we're both leaning in over the patient. There's a sudden swell of heat in my chest, and my heart starts drumming even harder. The next instant, a shocking thought strikes me with perfect clarity:

I think I'm attracted to Dylan.

Something between a gasp and a choke gets stuck in my throat. Actually, I don't *think* I'm attracted to Dylan Gillespie, I'm *certain* I'm attracted to him. I'm attracted to everything about him—his wit, intelligence, looks, kindness, and bravery. Since the first day I met him, I've been drawn to Dylan in a way I've never been drawn to a man before, and that magnetic draw has only gotten stronger ever since.

Panic begins coursing through me. I can't be attracted to Dylan. I can't get swept up in feelings for him—no matter how amazing they might be—when I'm still trying to determine how I feel about Chad. I believe relationships require loyalty, so I shouldn't walk away from Chad without at least trying to sort out things between us.

Right?

I tear my gaze from Dylan and stare down at the patient's wounds. Forcing myself to steady my breathing, I make myself concentrate on my task. I zero in on my first target for suturing: a long laceration on the patient's left forearm, which is oozing blood.

"Sir, your wounds have already been thoroughly irrigated, so I'm just going to do a quick cleaning of the area, numb it up, and then start placing stitches," I explain while I begin donning my gloves.

"No problem, babe," the patient replies, the odor of alcohol strong on his breath. He chuckles while looking me up and down. "You can do whatever you would like to me. I definitely won't mind."

I stop with one glove halfway on my hand. Dylan also pauses what he's doing, his slightly narrowed eyes shifting to the patient's face. The patient flashes me a grin, revealing a mouthful of missing and decaying teeth.

"Excuse me?" the girlfriend suddenly shouts, pointing an accusatory finger in the patient's face as she looms over him. "*Excuse me*?

What did you say to her? Did you call this girl, *babe*?"

The patient laughs and looks up at his girlfriend. "Oh, babe, I didn't mean it! I was just having fun! You know you're the only woman for me!"

The girlfriend flares her nostrils and retreats from the stretcher while shaking her head. "You know what? You've done this to me one too many times! I'm over this! I am *so over this*!" She slings her purse onto her shoulder. "I'm getting a ride home and eating the leftover brisket all by myself! You're on your own!"

"No! Not the brisket!" The patient cries, his voice cracking. He looks frantic while watching his girlfriend stomp toward the door. "Don't eat all the brisket without me! I love you, babe!"

The woman only shows him a hand before she marches out of the resuscitation bay without looking back.

There's a long, awkward pause, which is filled only by the beeping sound coming from the monitor. At last, the patient exhales a heavy sigh and says:

"This sucks, man. I really love brisket. I'm gonna miss it."

A laugh nearly escapes me, and I look over at Dylan. He meets my gaze with an unmistakable gleam of amusement in his eyes, and I can tell he has broken into a smile behind his mask. We watch one another for a second or two, and then we both resume suturing. Although I'm concentrating on what I'm doing, I find I also remain fully aware of Dylan. I notice his movements. His breathing. His eyes occasionally darting my way. His hands so near to mine as we work.

"How are things going?"

Dr. Santiago's voice snaps me to awareness. I sit up fast, and as I watch my attending come into the resuscitation bay, I realize I have no idea how much time has passed or how long I've been in here.

"I'm done suturing the wounds on this side," I inform Dr. Santiago while using scissors to snip the last stitch. "But it's Doctor Gillespie who has been handling the bulk of the work."

Dr. Santiago stops at the foot of the stretcher to survey the patient's repaired lacerations. He then says to me:

"Take your time finishing up. When you're done, come find me. One of my patients has an interesting CT finding I would like to show you."

"Will do." I set my instruments onto the tray. "Thanks."

Dr. Santiago turns to Dylan. "Great work in here. I'll inform Laura you're nearly done, so she can start prepping to get this patient transferred upstairs."

"Thanks, Jesse." Dylan places another stitch into the final laceration that needs repair, which is on the patient's right leg.

Dr. Santiago leaves the room. Dylan continues working. I slide my stool away from the stretcher and get to my feet, taking the chance to twist my torso and stretch out my back muscles, which have kinked up after being hunched over the patient for so long. I then clean up my work space, place the used instruments in the sink, and make sure all the needles are discarded in the sharps bin.

"Is there anything else I can help you with in here?" I ask Dylan while I remove my procedure gown and hair cover.

Before Dylan can answer, however, the patient pipes up:

"Yeah. Call my *ex*-girlfriend and see if you can convince her to save me a couple slices of the brisket."

I remove my mask, letting my smile show. "I'll see what I can do, sir."

I sense Dylan looking at me, and I check his way. Once again, there's humor in his eyes. A moment later, however, his eyes abruptly lose their luster. He clears his throat, lowers his head, and resumes suturing.

"Thanks again, Quinn," he says in a distinctly businesslike tone.

"You're welcome."

I watch him a few seconds more, but Dylan doesn't look up again, and so I turn away. As I exit the resuscitation bay, I'm instantly submerged in the non-stop ruckus of the main department. Above the noise, I hear someone call out:

"Quinn!"

Peering down the congested hallway, I spot Danielle coming toward me, and I give her a wave. Before I left the apartment today, Danielle mentioned she would be working a shift that overlapped with mine, and I've been looking forward to seeing her in the ED this afternoon.

As Danielle draws closer, the throng parts enough for me to see that there's someone walking alongside her. Based on the other gal's scrubs and crisply pressed, short white coat, I'm guessing she's also a med student. She's petite, she has big eyes and short, dark blonde hair, and she has a rather serious expression on her face.

Danielle stops in front of me and motions to the person who's with her. "Quinn, I'm super excited to introduce you to Rachel Nelson. Rachel is also a fourth-year med student, and she's going to be part of your emergency medicine residency class here at Lakewood. Isn't that cool?"

"Wow, really?" I smile at Rachel. "It's great to meet you, Rachel."

"It's wonderful to meet you, too." Rachel's serious expression quickly relents, and she shows a genuine, shy smile in return. "Lynn Prentis mentioned you were doing an ED rotation this month, and I've been looking forward to introducing myself." She tucks her hair behind her ears. "I'm on an elective nephrology rotation, and I was down here doing a consult on a patient when Danielle told me you were working. I'm glad to finally have a chance to say hello."

"Me, too," I reply sincerely.

"Oh, I almost forgot!" Danielle faces Rachel. "I wanted to let you know that Joel is arranging a shin-dig for my birthday on May first, and I'm hoping you and Austin will be able to save the date."

"May the first?" Rachel promptly whips out a phone from the pocket of her white coat and taps the screen a couple times. "Good news: we're both off that day. Our rotations wrap the day before, and we don't start our next rotations until the Monday afterward." She starts typing something on her phone. "I'm making a note that Austin and I should keep our calendars clear."

"Hooray!" Danielle does a clapping motion with her hands. "I'll text you with details . . . as soon as I have any idea what the details are. Joel is doing the planning, so I'm waiting for him to fill me in."

"We'll be looking forward to it." Rachel puts away her phone. She smiles again while her eyes shift between Danielle and me. "I need to go meet my team for afternoon rounds, but I'm excited for your party, Danielle, and I look forward to seeing you again, Quinn."

"Likewise," I tell her. "See you soon."

Rachel gives us a wave before she spins on her heels and scurries out the back exit of the department, checking her pager as she goes.

Danielle watches Rachel depart, and then she grins and tells me, "Austin Cahill is Rachel's boyfriend. The two of them had an epic clash on the first day of med school—about the usefulness of wood glue, of all things—and they wound up sparring almost every day after that. It was obvious they were totally attracted to one another, but it took them *forever* to figure it out." She's still grinning as she shakes her head.

"Thankfully, Rachel and Austin finally recognized how they really felt about each other. They started dating a month or so after Wes and Savannah did, and they've been practically inseparable ever since." She giggles. "I can't wait for you to see them together, Quinn. Rachel and Austin are the epitome of opposites attract. They couldn't be more polar opposite from one another, and yet they're somehow perfect together."

I remain quiet while my gaze traces the route Rachel took to leave the ED. Rachel and Austin . . . Savannah and Wes . . . Danielle and Joel . . . they're all successfully navigating devoted, stable relationships even though they're juggling the demands of work and medical training. They're not breaking up every time things get tough. They're not dragging their significant others through an on-again-off-again situation. They're prioritizing their relationships and making them work. So I don't understand why . . .

I emerge from my thoughts when I notice Danielle peering at me inquisitively. I quickly put on another smile.

"Thanks for introducing me to Rachel. It was awesome meeting her," I say before I do a quick scan of the department. "Now I think I'm supposed to go find Doctor Santiago. He said he had an interesting CT finding to show me."

Danielle gives me a thumbs-up. "Cool. I'm gonna go join the OBGYN team for rounds, since there aren't any ED patients for me to see at the moment. I'll talk to you soon, though."

Danielle gives me a last smile and heads for the exit. Before I can even collect my thoughts, an announcement blares out from the PA system:

"Code Blue. ETA ten minutes. Code Blue. ETA ten minutes."

I jump and whip around. Past the patients who are crowded along the corridor, I see several ED staff members hurrying toward one of the unoccupied resuscitation bays.

"How about a code, Quinn?"

Dr. Santiago appears at my side. He seems as unfazed as ever, despite the fact that he's about to supervise the ED team's efforts to try to bring someone back to life.

I attempt to appear equally unfazed. "Sure. I'm ready," I lie.

"Great. Let's go."

Dr. Santiago heads into the resuscitation bay, and I follow him inside. The huge room is packed and buzzing with commotion as everyone prepares to receive a patient in cardiac arrest. Kathy is readying the monitor. Hadi is prepping IV starts and bags of fluid. Another nurse, Carrie, is logging into the computer. Finn is wheeling the code cart into position, and a second tech is setting up the ECG machine. Soon, a pharmacist arrives, and he's trailed by the ED social worker, Dwayne. Next, one of the radiology techs enters the room and pushes a portable x-ray machine over to a corner to wait.

Henry Ingram, the third-year resident who interviewed me last December, enters the resuscitation bay and positions himself at the foot of the empty stretcher in the middle of the room. Henry is wearing black scrubs, and he has his hair pulled into a short ponytail at the nape of his neck. Something about Henry's aura is unconventional in a cool-and-in-control kind of way . . . and speaking of being in control, based on where he has put himself, he's going to be running this code.

Henry looks over at Dr. Santiago and does a double take when he notices me.

"Hey, Quinn," Henry says. "Nice to see you again."

I have to stop my mouth from falling open. Frankly, I'm not sure what surprises me more: that Henry remembers me, or that he seems so chill even though he'll be running the code. In contrast, though I'm only here to observe, I've been flogging my brain to make sure I recall every detail of each cardiac arrest algorithm.

"Hi, Doctor Ingram," I reply. "It's nice to see you again, too."

Henry's attention shifts to Dr. Santiago. "Would you like to let the soon-to-be Doctor Meyers run this one?"

I do a double take. Wait a sec . . . what did Henry say?

Dr. Santiago is nodding. "That's a good idea."

"Then I'll go assist Elly with her two septic patients." Henry steps away from the stretcher and puts his eyes on mine once more. "You'll do great."

Before I can formulate a coherent reply, Henry strides out of the resuscitation bay, leaving me staring after him.

My stomach sinks. I don't want to run this code. Not here. Not in front of everyone. If I screw up at all, the entire ED team will be witness, and word will spread like wildfire. Everyone will lose confidence in my capabilities. My reputation at Lakewood will be wrecked.

Hadi looks up from what he's doing. His brow furrows. "Where did Henry go? Isn't he running this thing?"

I cringe.

Dr. Santiago raises his voice so everyone is able to hear him. "Listen up: our visiting med student, and soon-to-be first-year resident here in Lakewood's ED, Quinn Meyers, will be running this code."

The resuscitation bay drops into silence as each and every person in the room looks over at me.

I shut and reopen my eyes. Unfortunately, everyone is still here. This isn't some sort of a hallucination. This is really happening.

Groaning to myself, I slide to the foot of the stretcher where Henry stood only moments ago. Everyone keeps staring, and it dawns on me that they're all waiting for me to do or say something. I have a sudden urge to run out of the room while screaming incoherently—heck, if

I'm going to obliterate my reputation here at Lakewood, I might as well become a legend in the process. Thankfully, though, the impulse passes, and I'm able to push aside my nerves enough to ask:

"Who will be administering meds?"

"That'll be me," Hadi replies.

"Who's recording?"

Carrie raises her hand. "I am."

I continue scanning the crowd. "Is pharmacy present?"

"Yes."

I turn to the techs. "You'll be alternating chest compressions?"

"Yep."

"Is respiratory therapy here?"

"Yes, I'm here!" A woman with red hair jogs into the room. "I'm Brenna from RT. Sorry I'm late."

I nod to her and resume looking over the group. "Airway?"

"That will be me."

To my surprise, Dylan steps out of the throng. This room is so full that I didn't even know he was in here. He goes to the head of the stretcher and begins checking intubation equipment with Brenna.

I turn to Dr. Santiago, about to say more, when the door of the resuscitation bay is suddenly slammed open. I jump and spin toward the sound.

My patient is here.

An EMS crew rushes in driving a stretcher with the coding patient upon it. One crew member is doing chest compressions. Another crew member is bagging the patient. The third EMT assists the techs with transferring the patient over to the ED stretcher. Before I've even fully processed what's happening, the lead crew member starts shouting report:

"Fifty-six-year-old male. History of an MI. Witnessed by his wife and son to collapse in the kitchen. Wife called nine-one-one and initiated CPR. Upon our arrival, the patient was found to be in pulseless v-tach. One IV placed in the right AC. He has received a total of three shocks and two doses of epi. Total downtime approximately twenty minutes."

The ED team makes fast work of taking over from the EMS crew: a tech begins doing chest compressions, Hadi places an additional IV in the patient's other arm, and Kathy connects the patient to the cardiac monitor. While they keep working, I look to the head of the stretcher and lock eyes with Dylan.

"Secure the airway, Doctor Gillespie."

Holding a traditional laryngoscope in his left hand, Dylan maneuvers the tool into the patient's mouth. Keeping his eyes on his target, Dylan picks up an endotracheal tube from the tray beside him and guides it into the patient's airway. Once the endotracheal tube is in place, Dylan removes the laryngoscope from the patient's mouth, and then Brenna quickly connects the end of the endotracheal tube that's sticking out from between the patient's lips to the compressible bag she has in her hands.

"Good color change," Brenna tells me as she begins administering oxygen and watches the colorimetric capnometer change from purple to yellow.

Dylan uses his stethoscope to listen to the patient's lungs. "Bilateral breath sounds anteriorly."

I turn to the tech. "Hold compressions."

The tech stops pounding on the patient's chest. The room gets tensely still as everyone looks to the monitor. To my dismay, the waveform that begins tracing across the screen confirms the patient is still in v-tach— ventricular tachycardia—a potentially lethal rhythm where the heart isn't properly pumping blood around the body.

"Is there a pulse with that?" I ask, though I fear I already know the answer.

Hadi palpates the patient's neck. "No pulse."

Every passing moment this man remains in pulseless v-tach increases his risk of sustaining permanent damage to his organs, and if we can't convert him back into a normal heart rhythm soon, we won't be able to revive him. But he can't die. He's too young. He has a wife. He has kids.

"Resume compressions, and prepare to shock once at one hundred fifty joules," I instruct.

The tech resumes pushing on the patient's chest. Brenna continues bagging the patient.

Hadi hangs IV fluid. At the same time, Kathy steps over to the defibrillator, which is sitting on top of the code cart, and presses the *charge* button. The defibrillator starts emitting its piercing wail, which rapidly rises in pitch before changing to a two-tone beep to indicate it's charged.

"Everyone clear," I order.

The tech stops compressions, and all the members of the team step back from the stretcher. While the machine keeps beeping, I make eye contact with Kathy once more.

"Administer the shock," I tell her.

Kathy pushes a red button on the machine that's marked with a lightning bolt. The patient's body momentarily arches as a burst of electricity is sent through the man's heart.

"Resume compressions," I say to the tech. I turn to Hadi and the pharmacist. "Administer one of epi."

As chest compressions start again, the pharmacist hands Hadi a syringe containing epinephrine. Within seconds, Hadi has the medication pushed through the patient's IV.

I view the clock, making a mental note of when this two-minute interval will be over and I'll need to order another rhythm check. Anxiously watching the seconds tick by, I begin racking my brain for what else I can do to save this man. Suddenly, an idea hits me, and I look over at Dr. Santiago.

"Can someone page interventional cardiology? Given this patient's history of an MI, we should probably get the interventionalist down here."

"I'll do that, Jesse, so you can stay and supervise," Dylan offers, already moving for the door.

"Thanks," Dr. Santiago calls after him.

Dylan leaves the room. I resume watching the clock, and once the rest of the two-minute interval passes, I lower my eyes to the team.

"Hold compressions."

The room again goes silent. Like everyone else, I've got my attention fixed on the monitor. I realize I'm nervously clenching my hands into fists at my sides as I wait. After an agonizingly protracted pause, the monitor blips, and a new waveform starts tracing across the screen. My eyes widen when I see the waveform appears to be a coordinated cardiac rhythm.

I turn to Hadi. "Pulse?"

Hadi feels the patient's neck, and he smiles. "There's a pulse."

I'm shaking as I raise my voice to address the whole team. "All right, everybody, we have return of spontaneous circulation. Until the cardiac team arrives, let's get him cooled and—"

The rest of my words are drowned out when a group of people enters the room. Leading the way is a tall gentleman who appears to be in his early sixties. His hair is neatly trimmed, he's dressed in green scrubs and a long white coat, and everything about him just screams he's an interventional cardiologist. With him is a woman whose badge indicates she's a cardiac ICU nurse.

She's followed by a man and a woman whose IDs indicate they're from the cath lab team. Dylan enters next. He's closely followed by Laura, who's talking on the phone with people who are prepping the cath lab.

The cardiologist glances at the cardiac monitor before setting his attention on me. "What do we have?"

"History of an MI two years prior," I reply, my words shaking from nerves and adrenaline. "Witnessed to become unresponsive at home. CPR started by family. On scene, found to be in pulseless v-tach and resuscitation efforts commenced. After ED arrival, he had one additional shock and one more dose of epi. We have return of spontaneous circulation."

"Great." The cardiologist steps closer to the stretcher. "We'll take it from here."

There's an explosion of renewed activity as the ED and cath lab teams prepare the patient for transport. Within moments, the patient is being pushed out the door with Brenna jogging alongside the stretcher as she keeps bagging him. The cardiologist follows, and the rest of the cath lab team swiftly trails after him.

An instant later, like a storm has passed, the resuscitation bay grows calm. Hadi quietly departs to help care for other ED patients. The techs begin cleaning up the mess created during the code. Carrie starts restocking supply carts. Dylan leaves to assess a new patient who just arrived by ambulance. Kathy commences with updating the patient's information in the computer. Someone from environmental services arrives to mop the floor. The radiology tech wheels the x-ray machine out the door, and the pharmacist departs behind him. As the room empties out, the change in atmosphere is so pronounced that if anyone walked in here now, they would never believe the intensity that gripped this place only minutes ago.

Out of the corner of my eye, I see Dr. Santiago coming toward me. I shift his way. Before either of us can say anything, however, Hadi pokes his head back into the resuscitation bay and calls out:

"Doctor Santiago, can you come again to Room Three?"

Dr. Santiago stops in his tracks. "You got it." Changing course, he strides out of the room while saying to me over his shoulder, "Feel free to pick up another patient, if they bring one in from the waiting room. However, given how full this place is, I'm guessing we're going to be on lockdown for a while."

I look over at the empty place where the patient's stretcher was not long ago. As I debrief the code in my head, the emotions of what occurred start sinking in fully. I can only hope that man will make it through his cardiac procedure and eventually return home to his family.

Lost in thought, I retreat from the stretcher and make my way out of the resuscitation bay.

"Quinn."

I hear Dylan's voice cut through the clamor, and my whole body warms at the welcome sound. I halt and peer around. When I locate Dylan in the throng and realize he's striding my way, my pulse accelerates.

Dylan reaches my side and tips his head in the direction of the resuscitation bay. "Are you doing all right? Running a code is never easy, especially when you're new."

I'm precariously close to getting lost in Dylan's gaze, but I manage to reply, "I'm doing all right. Thank you for asking, and thanks for your help in there."

"You're welcome." He shows a hint of a smile. "You—

"Hi, you two!"

This time, it's Danielle's voice I hear. Looking over Dylan's shoulder, I see her coming toward us. Her eyes are shifting between Dylan and me, and for a fleeting moment, a grin passes across her lips.

"I heard the announcement about the code coming in," Danielle remarks, stopping in front of me. She peers up at her brother. "How did it go?"

Dylan gestures my direction. "You should ask the person who ran it."

Danielle gasps and faces me again. Her eyes are big. "They had you run the code? How terrifying!"

I can't help laughing at her shocked expression. "Admittedly, yes, it was intimidating, especially at first." I motion to Dylan. "Thankfully, though, I had great help in there."

"What Quinn is too humble to mention is that she obtained return of spontaneous circulation and got the patient to the cath lab," Dylan adds evenly.

Danielle doesn't reply at first. Instead, she peers at both of us while the corners of her mouth curve upward once more.

"That's awesome," she finally states. "That's really awesome." Her smile gets bigger. "Hey, I have an idea: our shifts are all wrapping up about the same time, so what do you think about going out for dinner after work?" She looks at Dylan. "We could go to that great bistro you've always liked."

Dylan coughs. "I'm not sure. I—"

"Aw, come on. It'll be fun." Danielle nudges him. "Besides, we need to start introducing Quinn to some of the great eateries in the area. After all, she will be returning soon to live here for the next three years."

Dylan seems to take a moment before responding. "I'll have charts to finish after my shift, so I won't get out of here right on time. I would have to meet you there."

"That's not a problem." Danielle's smile is undeterred. She turns and says to me, "The bistro is in a really fun part of town. It's not far from where Rachel lives, actually. We can easily take the bus from here. What do you say?"

My mind is working fast. Dinner with Dylan sounds like a high-risk proposition, considering my feelings for him are hovering dangerously close to the surface. That being said,

Danielle will be there, so it's not as though this is a *date* with Dylan or anything like that. Besides, the thought of a good dinner is too enticing to resist.

"Sounds great," I tell Danielle.

Danielle appears pleased. "Excellent. How about we plan to . . ." she trails off when her gaze slides past Dylan and me to something—or someone—behind us. Her smile vanishes.

Dylan follows his sister's line of sight and checks over his shoulder. His posture stiffens, and he faces forward again. I can see the muscles in his jaw are tensed, and there's something stormy brewing in his eyes.

"I need to check on a patient," he informs us in a low voice before striding off.

With growing confusion, I peek at Danielle, but she's still glaring past me. Tracking her narrow-eyed stare, I discover she's zeroed in on a female who's standing at the far end of the corridor. The woman appears close to us in age. Her blonde ponytail is so long that it's nearly down to her waist, and she's dressed in the type of cute, fitted scrubs nurses typically wear. At the moment, she's chatting with Henry Ingram and showing him a smile. Interestingly, though, at least based on the rather solemn expression on his face, Henry doesn't appear particularly interested in whatever she's saying.

"Um, Danielle?" I whisper. "Is something wrong?"

Danielle doesn't have a chance to reply before her pager goes off. Tearing her eyes away from the mystery woman, Danielle pulls the buzzing pager out of the holder she has clipped to her waistband, and she checks her new message.

"Sounds like a patient is being transferred to the ED from clinic, so I need to go help," Danielle explains to me, returning the pager to its holder. Gradually, her smile returns. "I'll meet you here after our shifts are over, and we'll take the bus across town, okay?"

"Okay. See you then."

Danielle moves to depart, but not before throwing another fierce scowl in the direction of the mystery woman. Once Danielle does depart, I stealthily cast another curious glance at the woman myself. Her ID says her name is Lindze Gates, and she's a nurse on the cardiac floor.

Puzzling over what that might have been all about, I go to my workstation. I take a seat at the desk, shake the mouse to wake the monitor, and check the tracking board. Dr. Santiago's prediction was correct: this place is so full with active and boarding patients that the very limited space remaining is being used only for those who are the most critically ill or injured. This means the waiting room will get increasingly clogged with people who have less-urgent issues because there's nowhere to put them for treatment. In other words, it's going to be a long night for everyone.

I open the chart for the patient whose code I ran, and I'm hit with a punch of worry when I see there's already a note from the interventional cardiologist. To my immense relief, however, the note states the patient's procedure was successful; he underwent stenting of his left anterior descending coronary artery, and he was transferred to the ICU in stable condition. He's expected to have a good recovery.

Someone's laughter causes me to look over my shoulder. The sound came from Lindze, who's still talking at Henry with her engaging smile and animated hand gestures. Henry's rather deadpan expression hasn't changed. Eventually, he says something to her and walks off. Once he's gone, Lindze's gaze promptly leaps to the other side of the ED, and I realize she's watching Dylan, who's examining a hallway patient.

With my curiosity piqued even more, I peer at Lindze once again. At the same moment, Lindze shifts her eyes my direction and catches me staring at her. Before I can look away, Lindze spins on her heels and saunters off.

Twelve

Danielle and I step off the bus, and as it roars away from the curb, I look up and down the sidewalk with a smile. Danielle was right: this is a fun part of town. Shops and restaurants with cute facades line both sides of the street, and old-fashioned park benches and lampposts add to the charming ambience. String lights overhead stretch from one side of the road to the other, sparkling like stars against the evening sky. A live music performance can be heard coming from a nearby restaurant. Best of all, aromas of delicious foods are floating along on the breeze. My stomach growls.

"This is great," I tell Danielle.

Danielle grins in return. "I can't wait for you to see the bistro where you're . . . I mean, where *we're* having dinner. Come on, it's this way."

Danielle links her arm with mine, guiding me to the left to begin maneuvering the busy sidewalk. As we make our way down the block, she tells me:

"Having grown up around here, Savannah and I pretty much know all the best places to eat and shop. And we fully intend to show each and every one of them to you."

I inhale the scent of waffle cones as we pass an ice cream parlor. "It's great you and Savannah have been able to stay in the hometown area you love so much for college and med school."

"Definitely. I feel really fortunate. Not to mention, it has been awesome to have my best friend as my roommate all these years. Sometimes, I swear Sav is the only person who could put up with me." Danielle laughs good-naturedly. She then casts me a sideways glance. "Dylan, on the other hand, chose to go elsewhere for undergrad and med school. He could have attended practically anywhere, since his grades and test scores were so high; ultimately, he opted to do his higher education in Wyoming because it allowed him to play college football and then attend a med school that had a strong emphasis on wilderness medicine, which he loves." She continues eyeing me. "I'm glad he decided to return home for residency, though."

"That's great." I pretend to be admiring another storefront, acting as though hearing Dylan's name hasn't caused my heart to start pattering.

Danielle leads me down another street. "Anyway, I'm thankful I'll be staying in this area for residency, too, especially since Joel's job will keep him here for the foreseeable future." She sighs. "Before Match Day, I was worried I would match somewhere else, and then Joel and I would be stuck in a long-distance . . ." she trails off, and her face blanches. "I'm sorry. I forgot about your situation with Chad."

"No worries." I force a laugh. "Technically, Chad and I aren't in a long-distance relationship because he broke up with me, so it's all good, right?"

Danielle doesn't join in my laughter. Instead, her brow furrows. "I'm sure what you've been through with Chad has been heartbreaking and confusing."

My smile fades. "I'm not going to lie, it hasn't been easy. Then again, things with Chad have never been easy." I have to pause as my words replay in my mind, and I look away.

Danielle gives my arm a squeeze. "You're going to find the love of your life, Quinn, I'm certain of it."

I'm about to ask how she can be so sure when Danielle abruptly tugs me to a stop.

"Here we are!" she announces.

We're standing outside a narrow, two-story building that has a beautiful brick exterior and a striped awning over the entrance. The building's millwork is beautifully ornate, and lanterns and twinkle lights adorn the windowsills.

My smile relaxes. "Wow. This looks incredible."

"It's even better inside." Danielle uses one arm to open the restaurant door while pulling me across the threshold with the other.

Upon entering the building, we're met by a welcome rush of heat from a fire that's crackling in a stone fireplace near the entrance. Peering around, I see the interior of the restaurant is painted a gentle shade of blue, and charming photographs of European streets adorn the walls. Tables for two that are decorated with flickering candles line the wall at our right, while seating for larger parties is by the front windows. The sounds of patrons' conversations are being accompanied by instrumental music, the whirr of a coffee machine, and the soft clanking of glasses. As I finish taking in the sight, I conclude this place is cozy yet elegant, and based on what my nose is detecting, it's also a hub for precisely the types of comfort foods my taste buds are made for.

"What do you think?" Danielle inquires, though her pleased expression makes it clear she already knows exactly what I think.

"I think this is perfect." I inhale the scent of fresh dough coming from the kitchen. "And undoubtedly delicious."

Danielle does a little fist pump. "I'm so glad you like it."

I laugh and point toward the bar area, where a couple stools just opened up. "Should we go grab a seat?"

"Yes, but not over there." Danielle squints with concentration and scans the room. Her eyes eventually stop on a vacant table for two that's tucked in the very back corner of the restaurant. She motions to it. "Let's take that table."

Before I can reply, Danielle charges off to claim the little table, which is basking in the glow of the twinkle lights that are hanging in the window beside it. Danielle reaches the table and takes the seat facing the entrance. I catch up with her, remove my jacket, drop my bag at my feet, and sit in the chair on the other side.

"Good evening, ladies." A waiter shuffles up to the table. He sets down two glasses of water and hands each of us a menu. "While you are getting settled in, may I get you something to drink?"

Danielle looks at me. "What would you like?"

I survey the vast array of beverage options on the artistically decorated menu. "I'll have a lemonade with rosemary, please."

The waiter reaches into the pocket of the small apron he's wearing, and he pulls out a notepad and pen with such care that it's as though they're made of fine china. With painstaking deliberateness, he then proceeds to write down my drink order. When he's finally done, he sets his eyes back on mine.

"Would you like your beverage to be a standard size or a large?"

"Standard." I have no doubt I could guzzle down a large, but I'm also a med student who has to watch her budget.

The waiter resumes meticulously writing on his notepad.

"Aw, come on, get the large," Danielle interjects playfully. "The lemonade here is fresh, and it's so good."

I need only a microsecond to reconsider. "All right, I'm changing plans," I say to the waiter, deciding this isn't the time to be frugal. "I'll have a large, please."

The waiter pauses. For a long time. Flaring his nostrils, he crosses out what he previously wrote on his notepad with three slow, exaggerated swipes of his pen. He then begins writing something else, and he takes so long doing it that I'm actually beginning to wonder if he's practicing calligraphy. Eventually, he looks at Danielle.

"What would you like to drink, miss?"

Danielle doesn't even glance at the menu. "A large diet soda. It's one of his . . . *my* favorites."

"Are you sure about the size?" The waiter keeps his pen poised.

Danielle nods. "I'm sure."

The waiter writes another manifesto before telling us, "I will leave you to look over the menus, and I shall check in with you in a little bit."

He spins on his heels and heads toward the bar, cradling his notepad and pen against his chest as he goes.

With a contented sigh, I relax in my chair and take a drink of water. After such a wild, busy day in the ED, this outing is proving to be a welcome chance to decompress and hang out with Danielle. I'm about to ask how the rest of her shift went when I see Danielle's gaze leap over my shoulder in the direction of the entrance.

"There he is," she says.

My heart immediately wallops the inside of my chest. Dylan. Dylan is here. For a couple minutes, I had forgotten Dylan was coming. I sit up fast and stiffly glance over my shoulder, and in that moment, any residual sense of relaxation I might have been feeling vaporizes.

Dylan is standing near the fireplace, searching the bistro with his eyes. He's wearing a black jacket over his scrubs top. His hair is ruffled, and a hint of facial scruff is highlighting his jaw line. And his presence is as naturally commanding as ever. Watching him, I feel another rush within my chest, and I promptly face forward again, acting as though I'm immensely fascinated by the photo on the wall behind Danielle.

"Over here, Dyl!" Danielle springs to her feet and waves a bit too much gusto.

I have no idea what to do, so I keep staring at the wall while my pulse steadily rises. Soon, out of the corner of my eye, I see Dylan reach the table and come to a stop beside it. I gulp and raise my eyes to his.

"Hi," I say, my voice cracking like I'm a peri-pubescent boy.

"Hi, Quinn." Dylan shows me a slight smile. He then looks at his sister, who's still standing. "Should I get us a bigger table? Somewhere we can all sit down?"

"Nope. There's no need, actually." Danielle tugs her phone from the pocket of her jacket, which I realize she never bothered to take off. "There's an OB patient who's on her way to the ED for fetal monitoring, and I'm going back there to observe."

I do a double take. "What?"

"What?" Dylan echoes at the same time.

"Yep. I've unfortunately gotta go." Danielle is smiling as she slides farther away from the table. She motions to her vacated chair. "So you can take my seat, Dyl."

Dylan blinks a couple times, and then he slowly removes his jacket and sits down across the table from me.

Danielle puts her eyes on mine. "I got the message about the incoming patient while we were on the way here. Did I forget to tell you?"

"Yes." I cough. "Yes, you did."

"Whoops. Sorry." Danielle continues grinning while she puts away her phone. She looks between Dylan and me. "Well, the bus will be arriving at the stop outside at any moment, so I need to get going. Have a great time, you two!"

Danielle speeds for the exit without looking back. The next thing I know, it's just Dylan and me sitting at the cozy little restaurant table.

The cozy and, now that I think about it, rather romantic little restaurant table.

I peer at Dylan. His expression remains deadpan while he watches out the window until he sees his sister get on the bus. He then meets my gaze. I silently draw in a breath. Dylan's eyes are absolutely mesmerizing in the low light.

"All right, ladies, here we are." The waiter seems to appear out of nowhere as he bustles up to the table with a drink in each hand. He places the lemonade in front of me, turns, and stops with a frown when he sees Dylan. "The other young woman ordered a diet soda."

Dylan exhales. "I have a feeling that was for me."

"Hmm." The waiter hesitates, but he eventually relinquishes the drink and puts it on the table. He next retrieves the notepad and pen from his apron pocket, still handling them like they're explosive devices that can't be jostled. "Have the two of you decided what you would like to order for dinner?"

Dylan focuses on me and shows a platonic smile. "I realize you were expecting to have dinner with Danielle. Please don't feel obligated to stay on my account."

I stare back at Dylan while a million thoughts zip through my head in an instant. Dylan is graciously giving me an out. He's tactfully providing a way for me to leave without things feeling awkward. In other words, this is when I should politely agree that plans for the evening unfortunately got disrupted, and I should excuse myself and head home.

"Thanks," I tell Dylan. I look up at the waiter, and I hear myself say, "If you don't mind, I would like a couple more minutes to decide what I'm going to eat."

Dylan observes me, and then he picks up the menu that Danielle left behind. "I'll take a minute to look over the menu, too," he tells the waiter.

"Very well." The waiter's shoulders slump. He gently returns the pen and notepad to his apron pocket. "I will be back."

The waiter departs. Dylan and I again make eye contact across the table, and it suddenly feels as though the space between us is charged with electricity. I hurriedly clear my throat, refocus on the menu, and break the silence with the most harmless conversation topic I can think of:

"Have you come to this place a lot?"

There's a pause.

"I used to come here fairly often," Dylan answers in an uncharacteristically subdued tone. "I don't visit much anymore, though."

I lift my eyes. "Why not?"

Dylan sets down his menu. "Because I used to come here when I was dating Lindze."

Lindze.

Into my mind pops the image of the mystery woman Danielle was glaring daggers at in the emergency department earlier today.

"Lindze?" I dare to repeat. "Is she, by chance, one of the nurses at Lakewood?"

"Yes." Dylan picks up his menu once more. "We've actually known each other since we were kids, and we began dating in high school."

My mouth falls open, but I quickly recover myself and say, "I'm sorry. I didn't mean to pry."

"You're not prying." Dylan looks out the window. "Lindze and I dated exclusively for a few years, but when our senior year of high school rolled around and I was offered a college football scholarship, she broke up with me. I really wanted to go to Wyoming—they had a great school and a great football team, and a friend I had played high school football with was already part of the program. Not to mention, the med school there was where I hoped to go after college. Lindze, however, wanted to stay in this area for nursing school, and she didn't want to do the long-distance relationship thing, either." He restores his gaze to mine. "Though it stung, I couldn't entirely blame her for her decision. I knew a long-distance relationship would be difficult."

My breathing gets a little stilted. "Yes. That I . . . can understand."

Dylan peers directly into my eyes. "Chad, right?"

"Yes." I swallow. "Chad."

Dylan's brow furrows a little as he studies me. "I think it's my turn to apologize for bringing up a sensitive subject. I'm sorry, Quinn."

"You have nothing to apologize for." I watch the water droplets slide down the side of my glass. "Things with Chad have been hard, but I don't mind talking about them . . . with you."

I take an extra second before looking at him again. Dylan observes me in return with an expression that's impossible to decipher. Quiet settles over the table, but it's not an uncomfortable quiet. Rather, it's a pensive one. For reasons I can't explain, it feels natural to talk with Dylan like this.

"May I ask what happened after Lindze broke up with you?" I eventually inquire.

Dylan sits back in his chair. "Well, I didn't try to talk Lindze out of her decision to end our relationship. I obviously didn't want her to move somewhere she wouldn't be happy." He again looks right into my eyes. "More importantly, I knew I didn't want to be in a relationship with Lindze—or with anyone, for that matter—if she wasn't one hundred percent committed to it."

I open my mouth to reply but shut it again. There's a lump forming in my throat, and I fear if I try to speak, my voice will tremble with emotion and betray what I'm feeling.

But what, exactly, am I feeling?

An instant later, the answer hits me, cold and hard: I'm feeling doubt. I'm starting to doubt Chad and I ever really had the type of devoted, loving relationship I always told myself we did. I'm doubting it was only external circumstances that caused him to break up with me. I'm doubting the depth of Chad's feelings for me, and I'm even doubting my feelings for him. And in so doing, I'm doubting everything I've ever believed about what it truly means to be in love.

Dylan watches me for a few seconds, and then he diffuses the quiet by going on with his story. "Anyway, after graduating from high school, Lindze and I went our separate ways. She stayed in the area for nursing school, and I moved to Wyoming."

I manage to find my voice. "So is the breakup the reason why Danielle was shooting Lindze looks to kill earlier today?"

"No. Even Danielle wouldn't be that dramatic." Dylan chuckles, but his demeanor soon grows serious again. "Danielle's disdain for Lindze runs deeper than that."

"So the story with Lindze doesn't end there."

"No, it doesn't." Dylan resumes peering out the window. "Some years later, while I was in Wyoming and in the middle of med school, Lindze . . . returned to my life."

My eyebrows rise.

Dylan puts his gaze back on me. "Lindze had a series of boyfriends while she was in nursing school and then once she began working as a nurse at Lakewood. However, during my second year of med school, Lindze showed up on my doorstep and said I was the only man she had really loved. She wanted us to try again, even if it meant being in a long-distance relationship until I was done with med school."

"And you . . . agreed to try again," I venture carefully.

"Yes." He takes a drink. "I agreed to try again."

"Were you happy?"

"Hard to say. I thought I was happy, at least." Dylan shows a restrained smile. "In fact, Lindze was the reason I ranked Lakewood as my number-one choice for residency."

"Really?" My eyes get big. "Otherwise, you would have tried to stay in Wyoming for residency?"

Dylan nods. "Lindze made it clear she still didn't want to move, and she wasn't keen on continuing a long-distance relationship any longer than necessary. That forced me to make a choice. Ultimately, I chose to prioritize my relationship. I ranked Lakewood highest on my residency match list, hoping to get accepted into the program so I could be nearer to Lindze." He takes another drink. "Obviously, I did match at Lakewood, so as soon as med school was over, I returned here."

I start playing with the straw in my glass. "I'm going to guess this is where the story takes another turn for the worse."

"You could say that." Dylan sighs and rests his forearms on the edge of the table. "Not long after I started residency, Lindze blindsided me by breaking up with me again. In her words, there was another doctor she had feelings for." He takes a moment before adding, "Unbeknownst to her, she broke up with me only days before I was planning to propose."

I sense the color slowly drain from my face. "Oh, Dylan, that's terrible. I can't even imagine how that must have felt. I'm so sorry."

"Thanks. It was pretty devastating at first, but I soon realized it was for the best." Dylan's tone and expression give away nothing. "Like I said, I knew I didn't want to be in a relationship if the other person wasn't completely devoted to it, too."

Again, I'm unable to vocalize a reply as emotion swells within me once more.

"Please don't get me wrong," Dylan continues. "I wasn't disappointed to match at Lakewood. It's one of the best emergency medicine residency programs in the country, and it was otherwise going to be my second choice. I consider myself extremely fortunate to have matched here."

"Have the two of you decided what you are going to eat?" The waiter reappears with his notepad at the ready.

I pull my gaze from Dylan and distractedly point to the first thing on the menu. "I'll have the, um, chicken pot pie, please."

The waiter writes down my order like he's chiseling it into stone. He next looks to Dylan.

"And for you, sir?"

"I'll have the same," Dylan replies without even glancing at the menu.

The waiter records Dylan's order and gathers up our menus. "May I get you anything else while you are waiting?"

Dylan puts his eyes on me. I shake my head.

"No, I think that's everything," Dylan tells the waiter. "Thanks."

The waiter strolls away. I take another drink of lemonade, trying to give myself time to sort through my thoughts. At last, I say:

"I realize this is no consolation, but in case it makes you feel any better: Chad dumped me—for the third time in our on-again-off-again relationship—the night before I moved out here. I was totally blindsided, too. So I understand a little of how you feel."

Dylan's brows snap together. "No, that doesn't make me feel better. It only makes me think your ex-boyfriend is an idiot for dumping you."

"Thanks," I say with a sad, soft laugh. "And again, I'm immensely sorry for what you went through. It must be difficult running into Lindze at work. Especially if you . . . still have feelings for her."

Dylan finishes off his drink and sets the glass on the table. "I don't have feelings for Lindze, and I haven't had feelings for her in a very long time." His voice doesn't waver. "After she broke up with me, I realized Lindze wasn't who I thought she was. The woman I was in love with didn't exist, and I knew I was lucky to find that out before it was too late."

Growing pensive, I turn my head to peer out the window. After a time, I hear Dylan inquire:

"What about you?"

I look at him. "What do you mean?"

"I mean, what about Chad? How do you feel about him?"

There's a drawn-out pause when, once again, I'm shocked to discover I have no idea how to reply. Only a few weeks ago, I would have declared that Chad and I were in love, and that I was certain we would reconcile. Now, though, I'm not sure.

"On second thought, don't answer that question." Dylan has resumed searching my face with that probing gaze of his. "I didn't mean to put you on the spot. Your breakup is a lot more recent than mine, and I certainly understand if you're not convinced things are really over with Chad."

"What?" I shake my head, like doing so will knock my thoughts into place. "You didn't put me on the spot. It's just that I . . ."

"Still care about him," Dylan finishes for me.

I rub my forehead. "Of course I care about him, but that doesn't mean . . . that is, I'm trying to figure out how Chad really feels about me, how I really feel about him, and what I really want."

Dylan crosses his arms over his chest. "How Chad feels about you shouldn't be a mystery. If Chad truly cares about you, he—"

"Here you are." The waiter approaches with our food.

The next thing I know, I'm staring down at the steaming-hot chicken pot pie the waiter places on the table in front of me. The aroma of its flaky, perfectly baked crust fills my nostrils, and I can see fresh vegetables and pieces of chicken bubbling in their juices inside it.

But I don't want a bite. My appetite is gone. I can't remember the last time I lost my appetite.

"Quinn?" Dylan asks after the waiter departs.

I hesitate before raising my eyes to his.

Dylan sighs and sets down his fork. "I realize it's not my place to try to give you relationship advice. I guess it just makes no sense to me how a guy could break up with you. You're smart, funny, beautiful . . ." He clears his throat and glances away. A second or two goes by, and then, like a switch gets flipped, emotion again disappears from his face. "What I'm trying to say is that I've learned love is unpredictable and hard. Ninety-nine percent of the time, it leads to heartache. Frankly, it's not worth it."

I draw in a sharp breath. "You don't really believe that."

"I do believe it. I have absolutely no desire to waste my time pursuing romance." Dylan leans forward and lowers his voice. "If someone I thought I knew so well—someone I had known since childhood—was able to blindside me the way Lindze did, I'm never going to trust I understand anyone's real character again. I've been fooled once by what I thought was love, and I'm not going to get fooled again."

I stare at him. "You know, you view things more similarly to Chad than you probably realize."

Dylan arches an eyebrow. "I highly doubt that."

"I'm serious. Chad broke up with me this last time because he didn't want our relationship complicated by the long-distance aspect. It had nothing to do with how he felt about me." I'm ignoring the voice in my head that's telling me I'm attempting to convince myself as much as I'm trying to convince Dylan that what I'm saying is true. I hurriedly go on. "In other words, Chad gave up on relationships when things got hard, and if you think about it, you've kind of done the same thing."

Dylan is shaking his head. "There's a big difference between choosing not to give one's heart away, and breaking up with someone because conditions aren't perfect. In the first scenario, I'm being smart and careful. In the second, by not being willing to commit unless things are exactly how he wants them, Chad is proving he doesn't really love you."

It takes one long, terrible second for me to process Dylan's words. Then a sickening sensation rises up inside me. My face flushes. Tears sting my eyes.

"I can't believe you said that," I whisper unsteadily. "Who are you to judge whether or not Chad loves me? You know nothing about Chad, and you know nothing about my relationship with him. You're in absolutely no place to declare whether or not he loves me."

Dylan sits up taller. "Quinn, that's not what I meant. What I was trying to say—"

"Please don't try saying anything else. You've said enough." I pick up my bag, find my wallet, yank out some cash, and slap the money on the table. "If you'll excuse me. I think it's best if I go."

I stand, throw on my jacket, and sling my bag onto my shoulder. I take a step to leave but Dylan puts a hand on my arm.

"Quinn, please give me a chance to explain what I meant."

"Don't worry about it," I reply coldly. "Since you've given up on relationships, I wouldn't expect you to understand anything about those of us who haven't." I shake my arm from his hold. "Goodbye, Dylan."

His jaw muscles are tensed. "At least let me drive you to the apartment."

"No, thank you. I would rather take the bus. Goodnight."

Weaving past the other tables, I make it to the front of the bistro and charge outside into the cold night air. My stomach is churning. My breathing is shallow. Everything feels totally wrong, like a puzzle got knocked to the ground and all the pieces are out of place, but I have no idea how to put the pieces back together. I'm not sure what hurts the most: that Dylan said what he did, or that what he said might be true.

I reach the bus stop, pull out my phone, and check the time. When I look up again, I notice Dylan standing outside the restaurant. To anyone else, it would appear as though he's scrolling through messages on his phone. However, I can see the stiffness in his posture, and I catch his eyes occasionally flicking my way. He's watching to make sure I get on the bus safely.

I quickly look away from Dylan and stare at the pavement beneath my feet. The seconds seem to drag on before I finally hear the rumble of an approaching bus. Raising my head, I anxiously peer down the road, and I exhale with relief when I see it's a bus that follows a route I can take back to the apartment. The bus stops at the curb with its breaks squealing, and as soon as its doors open, I hurry up the stairs. Breathing hard, I drop down onto a seat. The bus doors close. Only once the bus is pulling away from the curb do I dare to glance out the window. Dylan is gone.

Thirteen

"Hello, Ms. Arrondo. My name is Quinn Meyers. I'm a fourth-year medical student, and I'll be helping to care for you while you're in the emergency department. Please tell me what's going on."

Ms. Arrondo, a fifty-nine-year-old patient, puts a panicked gaze on me. "I'm having . . . chest pain."

I step aside to allow the EMS crew to depart the exam room with their now-empty stretcher. I then refocus on my patient, who's situated on the ED stretcher in the middle of the room. Finn is putting stickers on Ms. Arrondo's chest in preparation to obtain an ECG, and Hadi is getting the patient connected to the monitor.

I step closer to the foot of the stretcher. "When did your chest pain start?"

Ms. Arrondo seems to be working to breathe as she peers up at the clock, which shows it's about one in the morning.

"The pain woke me up . . . a couple hours ago." Ms. Arrondo pauses to catch her breath. "At first, I thought it was heartburn, but the pain . . . kept getting worse. I then started feeling short of breath, and it seemed . . . my heart was racing. That's when I decided to call nine-one-one."

I glance at the monitor. Ms. Arrondo's latest set of vitals show her heart is beating fast, and her oxygen saturation level is a little low. I next look over at Finn, who has the ECG machine ready. I then concentrate on Ms. Arrondo once more.

"I'm glad you came in." I'm speaking calmly, though my concern for this patient is mounting. "The first thing we're going to do is get an ECG. Hadi will then place an IV and draw some blood."

"Okay." Ms. Arrondo rests her head on the pillow.

Hadi lowers the back of the stretcher so the patient is lying flat. Finn waits a couple seconds for the motion artifact to clear from the screen of the ECG machine, and then he pushes a button on the device. Soon, the twelve-lead ECG is processed, and a paper copy prints out. Finn hands the paper to me.

I take a few seconds to review the ECG. It confirms Ms. Arrondo's pulse is tachycardic; even more concerning is the subtle waveform abnormality I notice in lead three. My worry for her ticks up another notch.

I raise my eyes to Finn. "Thanks."

"No problem." Finn pushes the ECG machine out of the room.

I fold up the ECG and slip it into the pocket of my white coat. "Ms. Arrondo, while

Hadi gets your IV placed and starts fluid, I'm going to do my exam." I step to the sink to wash my hands. "Once I'm done, I'll place orders for blood work and imaging of your chest. I'll also order medication that will make you more comfortable while we're sorting out what's going on."

"Thank you," Ms. Arrondo tells me, sounding winded.

Hadi raises the back of the patient's stretcher so she's sitting up again. While he gets to work on the IV, I start examining the patient. I listen to her fast-beating heart, and I detect a faint expiratory wheeze on the right when I ascultate her lungs. The rest of her exam is unremarkable.

Once I'm done, I drape my stethoscope around my neck and check the little point-of-care machine that's sitting on top of the supply cart. The machine has been whirring quietly for the past several minutes while it processes a sample of Ms. Arrondo's blood. Soon, the machine lets out a beep, and it displays on its screen the patient's troponin result. The level of troponin—a cardiac enzyme—in Ms. Arrondo's bloodstream is elevated to an indeterminate range. In other words, the level is higher than what's considered normal, but it's technically not abnormal . . . at least, not yet.

I face my patient once more. "I'll return soon, Ms. Arrondo, but before I go, is there anything else I can get for you?"

"No, I'm . . . all right." Her wince of discomfort betrays her. "I appreciate you asking, though. Thank you."

I meet Hadi's gaze.

"Aspirin?" he asks, reading my mind.

"Yes, please." I move to leave the room. "I'll go enter orders into the computer."

I give Ms. Arrondo a smile before I slip out of the room. As I close the curtain behind me and scan the department, I have to shake my head. Even though it's in the middle of the night, this place is busier than I've ever seen it before. Each exam room is occupied with a critically ill patient, countless other patients line the corridors, and a seemingly endless parade of ambulance crews continues delivering even more people who need to be seen. Meanwhile, nurses, techs, secretaries, respiratory therapists, pharmacists, social workers, residents, and attending physicians are racing in every direction to take care of patients as fast as they can. The air is permeated with the non-stop sounds of conversations, ringing phones, overhead announcements, shouting patients, alarming medication pumps, pagers going off, walkie talkie chatter, the rumbling of the portable x-ray machine, ambulance sirens outside, and EMTs giving report. It's a madhouse in here, but from what I've heard staff members say, this is just another typical Friday night here in Lakewood Medical Center's emergency department.

A pit forms in my stomach, and I again find myself wondering if I really have what it takes to succeed here as a resident. It's one thing to get through a few shifts as a visiting med student—I'm not part of core staffing or relied on to help carry the patient load, and I'm not necessarily expected to manage patients who are severely ill. However, in a couple months, I'll be playing an entirely different ballgame. I'll be expected to manage multiple sick patients simultaneously, and I'll be expected to manage those patients with less supervision. I'll also be expected to capably perform all sorts of procedures, including doing central lines, intubations, chest tube insertions, cardioversions, dislocation reductions, and lumbar punctures. On top of that, I'll be part of core staffing, which means I'll be responsible for helping to keep patients moving efficiently through the department.

Blowing a loose curl from my face, I do my best to push aside my jitters, and I weave a path to my workstation. When I reach my desk, I drop down onto the chair and wiggle the mouse to cause the log-in screen to appear. I've gotten pretty adept at logging into the system, so it isn't long before I've got the orders placed for Ms. Arrondo.

I look up and peer around the department again, trying to locate Dr. Santiago so I can tell him about my latest patient. This place has been so busy that I've barely had a chance to talk to him since my shift started two hours ago. In fact, because it has been so busy, Jesse has not only been supervising, he has also been seeing patients on his own. In the couple hours I've been here, I've already seen Jesse run a code, manage a trauma patient, care for a child with second-degree burns, admit someone who overdosed on aspirin, and intubate a man with a hemorrhagic stroke. Observing him has been a daunting reminder of the extremely high caliber of people who work in this place . . . and that I'll eventually be expected to perform like one of them.

I spot Dr. Santiago stepping out of a patient's room. Before the room's curtain has even shut behind him, he's approached by three nurses who appear to be asking him questions about other patients. I hesitantly get to my feet. I don't want to bother Dr. Santiago when he has so much going on already, yet he should hear about Ms. Arrondo sooner versus later, and based on the way things are going around here, if I don't catch up with him now, it will be a long time before I have another chance. So I leave my workstation and head across the department toward him. He looks over at me as I approach.

"Hey, Quinn. How are things—"

"Doctor Santiago, please come to Room Thirteen," someone says over the PA system. "Doctor Santiago, please come to Room Thirteen."

At the same moment, out of the corner of my eye, I notice someone emerge from another exam room. My heart thuds when I realize it's Dylan. Tonight's shift has been so busy and hectic that I didn't even know he was working.

I haven't seen Dylan since that night at the bistro over a week ago, but I've been thinking about what happened—and I've been thinking about him—a lot.

That evening, after I left the bistro, I returned to the apartment, and I found Danielle and Savannah in the main room, pretending to be studying and not waiting up for me. Considering Danielle was already in her pajamas, and there was a plate with remnants of her finished dinner on the floor by where she sat, I had a sneaking suspicion her story about needing to observe an OB patient at the hospital had also been a ruse. I didn't call her out on it, though. I knew she had nothing but the best of intentions by trying to set me up with her brother.

When I entered the apartment, Danielle popped off the couch and gleefully asked how dinner with Dylan had gone . . . but once she got a look at the expression on my face, her smile disappeared. Wearily plunking myself down on the chair by the fireplace, I did my best to explain to Danielle and Sav what had happened. It wasn't easy, though, because I was still struggling to understand it myself. I knew Dylan hadn't intended to insult or hurt me. So why, really, had his remarks wounded me so deeply? And why was it increasingly feeling as though my mind was insisting on one thing while my heart was telling me another?

After I finally did finish telling the gals what had happened at the bistro, Danielle and Savannah graciously didn't inundate me with advice or opinions. Instead, they gave me dessert. Nothing more was said on the matter, except when Danielle muttered something about how her brother was the biggest idiot on the planet. After dessert, I thanked them and retreated to my room. And I called Chad. I'm not sure why. I suppose I was desperate for reassurance that I was doing the right thing by staying open to the idea of possibly getting back together with him. The call never happened, though, because Chad didn't answer.

I snap to attention when I realize Dylan is coming toward Dr. Santiago . . . and toward me. Dylan notices me standing with the nurses, and he does a double take and halts. I swallow hard. There's a distinct pause while we hold one another's gazes.

"I'm sorry, Quinn, but it sounds like I need to go check on Room Thirteen," I hear Dr. Santiago say.

I tear my gaze from Dylan and look at my attending. "No worries. I understand."

Dr. Santiago motions to Dylan. "While I'm tied up, why don't you staff your new patient with Dylan? He can supervise you until I'm available."

I open my mouth to reply, but my throat is suddenly so dry that no sound can come out.

Dr. Santiago doesn't seem to notice my discomfiture, and he turns Dylan's way. "Would supervising Quinn be all right with you?"

Dylan's expression reveals absolutely nothing. "Sure."

"Thanks," Dr. Santiago tells us both, and then he strides away.

The nurses disperse, leaving Dylan and me alone. I keep staring in the direction Dr. Santiago went while I tell myself to get a grip. I can work with Dylan. I can be professional around him, and I have no reason to worry about what Dylan thinks of me in anything other than a professional capacity. He has made it clear he's not interested in romance, and so he'll never be anything to me other than Danielle's older brother and another resident in this emergency department.

"Hi, Quinn," Dylan says.

I look up at him. Dylan's expression remains impossible to decipher. Aware that I'm up against the ultimate master of masking emotion, I throw back my shoulders and try to make my expression equally cryptic.

"Hi, Dylan," I reply.

Dylan is searching my face. "Do you have a new patient?"

"Yes." I maintain my aloof air. "I have a fifty-nine-year-old woman who woke about three hours ago with chest pain. She developed shortness of breath and palpitations, and she called nine-one-one. Upon EMS arrival, she was tachycardic and mildly hypoxic. Exam was notable for tachycardia and a faint, right-sided expiratory wheeze. ECG shows a waveform abnormality in lead three. Initial troponin is indeterminate. A PE is at the top of my differential. Labs, meds, and imaging have been ordered. Aspirin was administered." I glance in the direction of Ms. Arrondo's exam room. "And it looks like she's being taken for her CTA right now."

Dylan follows my line of sight to the other side of the department. A radiology tech is pushing Ms. Arrondo on her stretcher toward the radiology suites, where she'll undergo a CT angiogram to look for a pulmonary embolism, or "PE," which is a clot lodged in the lungs.

"Sounds like you've got everything off to a great start." Dylan shifts my way once more. "Is there anything else you want to go over with me?"

Is that a serious question? I nearly ask aloud. Instead, I shake my head. "No. My other patients are dispositioned. So while Ms. Arrondo is getting her CTA, I was going to see if there's a new patient waiting."

"All right." Dylan peers into my eyes in a way that makes me think he's able to read my thoughts. "Please let me know how I can help."

A strange laugh almost escapes my lips before I turn away. I charge across the department and return to my workstation. As I take my seat, I slowly breathe in and out a couple times to settle my racing heart. I remind myself yet again that it doesn't matter if I'm drawn to Dylan. He isn't interested in romance, and I still need to sort out things with Chad.

I slip off my short white coat, hoping that doing so will help me cool down. After hanging my coat over the back of my chair, I straighten my scrubs top and focus on the patient tracking board. There's one new patient who's waiting to be seen. The board indicates the patient is a thirty-four-year-old male in Hallway Seven. Oddly, his name isn't listed, and his chief complaint is indicated only as, "*???*"

I use the computer mouse to click the patient's room number on the tracking board, assigning myself as his care provider. I then get up and weave through the chaos toward the room designated as Hallway Seven, which is nothing more than a stretcher jammed into a small nook next to a sink and a paper towel dispenser.

As I draw closer to the nook, I fix my attention on the man seated upon the stretcher. He's wearing flannel pajamas and fuzzy slippers. His hair is smashed into an impressive degree of bed head. His round glasses are magnifying his eyes, which lock on me as I approach. I note he's gripping something in his hand.

"Good morning, sir." I stop beside the stretcher. "I'm Quinn Meyers. I'm a fourth-year medical student who will be assisting you. Before we discuss what brings you in today, may I please get your name?"

"Harris. But you can call me Harris."

I shift my stance. "Thank you. And so I can ensure the medical record is accurate, may I also get your last name?"

"Harris."

I take a moment to deliberate how stupid I want to sound. "I apologize for my confusion, sir, but I do want to ensure your information is correct in our charting system. Is your first name Harris, or is your last name Harris?"

"Both."

I wet my lips. "Both your first name and your last name is Harris?"

"Yes. I'm Harris Harris."

I peer at him. He peers back. As best as I can tell, he's completely serious. So all I can do is reinforce my smile and go on:

"Thank you, Mr. Harris. I—"

"Call me Harris."

"Right. Harris. So, um, Harris, please tell me what brings you into the emergency department this early in the morning."

Harris Harris's magnified eyes narrow behind his glasses. "I need to speak with the doctor who attempted to drug me with recreational substances."

My mouth drops. "What?"

Harris Harris shakes what he's holding in his hand. It sounds like a baby rattle, and I realize it's a prescription bottle filled with pills. He keeps shaking the bottle as he says:

"I demand to speak with the doctor who attempted to administer marijuana to me without my consent."

I blink several times. "Sir—"

"Call me Harris."

"Harris. Of course." I glance at the bottle Harris Harris continues holding in his vice-like grip, but I can't read the label. "Harris, are you saying someone prescribed you—"

"I'm saying the doctor who saw me yesterday morning diagnosed me with a bacterial sinus infection and stated he would start me on antibiotics." Harris Harris peers suspiciously around the department before returning his glare to me. "I filled the prescription yesterday afternoon and took my first dose at that time. I then set my alarm to take my next pill precisely twelve hours later." He shakes the bottle with more fervor. "When I got up at one this morning to take my second dose, that was when I noticed what the label on the bottle said." He leans toward me. "The doctor told me I would be receiving antibiotics, but do you know what I was actually prescribed?"

I hesitate. This feels like a trick question.

"Pot! The doctor prescribed pot!" Harris Harris declares, thankfully not waiting for my reply. "I'm not a physician, but I'm not stupid. Marijuana isn't an antibiotic." He begins shaking his head. "I'm horrified to discover an institution such as this is administering recreational drugs to patients without their consent, and doing so under the guise of treating bacterial infections!"

I manage to recover from my shock enough to motion to the bottle in Harris Harris's hand. "Sir—"

"Harris."

"Harris. Right." I rub my forehead. "Harris, would you mind if I took a look at that pill bottle?"

"Not at all. You'll see right on the label, plain as day, that the doctor prescribed pot." Harris Harris holds out the bottle for me to take, but his gaze suddenly flicks over my shoulder, and he swings his arm to point past me. "That's him! That's the doctor who surreptitiously attempted to drug me with marijuana!"

I turn around. Harris Harris is pointing directly at Dylan.

Of course he is.

Dylan is on the other side of the department, standing beside his workstation and talking on the phone with a serious expression on his face.

"Yes. That's him. That's Doctor Gillespie," I hear Harris Harris utter in a low, oddly sinister tone. "He may think he has everyone fooled, but he hasn't fooled me. I'm onto his clandestine life."

Still with the phone to his ear, Dylan happens to glance our direction. He does a double take when he notices both Harris Harris and me gawking at him from across the department. Dylan focuses on Harris Harris with a look of recognition, and then he fixes his gaze on me with a slight quirk of one eyebrow. I answer Dylan's unspoken question with a subtle shrug and a tip of my head toward the bottle Harris Harris is clutching. Dylan nods, says something into the phone, and hangs up. He then begins striding toward the nook.

"Ah, so Doctor Gillespie has the audacity to come over here, does he? He's going to attempt to cover up his nefarious activities by spewing more lies and deceit?" Harris Harris chuckles victoriously. "Well, wait until Doctor

Gillespie hears what I have to say. He's about to find out his days of being a drug lord are over."

I don't reply because I have absolutely no idea what to say. So instead, I simply back up a few steps, making room for Dylan to join me in the nook beside Harris Harris's stretcher. Dylan shoots me another glance before he concentrates on the patient.

"Good morning, Harris." Dylan says in his deep voice. "What brings you again to the emergency—"

"Give up, Doctor Gillespie!" Harris Harris's shout carries over the ambient din, causing other patients to look our way. "Or are you even a real doctor?"

Dylan blinks, his expression going completely deadpan. "Yes, Harris, I'm a real resident physician."

"Well, it doesn't matter, because your medical career is about to come to an end!" Harris Harris shakes the pill bottle like a maraca. "Yes, *Doctor* Gillespie, your little charade is about to come toppling down!"

The entire corridor has fallen silent. I glance around, not sure whether to laugh or cry when I count the number of patients, visitors, and ED staff members who are watching the fiasco. I glance up at Dylan. He returns my look, and I realize he's fighting to contain a grin. Suddenly, I have to bite the insides of my cheeks to keep myself from smiling in return.

Dylan readopts his serious expression, draws himself up to his full height, and resumes speaking to Harris Harris. "I'm sorry something has upset you, though I must admit that I'm not clear what *charade* you're referring to."

Harris Harris scoffs. "I would expect you to say that. Well, I'm happy to refresh your memory." He uses his free hand to point to the pill bottle he's holding. "I'm referring to the fact that you prescribe pot instead of prescribing antibiotics. I'm referring to the fact that you live a secret life as a drug lord!"

Several of the eavesdropping patients gasp. Others start whispering.

Dylan's expression doesn't change. He gestures to the pill bottle. "Harris, is that the medication you're referring to?"

"Of course it is." Harris Harris clutches the bottle to his chest. "And don't think for a moment I'm going to surrender it over to you. This is evidence, and you would give anything to confiscate and destroy it."

Dylan scratches his head. "Well, then, Harris, I'm not sure how to help you. I think I know what's going on, but in order to be sure, I do need to check the—"

"No! Never!" Harris Harris leans as far away from Dylan as the cramped nook allows. "You'll never take this from me!"

Several people in the corridor have started recording the encounter on their phones. Before Dylan and I wind up in the next online viral video, I step closer to Harris Harris, put on what I hope is an I-don't-want-to-destroy-any-evidence smile, and say:

"How about I look at the bottle, Harris? I'll read the label to Doctor Gillespie, and I'll give it back to you as soon as I'm done."

Harris Harris observes me for a second or two. "Fine."

Harris Harris gives me the bottle, and I turn it over in my hand so I can read the label. Sure enough, the medication was dispensed by a pharmacy yesterday, and Dr. Dylan Gillespie was listed as the prescribing physician. I shift my eyes to the name of the medication:

Amox/Clav Pot

I raise my gaze to Dylan.

"Generic Augmentin?" Dylan asks me.

"Yep," I reply.

"What? What is this?" Harris Harris's eyes begin leaping between Dylan and me. He points an accusing finger in my face. "You're in on this, too? You're his drug runner?"

I hear more patients gasp while the rest continue recording the encounter, blatantly ignoring the techs and nurses who are telling them that filming in the ED is prohibited. I sigh. This conversation is going to be all over social media by breakfast. Needless to say, becoming known because I'm a rumored drug mule isn't the way I wanted to establish my reputation around here.

Now it's Dylan's turn to rub his forehead like it's starting to ache. "No, Harris, Quinn isn't a drug runner."

Harris Harris is still skewering me with his gaze as he snatches the pill bottle from me. "Then how do you know what this label means?"

"Because, in this case, *pot* is short for potassium," I explain, doing my best to ignore the cameras. "The generic name of your antibiotic is *amoxicillin-clavulanate potassium*. However, because the name is too long to fit on the label, it was abbreviated. *Pot* was used instead of *potassium*."

Harris Harris stares at me for an immensely long time. "You don't say." He examines the label again. "You know, I actually knew *pot* stood for *potassium*. I mean, it's not like a doctor is going to prescribe marijuana when a patient needs antibiotics." He snorts a laugh and stands up. "Can you believe some people might not understand that?"

With a shake of his head, Harris Harris casually pushes past Dylan and me and strolls for the exit. With looks of disappointment, everyone in the corridor begins putting away their phones.

Dylan watches the patient go, and then he shifts my way and lets his grin show. "Another satisfied customer."

A snicker rises up inside me, and I break into real laughter. "I'm just relieved to hear you don't live a secret life as a drug lord."

Dylan starts laughing along with me. "Glad we got that cleared up."

Our laughter gradually dies away, and our eyes meet once more.

"Hey, Dyl!"

A woman's call carries through the air, causing Dylan's gaze to flick past me in the direction from where it came. Instantly, his expression becomes stone-like. Following his stare, I turn around.

Lindze is strolling our way. As before, she's dressed in cute scrubs. Her long hair is twisted up into a bun, and she has on enough makeup to appear totally put-together without looking like she overdid it for working in the middle of the night. She glances at me only for a second before she gets to Dylan's side and shows him a smile.

"You're on a run of overnights again?" Lindze asks him with the air of familiarity.

Dylan offers a slight nod. "Just one shift tonight, and then I'm off for a while."

"I'm off after this shift, too." Lindze rests a hand on Dylan's forearm, appearing completely comfortable doing so. "We should go out and grab breakfast after our shifts are done later this morning."

Dylan swallows. "I appreciate the offer, but—"

"Think about it. It might be nice to catch up." Lindze leans closer to him. "I'll find you after work to see what you decide."

Lindze walks off, headed for the room of a patient who's being admitted to the cardiac ICU. I peer up at Dylan. He's still staring in the direction Lindze went, and his gaze, which was so warm and engaging only moments ago, has grown stormy and distant. A long time passes before he turns my way. He almost seems to be peering through me when he says:

"Please excuse me, Quinn. I need to go check on a patient, but let me know when anything else comes up I can help with."

"I will. Thanks." I'm struggling to ignore the cold emptiness that has replaced the delight I was feeling only minutes ago. "I'll review Ms. Arrondo's CT scan, and if she does have a PE, I'll admit her to the medicine service."

"Great," Dylan replies, and then he strides away.

I remain in the nook, attempting to sort out what happened, but I can't. My mind is strangely blank. Almost robotically, I return to my workstation. I log into the computer and open Ms. Arrondo's chart. The CTA of her lungs confirms she unfortunately does have a pulmonary embolism, and based on the size and location of the clot, I'll need to admit her for monitoring and further treatment.

I go to Ms. Arrondo's bedside and inquire how she's doing. Thankfully, she reports feeling better. Her latest vitals are improved, and her repeat exam is stable. I update her on the CT results and recommended plan for care. She graciously agrees and expresses her appreciation.

Still in a mental haze, I depart Ms. Arrondo's room and update Hadi on the plan for our patient. I then return to my computer. I place orders for the blood-thinning medication Ms. Arrondo needs, and I add orders for a repeat troponin and ECG. Next, I page the on-call resident for the admitting medicine service. A few minutes later, a second-year resident named

Tara Hess returns the call, and she kindly accepts the patient for care. I place the admission order in the computer, and I notify the charge nurse that Ms. Arrondo has been admitted.

Then I find myself staring numbly at nothing.

I shouldn't be bothered by what took place between Dylan and me. Dylan has chosen to shun romance, and so it's only a recipe for self-induced heartache to remain swept up in feelings for him. Besides, before Dylan flipped my world upside-down, there was Chad. There still *is* Chad. And Chad and I need to talk.

A surge of aching emotion fills me, and I exhaustedly drop my head in my hands. Doing this rotation has proven to be the biggest mistake of my life. Moving here caused Chad to break up with me. Meeting Dylan has led me to question everything I've ever believed about love. Working at Lakewood has destroyed my confidence that I could ever fit in here.

I raise my head and scan the department through tear-filled eyes. Lakewood isn't the right place for me, for more reasons now than ever before.

Maybe I should leave. I could explain to Dr. Santiago that I've realized I don't fit in and there's no point in me sticking around. Later this very day, I could start driving home to everything that's familiar . . . everything I understand. I could look into changing where I do residency. I could talk with Chad and finally sort out how I feel about him. And I could leave behind Dylan and all the angst I've felt since meeting him.

I should leave Lakewood Medical Center. Now. Right now.

I push back from my desk and stand up on shaking legs, ready to search out Dr. Santiago to tell him I'm leaving. Just then, an announcement booms out from the overhead speakers:

"Mass-casualty incident alert. Mass-casualty incident alert."

A pulse of total silence rocks the department. The next moment, several ED staff members start racing toward one of the resuscitation bays. As I watch them, a new flood of adrenaline begins flowing through me. I glance at the exit and then back at the resuscitation bay.

I can't leave now. Not yet. Not when several patients who have been critically injured are about to get brought in for emergency care. I may not fit in here at Lakewood, but for the next few hours, at least, I want to try to help. Somehow.

Drawing in a breath, I cinch my ponytail tighter, leave my workstation, and march toward the fray.

Fourteen

I enter the resuscitation bay and immediately get swept up by a tornado of activity and noise. Darting over to a corner to get out of the way, I watch with widening eyes as doctors, nurses, ED techs, pharmacists, respiratory therapy, and radiology techs rush to prepare for the simultaneous arrival of several critically injured patients.

As the commotion continues, I nervously peek out the open door of the resuscitation bay to view the rest of the department. Sick patients are in every room, and countless others line the corridors. Meanwhile, ambulance crews keep wheeling in even more people in need of care. This place is already far beyond capacity, and the arrival of several mass-casualty patients is imminent. It won't be long before every resource around here—from available personnel to supplies to blood products for transfusions—will be in short supply as the ED team races to save numerous lives at the same time.

The intense, coordinated chaos in the resuscitation bay ratchets up another notch as ED techs wheel stretchers and code carts into position, nurses prepare IV starts and bags of fluid, radiology techs ready the portable x-ray machines, and doctors work with respiratory therapy to test the intubation equipment. Soon, the social worker and two secretaries scurry in, and they head to the corner opposite me to watch until they're needed. Moments later, the conspicuous arrival of residents from the surgical service adds to the pandemonium—I recognize Jay Moen as the upper-level resident among them.

"Laura?" Dr. Santiago's voice carries over the din. "What do we know so far?"

A hush falls over the room. Like everyone else, I spin toward Dr. Santiago. He's standing smack in the center of the resuscitation bay between two empty stretchers. I have no idea how Dr. Santiago can appear so calm, but he seems in complete control as he looks toward the doorway. Following Dr. Santiago's line of sight and peering through the crowd, I see the charge nurse, Laura, entering the room; she's holding a blue sticky note in her hand that has something scribbled upon it.

"Okay, everyone, listen up," Laura barks loudly enough for all to hear. "Sounds like we're dealing with a two-car MVC. The driver of Car One is believed to have been under the influence when he swerved into oncoming traffic and struck Car Two at a high rate of speed. Car One had three male occupants, all believed to be in their twenties. On-scene assessment by EMS labeled the driver of Car One as green, one passenger as yellow, and the other passenger as red. Each patient is coming by ambulance, and all of them should be here any minute."

Laura stops to check her notes. I glance around the room, which has become pin-drop silent. Everyone is staring at Laura with focused gazes and concern etched in their faces while they wait for her to continue. I can guess what they're all thinking: three patients will be arriving in rapid succession, and at least two of them need life-saving interventions. Meanwhile, the third patient, the one labeled as green—the color assigned to those deemed the least injured in a mass-casualty incident—can't be ignored, for he could also have life-threatening injuries that just haven't manifested yet.

Laura looks up from her notes and resumes speaking fast. "Car Two had two occupants, a husband and wife who are both believed to be in their mid-to-late eighties. The driver, the male, was labeled as yellow. The female was labeled as red." She pauses, her expression grim. "Their ambulances should also be arriving shortly."

The tension in the room spikes. Members of the team begin exchanging glances. As I finish processing Laura's words, a sense of dread washes over me. In addition to the three patients from the first vehicle, the two elderly patients from the other car will also be arriving in need of emergency care. As if the prospect of receiving two more severely injured patients wasn't daunting enough, it's made even more so because these victims' advanced ages put them at particularly high risk of sustaining—and succumbing to—their injuries. My stomach churns.

Apprehensive silence still grips the room as everyone returns their attention to Dr. Santiago. Wasting no time, he surveys the group of providers while issuing orders:

"We'll divide into teams. The yellow and red patients from Car One will be brought in here. Doctor Ingram will lead the team that manages Patient Red. Doctor Vincent will manage Patient Yellow."

There's a surge of activity and talking among the group as Henry Ingram and Elly Vincent emerge from the crowd. They each position themselves at the head of one of the empty stretchers in the middle of the room. Promptly, two nurses and a tech move closer to Elly, designating themselves as the team members who will be working with her. Two other nurses and a tech go over near Henry's stretcher to indicate they'll be on his team.

"The patients from Car Two will be cared for in Resus Three," Dr. Santiago goes on, motioning in the direction of the adjacent resuscitation bay. "Doctor Gillespie will manage Patient Red. Doctor Reed will manage Patient Yellow."

Dylan steps forward, his brows pulled low and the muscles of his jaw working. He makes eye contact with Grant Reed, who has also appeared from the throng. Without a word, Dylan and Grant stride out the open door, headed for the adjacent resuscitation bay with only minutes to prepare before their critically wounded patients arrive. The remaining nurses and techs hurry after them while deciding amongst themselves who will join Dr. Reed's team and who will assist Dr. Gillespie.

Dr. Santiago next turns to the surgery residents. He orders two of them—an intern named Erik Prescott and another intern named Brittany Chen—to stay in here to assist Henry and Elly's teams. Jay Moen gets assigned to help Dylan and Grant next door.

With the care teams established, everyone swiftly resumes preparations, and the palpable energy in the room continues to intensify. Conversations between staff members are loud and fast, and updates are ringing out from the PA system. A radiology tech heads for the resuscitation bay next door with one of the portable x-ray machines, and the other radiology tech gets the second machine ready for use in here. The social worker is making calls to mobilize the additional resources he needs. Brenna from respiratory therapy is also on her phone, and I can overhear her telling one of her colleagues to go to the other resuscitation bay as quickly as possible.

"Quinn," Dr. Santiago unexpectedly calls out.

I jump and spin his way.

"You'll take care of Patient Green from Car One, and you'll manage him in Room Nine," Dr. Santiago tells me. "We'll grab one of the nurses and a tech from the main department to assist you."

There's another sharp break in the action as everyone stops what they're doing to look my way. I sense myself go pale. Me? In charge of one of the mass-casualty patients? No. There's no way. Managing a trauma patient is challenging enough; managing a trauma patient as part of a mass casualty—especially as a med student in a hospital where I'm not familiar with personnel or protocols—is an even more complicated manner. It doesn't matter that the patient was labeled as green, either; it's no guarantee he's out of the woods. There's still a chance the patient sustained occult injuries that I might not be qualified to recognize or manage.

"Quinn?" Dr. Santiago prompts.

Heart racing, I glance around the room, meeting the stare of each person who's watching me and waiting for my reply. In the split-second of total quiet, I sense something stir within me. The ED team is being called upon to treat numerous victims of a mass casualty, and every person here is going to be pushed to his or her limit. So I need to step up to the plate, too. I need to stop cowering. I need to stop doubting. For right now, at least, I'm part of Lakewood Medical Center's team.

I put my eyes on Dr. Santiago. "Okay. I'll do it."

Dr. Santiago nods before he turns and starts speaking with Henry. Everyone else resumes what they were doing. While organized chaos takes over the resuscitation bay once more, I peer out the door and locate the room labeled as Exam Nine. I can see why Dr. Santiago chose it for my patient: it's close enough to the resuscitation bays that Dr. Santiago will be able to circulate rapidly between all the rooms where the mass-casualty patients are being treated, so he'll be able to keep a close eye on things as they unfold.

"Jesse, how can I help?" Dr. Tammy Sanders, another ED attending, is hurrying into the room.

"Unfortunately, I need to ask you to manage the rest of the department; I anticipate being tied up with these trauma patients for a while." Dr. Santiago's slightly furrowed brow is the first hint of unease I've seen from him. "What's your staffing like out there? How many residents do you have working with you tonight?"

"I've got Maurine Endot, and I'll pull Xavier Tan over from Fast Track to help us in the main department. Wilma should be able handle Fast Track alone," Dr. Sanders replies. She gives Dr. Santiago a reassuring smile. "We'll make it work."

"Thanks," Dr. Santiago tells her.

Dr. Sanders quickly departs, and as she disappears from view, a secretary's voice rings out over the PA system:

"First ambulance is here. First ambulance is here."

My body lurches, and I lunge to a cart to grab some PPE, but I don't even have time to don a gown or gloves before an EMS crew bursts into the resuscitation bay pushing a stretcher. I stagger out of the way while taking in the haunting sight of a young man who's covered in blood and lying motionless on the backboard that's secured to the stretcher.

"Who do you have?" Dr. Santiago calls out.

"Patient Red from Car One," an EMS crew member shouts in reply.

There's an explosion of activity as Henry Ingram's team jumps into action. The nurses and tech transfer the patient over to their empty stretcher, and the lead EMS crew member starts giving Henry report. With incredible coordination and speed, Henry's team gets the patient connected to the monitor and stripped down to fully expose his injuries. Hadi places an IV in each of the patient's arms. No more than another minute or two passes before Henry has the patient intubated. As Brenna connects the patient to the ventilator, the radiology tech sets up to obtain a chest x-ray.

"Second ambulance is here Second ambulance is here."

The announcement rings through the air, and I whip around to view the doorway again. I have to leap aside as another EMS crew charges into the room. They, too, are wheeling in a young man who's strapped to a backboard on top of the stretcher. This young man is also terribly bloodied and bruised. He's moving slightly, and I hear him letting out weak, incoherent moans.

"Patient?" Dr. Santiago asks from his position near center of the room.

The lead crew member wipes his brow while he loudly responds, "Patient Yellow from Car One."

Elly is holding up her hand so the EMS crew can locate her in the throng. As the lead provider starts giving Elly report, her team works with equal skill and quickness as their colleagues. The patient is transferred to the ED stretcher and connected to the monitor. The nurse, Pete, places two IVs. Elly starts assessing the patient's airway while Brenna hurries to her side, ready to assist if the patient needs to be intubated.

"Third ambulance is here. Third ambulance is here."

My head is spinning as I tear my attention from Elly and shift toward the door once more. No one enters this time, but above the pounding of my own heart, I hear a racket right outside the room. The third EMS crew must be taking one of the elderly patients into the adjacent resuscitation bay where Dylan, Grant, and their teams are waiting.

I suddenly realize my patient will also be arriving at any moment.

A hefty punch of fresh adrenaline sets my heart rate soaring. With trembling hands, I throw on a procedure gown and face shield, and I grab a pair of gloves. I make a fast move for the door, about to sprint to Exam Nine, when another ear-piercing announcement blares out from the overhead speakers:

"Fourth ambulance is here. Fourth ambulance is here."

I hear another clamor outside the room, and I halt before reaching the doorway, not wanting to clog the corridor while the EMS crew is taking their patient into Dylan and Grant's resuscitation bay. During the one moment I restlessly wait, I send up a silent, anxious prayer to the Universe that the elderly husband and wife will somehow defy the odds and survive . . . that everyone involved in this terrible crash will live.

As fast as it came on, the noise in the corridor fades. The fourth crew has entered the other resuscitation bay, and my path is clear. I resume rushing for the exit, but I have to stop again to avoid crashing into Laura, who's coming back into this room.

"Doctor Santiago," Laura yells so he can hear her. "This last EMS crew has informed us that Patient Green from Car One refused medical transport and care. He was left on scene, and he's in the custody of the police."

I become very still as Laura's words process in my head. The fifth patient isn't coming. *My* patient isn't coming. In other words, I won't have to manage one of the mass-casualty patients after all. I've been let off the hook.

Yet I don't feel relieved. To the contrary, what I feel is an ongoing, nearly overwhelming desire to assist the ED team and help these patients in whatever way I can. I may only be a fourth-year medical student, but I want nothing

more than to do my part. Because I know—
somehow, amidst this frantic, chaotic, stressful
moment, I know more than I've ever known
before—that being part of Lakewood's
emergency medicine team is what I want, both
today and for residency. I'm determined to learn,
work hard, support the program, and make a
difference in the lives of patients who come here
for care.

I look over my shoulder at Dr. Santiago.
"How else can I help?"

"Go assist in Resus Three," he replies.

I dart past Laura, exit the room, and make
an immediate left into the adjacent resuscitation
bay. The huge room is identical in size and
layout to the one I just left behind, and at the
moment, it's also as equally loud, crowded, and
infused with intense energy while efforts to save
the two elderly patients are underway.

I stop to get my bearings. Up ahead on my
left, one of the care teams is closely surrounding
a stretcher. Through the flurry of fast-moving
activity, I catch a glimpse of Dylan. His gaze is
fixed with concentration as he intubates the frail-
appearing, elderly woman who's lying on the
stretcher before him. My eyes leap to the
monitor. The woman's blood pressure is
ominously low. With growing concern, I return
my attention to the team and watch the
respiratory therapist connect the sedated,
intubated patient to the ventilator. I can see the
injured woman has fresh bruises and cuts all over
her body. Dried blood is visible in her wispy,
white hair, and more blood stains are on her

clothes, which were cut off and now litter the ground. The woman is so tiny. So fragile. Does she have any chance of surviving?

I have to force myself to shift my gaze to the other side of the room. Grant Reed and his team are working with rapid, coordinated actions to get their patient stabilized. Grant is examining the patient. Kathy is drawing blood from one of the patient's IVs. Another ED nurse, Tom, is hanging IV fluid. Finn is setting up to get an ECG, and the radiology tech is preparing to obtain x-rays. The patient on the stretcher—the elderly man and spouse of the woman who was just intubated—appears to be moving, which is a small relief.

"Quinn?"

I'm yanked to attention when I hear Dylan's voice. I swivel around to face him. He's still positioned at the head of the woman's stretcher. As our eyes meet, I realize Dylan is the highest-ranking emergency medicine physician in the room, so he's in charge of what happens for the time being.

I take a step toward him, raising my voice so he can hear me. "Patient Green from Car One isn't coming, so Doctor Santiago sent me in here to—"

"Doctor Reed," someone barks from the doorway.

Dylan's eyes leap past me. I check over my shoulder to see who he's looking at. Laura is coming into the room, and she's heading directly toward Grant.

"Doctor Reed, we need you out in the main department to manage the boarding patients," Laura states, reaching Grant's side. "Carrie informed me that a couple boarders are becoming unstable. The intensivist was paged, but he claims he's so tied up in the unit that he can't come down to help. Meanwhile, Doctor Sanders is intubating a hemorrhagic stroke, Maurine picked up a STEMI, and Xavier is managing someone with urosepsis." She exhales hard. "So Doctor Santiago has asked that you oversee care of the boarding patients until an inpatient provider is able to assist."

Grant's eyes flick to Dylan's side of the room. "Who's going to help Dylan manage the patients in here?"

"Quinn will do it," I hear Dylan state.

I pause, and then I join Laura and Grant in turning Dylan's direction.

"Grant, give Quinn report," Dylan continues steadily. "Quinn, take over managing Patient Yellow so Grant can manage the boarders."

Everyone eyes me, and I can almost feel their uncertainty hovering in the air. Frankly, I don't blame them for being wary. I'm only a fourth-year med student—and a visiting med student, at that. I'm not the one who would typically care for a seriously injured trauma patient. Yet this situation is anything but typical. If there was ever a time to prove to Lakewood's ED staff that I belong here—if there was ever a time to prove to myself that I can truly be an

asset to Lakewood's emergency department—
that time is now.

I clear my throat and say to Grant, "Please
go ahead with report."

Grant slides away from the stretcher,
making room for the radiology tech to maneuver
the x-ray machine to the patient's side.
Motioning to the elderly gentleman, Grant
begins giving me report:

"This is Ivan Langton. Eighty-seven years
old. Restrained driver of an SUV hit head-on at a
high rate of speed. Vehicle spun into the median.
Airbags deployed. Unknown LOC. Awake upon
EMS arrival with a GCS of fourteen. Mr.
Langton's confusion cleared en route to the ED."
Grant checks the monitor and returns his blue
eyes to mine. "Upon arrival, the patient was on a
backboard and in a c-collar. He was protecting
his airway. Tachycardic in the one-teens. Mildly
hypoxic. Complaining of chest wall pain. Two
large-bore IVs placed. Blood drawn. Initial
bedside troponin within normal limits. Point-of-
care chem panel shows normal renal function.
Scout x-rays being obtained. Finn is about to get
an ECG."

My mind races to file away all the
information. "Got it. Thanks."

Grant gives me a tip of his head, and then
he quickly leaves the room with Laura at his side.
I blink and realize I'm now in charge of
managing Mr. Langton's care.

There's a chirp from the portable x-ray
machine as the radiology tech finishes getting

the images. I go to the tech's side and take a look at the pictures on the machine's little monitor. Thankfully, from what I can discern, at least, Mr. Langton's cervical spine, chest, and pelvic x-rays don't show any obvious acute abnormalities.

While the radiology tech hurriedly maneuvers the machine across the room to take x-rays of Dylan's patient, I turn toward Mr. Langton once more. I discover Kathy, Tom, and Finn are all watching me . . . waiting for me to take charge. Trying to appear as though I know what I'm doing, I position myself at the head of the stretcher and commence with my initial assessment of the man who's lying upon it.

Mr. Langton is tall and thin. He looks in good health for his age—and in a way, that makes his currently battered state even more heart-wrenching. Mr. Langton is awake, though he's keeping his eyes closed. His nose is swollen and discolored, and there's dried blood around his nostrils, so I'm guessing he sustained a nasal fracture when his airbag deployed. I see the cervical collar the EMS crew put on him has already been changed to one that's more cushioned. The patient was also already rolled off the backboard, so he's lying on the mattress of the stretcher, which will be a little softer against his back and hips. Mr. Langton is breathing normally, and the rise and fall of his chest is symmetric, though there is bruising running diagonally across his chest wall in the distribution of a seatbelt. His abdomen doesn't show any bruising or obvious distention. I don't see any deformities of his arms or legs, though his extremities are marred with bruises and skin tears.

I peer up at the monitor. Thankfully, Mr. Langton's vitals remain stable. I shift my attention back to Mr. Langton's face, and as I do, he opens his eyes and stares straight up at me.

"Mr. Langton, my name is Quinn Meyers," I tell him in a calm tone. "I'm a fourth-year medical student, and I'll be taking over for Doctor Reed, who was caring for you when you first arrived. How are you feeling?"

"Don't worry about me." Mr. Langton attempts to turn his head to look toward his wife's side of the room, but he can't because of the collar around his neck. He focuses on me again, and his gaze becomes desperate. "Please make sure my dear Ethyl is all right."

A lump fills my throat, and I peek across the resuscitation bay at where Ethyl Langton remains intubated and connected to the ventilator. She looks so small and vulnerable, surrounded by machines, IV lines, and hanging bags of medications and fluid. As I watch, the tech on Dylan's team goes to the head of Mrs. Langton's stretcher and begins driving her out the door. Dylan, one of the nurses on his team, and the respiratory therapist follow close behind. Undoubtedly, they're taking Mrs. Langton to the radiology suites for her CT scans.

I again look down at Mr. Langton. "Your wife is being cared for by an excellent team, and they're doing everything they can to help her."

"May I see her? May I talk to her?" Mr. Langton's words shake. "I don't want her going through this alone. She's my sweetheart, and I want her to know I'm here with her."

I manage to keep my own voice steady. "They've taken your wife to get some CT scans, so she isn't in here at the moment, but I'll tell you when she returns." I gently rest a hand on Mr. Langton's shoulder, hoping it somehow offers a tiny bit of comfort. "In the meantime, I want to make sure you're all right, too. I'll finish my exam, we'll get an ECG and send off some labs, and then we'll get you to the CT scanner."

"Do whatever you think is necessary." Mr. Langton fixes his gaze on the ceiling. Though his demeanor is stoical, a tear is running down the side of his face. "Just make sure Ethyl is all right. Please. She's the love of my life."

I feel the sting of emotion as I put my stethoscope in my ears. After I listen to Mr. Langton's heart and lungs, I step aside to allow Finn to obtain the ECG, which he hands over to me. Thankfully, I don't see any acute abnormalities on it. Tucking the ECG into the pocket of my scrubs, I resume examining my patient while Finn starts to clean Mr. Langton's wounds. Once my exam is completed, I go to the computer and enter orders. I then say to the team:

"Finn, please take the blood to the lab. Tom, please grab the PRN medications so we have them ready if Mr. Langton needs them. In the meantime, Kathy and I will get Mr. Langton to CT."

"You got it." Finn swaps out his gloves for a clean pair, gathers up the tubes of blood, and hurries away.

Tom is also moving for the door. "I'll go get those meds."

Kathy and I start preparing to transport Mr. Langton to the radiology suites, and it isn't long before we have him connected to the portable monitor and his IV fluids hanging from the pole on the stretcher. With Kathy walking alongside me, I drive the stretcher out of the resuscitation bay and start maneuvering it along the jam-packed corridor. Through the crowds, I see Dylan and his team up ahead and coming our direction. They've just left the radiology suites, and they're bringing Mrs. Langton back to the resuscitation bay.

"Sir, your wife is returning from CT." I tip down my head so Mr. Langton can see my face.

Mr. Langton's brow furrows. "How is she? Is she all right?"

I choose my words carefully. "I don't believe they have the results of her scans yet, but the radiologist should be reading them shortly."

Mr. Langton draws in a stuttering breath. "Oh, my dear Ethyl," he whispers, not knowing we're now passing Dylan and his team, and his wife's stretcher is only inches away. "She's the love of my life. She means everything to me. I'm not going to leave her."

My eyes track over to Dylan before I even realize it, and I discover he's looking at me. We continue watching one another as we go in opposite directions, and then Dylan is gone from my view . . . but the feeling that was generated by his nearness remains.

Kathy and I reach the end of the corridor, and we guide Mr. Langton's stretcher into the CT control room. The techs promptly hop into action, driving Mr. Langton into the adjoining room that houses the CT scanner itself. Moving with the speed of experience, the techs get Mr. Langton transferred to the bed that runs through the center of the scanner, which basically looks like a giant ring standing on its side, and then they return to the control room.

One tech pushes a few buttons on his computer, and through the window that looks into the CT room, I see the scanner light up. Within moments, Mr. Langton's CT images start appearing on the computer monitors. I lean in to view the images more closely. I'm relieved that I don't see evidence of a head bleed, and that Mr. Langton's cervical spine also looks all right. I do think there's a nasal fracture, as suspected. As the rest of the images load, I don't identify any other injuries, but I won't feel at ease until I've seen the official report from a radiologist.

The scanner goes dark. The techs jump up from their chairs, head into the adjoining room, and transfer Mr. Langton to the ED stretcher once more. With Kathy at my side, I drive Mr. Langton out of the radiology suites and back along the corridor. Soon, I'm parking his stretcher in its former place in the resuscitation bay.

With the patients stabilized and their initial workups complete, the resuscitation bay settles into a strange, subdued-yet-vigilant quiet. Other than conversations being spoken in low voices, all I hear is the repeating beep of the monitors and the faint hiss of Mrs. Langton's ventilator. Finn has resumed cleaning Mr. Langton's wounds, and Tom is using the portable monitor to cycle a fresh set of vitals. Kathy is entering notes into the computer. Meanwhile, on the other side of the room, Dylan is speaking to one of the nurses while the respiratory therapist is making adjustments to the settings on Mrs. Langton's ventilator.

"May I see Ethyl now?" Mr. Langton's soft, heart-wrenching plea somehow fills the resuscitation bay. "I don't want her to be alone."

Everyone seems to pause. I look over at Dylan. He meets my inquiring gaze and nods.

I focus on Mr. Langton once more. "Yes, you can see her now. Your wife is connected to a breathing machine, so she won't be able to speak, but you're welcome to talk to her all you want."

"Thank you." Mr. Langton's eyes brim with fresh tears. "Bless you."

Tom releases the break on Mr. Langton's stretcher, drives it across the room, and positions it right next to his wife's stretcher. Still flat on his back, Mr. Langton tremblingly reaches out and searches until he finds Mrs. Langton's limp hand, which he cradles in his.

"I'm here, Ethyl." He gives his wife's hand a squeeze. "I'm not going to leave you, sweetheart. I love you."

I draw a stuttering breath while fighting to hold back tears of my own. The room becomes poignantly quiet as both teams stop to watch Mr. and Mrs. Langton in respectful silence.

"Ethyl and I fell in love the moment we met." Mr. Langton smiles reminiscently while gazing up at the ceiling. He continues holding his wife's hand. "As soon as I saw her, I knew I didn't want to go another day without the blessing of having her at my side." His eyes shift to me. "That's true love, you know. When two people love one another, they want nothing more than to be together. They understand being together is the most precious gift of all."

My vision blurs with the tears I can no longer hide. While I inhale and exhale to steady my emotions, I sense someone watching me. As if drawn there, my eyes shift to Dylan.

"Hey, everyone." Laura walks into the room, shattering the stillness. "I've got Doctor Moen working on inpatient bed assignments, and I need an update on the status of . . ." She halts when she sees Mr. and Mrs. Langton. "What's going on?"

I turn from Dylan to face Laura. "Mr. Langton wants to stay with his wife," I explain simply.

Laura arches an eyebrow. "Well, obviously, we would like to accommodate that, however there are policies—"

"I'll ask Doctor Moen to have the SICU make arrangements for the Langtons to be in the same room," Dylan interjects calmly. His eyes briefly return to mine before he goes on to address Mr. Langton. "Sir, whether you're admitted or staying as a guest, we'll make sure you're able to remain with your wife."

Mr. Langton's jaw quivers with emotion. "Thank you for understanding."

"You're welcome, sir," Dylan tells him. He looks at me again before departing the room.

Laura watches Dylan go, and she shakes her head. "I sure hope the bed manager in the SICU won't mind," she remarks before trailing Dylan out the door.

"Quinn?" Kathy calls, motioning to the computer she's working at. "It looks like Mr. Langton's labs are starting to result."

Leaving Mr. Langton's bedside, I join Kathy in viewing the lab results displayed on the computer monitor. Thankfully, other than a slightly low potassium level, Mr. Langton's labs are stable with priors. Yet the knots in my stomach are only tightening as I next click on a tab to review the radiologist's reports of Mr. Langton's CT scans. The radiologist has confirmed Mr. Langton's head and cervical spine are okay, and that he does have a nasal fracture. He may also have a tiny contusion of his small bowel. Miraculously, though, the rest of his imaging was deemed to show no acute injuries.

Once I finish reading the radiology reports, I finally release the breath I was holding.

Mr. Langton didn't make it through the crash unscathed, yet he was remarkably lucky. I think he'll make a good recovery.

There's a smile on my face as I return to Mr. Langton's bedside. "Sir, the radiologist notes you have a broken nose and possible bruising of your bowel, so I would like to admit you for further monitoring and care. The great news, though, is that no other injuries were seen on your CT scans, and since your head and neck are okay, we can sit you up, if you would like."

"Yes, please," Mr. Langton says. "Thank you."

"You're more than welcome." I lift the back of Mr. Langton's stretcher so he's sitting up. I note he still doesn't let go of his wife's hand.

"How are Ethyl's results?" Mr. Langton asks. "And when does she get to wake up?"

I glance at Mrs. Langton, who remains dwarfed by machines while sedated and connected to the ventilator. I have no idea what her results show or what her prognosis might be. Almost reluctantly, I look at Mr. Langton again. His gaze is pleading. What can I possibly tell him? I don't want to worry this sweet man unnecessarily, but I also don't want to give him false hope. What if it turns out there's only devastating news about his beloved wife?

"I'm not sure if your wife's results are back yet," I begin carefully, "but—"

"Mr. Langton, I believe your wife will be able to come off the ventilator before the day is over," I hear Dylan say.

With a silent gasp, I look toward the doorway. Dylan is entering the room with Jay Moen at his side.

"We've been looking over your wife's CTs with the radiologist." Dylan comes up next to me while he continues speaking to Mr. Langton. "Your wife has two non-displaced rib fractures, but the underlying lung appears normal. More notably, she has a small bleed in her head called a subarachnoid hemorrhage, and so she needs to be admitted for monitoring. She'll undergo another CT in a few hours to ensure the bleed isn't getting bigger." He pauses, which gives Mr. Langton time to process the news. "If everything looks good on the repeat CT, and your wife otherwise remains stable, Doctor Moen and his team will wean your wife off the sedating medication she has been receiving. Once she's fully awake, they'll remove the breathing tube and get her off the ventilator." He puts a hand on Mr. Langton's shoulder. "Though we're still early in the process, I believe your wife will be all right."

Smiling tearfully, Mr. Langton clings to his wife's hand, leans closer to her, and says in her ear, "Did you hear that, Ethyl? You're going to be all right." He lifts his wife's hand and kisses it tenderly. "And I won't leave you until we both get to go home."

Dylan puts his eyes on me, and I return his look. Holding one another's gazes, we break into smiles of our own.

Jay Moen's pager suddenly goes off. He reads his new message and says, "The SICU is readying a bed for Mrs. Langton. What's the disposition plan for your patient, Quinn?"

I turn to Jay. "Mr. Langton sustained a bowel contusion, so I would like to formally admit him to your service for monitoring. He'll need an internal medicine consult, and he would probably also benefit from an inpatient ENT consultation for his nasal fracture."

"Sounds good." Jay glances at Dylan. "What do you think?"

"I completely agree," Dylan replies to Jay, though he's still watching me.

"Great. I'll update the SICU. After that, I'll return to clear Mr. Langton's cervical spine and get that collar removed." Jay heads for the door, but he stops and looks back at me. "Nicely done, Quinn." He gives me a casual salute before he exits the resuscitation bay.

I stare after him, taking a moment to let that sink in. Maybe, just maybe, I'll make it here at Lakewood after all.

Another moment passes, and then I become extremely aware of Dylan, who's still standing right beside me.

"I'll go update Doctor Santiago about the plans for our patients," I tell him quickly.

Without waiting for Dylan to reply, I head for the door.

"Quinn?" I hear him call after me.

I halt, take a split-second to catch my breath, and peer over my shoulder. When my eyes meet Dylan's again, my heart starts drumming harder.

"Great job." Dylan's handsome smile returns. "Lakewood is lucky to have you here."

I grin as a thrill fills my chest. "Thanks."

I turn and leave the room, feeling as though I'm walking on air.

Fifteen

I step outside, and as the doors of the emergency department slide shut behind me, I inhale a refreshing dose of morning air. There's something weirdly gratifying about finishing an overnight shift; it's like completing a tough workout—or, I suppose, like crossing the finish line of a marathon, although I'm not sure about the marathon because I've never run one and have absolutely no intention of ever doing so. Anyway, there's a sense of satisfaction in knowing that because I toughed it out and worked through the night, I get to go home and sleep while everyone else is only starting their work day. Granted, when I wake up later this afternoon having no sense of what time it is, and my circadian rhythms remain totally messed up for another few days, I won't be quite as pleased. For the moment, though, I'll savor the feeling of conquering an overnight shift.

I zip up my coat, hike my backpack onto my shoulder, and start making my way toward the bus stop, going in the opposite direction of countless hospital employees who are yawning, gripping coffee cups, and trudging toward the hospital to begin their morning shifts.

"Quinn?"

It takes me a second to convince myself I really heard Dylan's voice, and then I spin around. There's a conspicuous flutter in my chest when I spot him exiting the building, and the fluttering grows stronger when Dylan begins walking my way. I have no idea how he manages to do it, but although we just finished a brutal overnight shift, Dylan looks hotter than ever. There's something immensely attractive about the hint of facial scruff he developed overnight, and the way his hair appears as though he ran his hand through it a few times. He appears casual yet in-control with his jacket over his scrubs top and his messenger-style bag on his shoulder. Most striking of all, the morning sunlight is causing his green eyes to sparkle in a way that makes the fluttering in my chest evolve into full-on pounding.

Dylan reaches my side. "Were you planning to take the bus to your apartment?"

I nod in reply because, apparently, my voice has suddenly decided to skip town.

Dylan glances toward the bus stop before looking at me again. "May I drive you home, instead?"

"What?" I eke out, my voice making an awkward return. "I mean, aren't you going out to breakfast with Lindze?"

Dylan becomes very still, and then he slowly shakes his head. "No, I'm not going out with Lindze. Not today. Not ever." Keeping his eyes on mine, he takes a step closer. "I would really like to drive you home, if you would allow me."

A hundred thoughts clash inside my head in an instant. I know Dylan has decided not to pursue romance. I also know I need to sort out things with Chad. Yet I cannot deny the magnetic energy that's swirling between Dylan and me at this very moment. So while part of me wants to refuse Dylan's offer—frankly, the less time we're together, the less angst there will be for me—the other part of me wants nothing more than to spend a few more minutes with him.

"I appreciate you offering," I hear myself saying diplomatically, "but I don't want to inconvenience you, and—"

"It would be my pleasure," Dylan adds.

I sense heat seeping into my cheeks as my internal battle declares its victor. "Then a ride would be great. Thank you."

Dylan shows a smile before tipping his head in the direction of the parking garage. "My truck is in there."

Falling into silence, we head for the garage. Though we don't speak, however, the energy brewing between us seems to be communicating plenty. I try telling myself I'm simply experiencing the I've-been-up-all-night buzz, but I know what I'm feeling is due to much more than that. I need to distract myself. I have to say something. Anything. STAT.

"I've got some good news," I blurt out. "Before I left the ED, I looked through Mr. Langton's chart to get updated on how he's doing in the ICU."

Dylan turns his head to view me. "Hopefully, all is still going well?"

"Yes, I'm extremely happy to say. Mr. Langton continues doing so well, in fact, the admitting team is anticipating he'll be discharged to home in one or two days." I smile. "However, per the nursing notes, he has made it quite clear he's not leaving without his wife at his side."

Dylan focuses his gaze straight ahead, his expression serious. "Mr. Langton is a good man."

I study Dylan's profile, very aware that the draw I feel toward him is only growing stronger. "Yes, he is."

Dylan stays silent for a second or two before looking at me again. "I've got some good news to add to that: Ethyl Langton has been extubated. She's off the ventilator and breathing on her own."

"Really?" I exclaim with delight. "That's awesome!"

Dylan shows a smile. "Her repeat CT showed the subarachnoid was stable, if not slightly decreased in size. Over the course of the morning, her vitals remained solid, and her next round of labs also looked good. The ICU team was able to extubate her without difficulty." A glimmer of levity appears in his eyes. "Not surprisingly, she has already informed everyone she fully intends to go home with her husband,

and she won't stay in the hospital a minute without him."

I tip back my head and laugh. Soon, though, my laughter fades, replaced by a more pensive mood. "Mr. and Mrs. Langton were certainly an amazing example of a loving, devoted couple. I . . ." Blushing again, I let the rest of my words die on my tongue.

Dylan doesn't reply. He removes his keys from the pocket of his jacket and points the key fob to our left. There's a chirp from his black pickup truck. Stepping ahead of me, Dylan opens the passenger-side door.

"Thanks," I say in nearly a whisper as I brush past him to climb inside the truck.

While I fiddle with the seatbelt, Dylan shuts my door, walks around the front of the truck, and gets into the driver's seat. He snaps his seatbelt, starts the engine, and navigates out of the parking lot. As more seconds pass, the silence in the cab intensifies to the point that I'm actually starting to worry Dylan can hear how hard my heart is pounding.

"Quinn, there's another reason I wanted drive you home," Dylan finally states.

My pulse bumps up another notch. I shift in my seat to face him. And I wait.

Dylan adjusts his grip on the steering wheel and keeps looking out the windshield. "I want to apologize for what I said to you at the bistro the other night." He pauses to swallow. "You were right: I had no business saying the things I did, and I'm sorry."

"You don't need to apologize. You have every right to your opinion, and you had the right to express it." I peer out my window. "Admittedly, your remarks stung, but I also knew you were only trying to help." I look at him again. "I'm sorry I walked out on you that night."

"I don't blame you for leaving." Dylan pulls his eyes from the road to meet mine. "Yes, I was trying to help, but I didn't go about it in the best way. I guess it was making me insane to think you might be getting misled or hurt by someone whose devotion isn't sincere. You deserve infinitely better than that, Quinn." He peers out the windshield once more. "Regardless, it was wrong of me to assume I knew anything about your situation with Chad, what conversations the two of you have had, or how you . . . feel about him." He clears his throat. "So again, I'm sorry."

Chad.

His name hits my ears, and I'm rocked to the core when I realize I don't feel much of anything in response. In fact, I haven't felt any spark or excitement when thinking about Chad for days . . . for weeks. Staggeringly, at some point along the way recently, though Chad remained in my mind, he stopped controlling my heart. It happened so gradually, though, I didn't recognize the change until now. Why—how— has the man who monopolized my heart for so long faded into the distance?

Perhaps living far away from Chad these past several weeks has helped me view him more objectively, thereby making it easier to admit his approach to relationships is vastly different than what I want. Time away from Chad has helped me come to terms with reality rather than continuing to make excuses to justify his behavior.

Or maybe it has been eye opening to observe couples like Danielle and Joel, and Savannah and Wes—couples who are clearly dedicated to making their relationships work. For me, they've come to represent how people who are genuinely in love will find a way to prioritize and strengthen their relationships, even when life puts challenges in their paths.

Or it could be that I learned an incredible lesson from Mr. Langton this morning. Without knowing it, in the middle of that loud, chaotic emergency department, Mr. Langton quietly exemplified what lasting, selfless, and unfailing love truly means. It's a lesson I'll never forget

Or maybe this change in me happened because I met Dylan.

Though I tried to deny it, in that first moment I met him, Dylan ignited something within me that I had never experienced for a man before. And since that time, my feelings for Dylan have only expanded and richened. As I've observed him, spent time with him, learned more about him, and been cared for by him, my heart has been opened to what being in love could really be like. What it should be like.

Because I've fallen in love with Dylan Gillespie.

I nearly gasp aloud as the thought hits me.

I am in love with Dylan.

For one glorious moment, the epiphany is elating, and it sends my heart soaring. An instant later, however, the wildly beautiful and ecstatic feeling that's coursing through me disappears, replaced by something heavy and cold.

I've fallen head-over-heels for a man who has sworn off love.

Is that why Dylan made his feeling so clear to me the other night at the bistro? Was he sensing I was developing feelings for him, and he wanted me to understand that my feelings would never be reciprocated? The thought is both humiliating and completely heartbreaking.

When I sense the truck slowing, I emerge from my racing thoughts and see we're pulling into the parking lot of my apartment building. A blast of panic hits me. In only a few moments, I'll have to speak to Dylan again. But what am I supposed to say? How am I supposed to behave around the man I just realized I'm completely in love with, especially when that man has made it abundantly clear he has no interest in romance? I dig through my brain for answers, but my mind is empty. It's a pit of nothingness.

Dylan pulls the truck into a parking stall and turns off the engine. There's a beat before he removes the keys from the ignition and turns my way. I hurriedly unbuckle my seatbelt with my shaking hands.

"Thank you for the ride," I tell him.

"You're welcome."

I open the door, slide out of the truck, and show a strained smile. "Thanks again."

I swing the door closed and start charging toward the building's main entrance. A moment later, my insides leap when I hear the unmistakable sound of Dylan getting out of his truck and shutting the door.

"Quinn?"

I nearly trip as I force myself to stop. Doing my best to slow my rapid breathing, I turn back around.

Dylan comes across the parking lot and stops in front of me. I raise my eyes to his. Every instinct is drawing me to him, yet every thought is reminding me there will never be anything romantic between Dylan and—

"Quinn," Dylan says, peering at me closely. "I realize this isn't the best time or place to tell you this, but I think I'm going to go crazy if I wait any longer."

I draw in a swift, stunned breath. Is it possible? Is Dylan about to say what I think he's going to say?

Dylan steps closer. "Quinn, I—"

"Quinn?" someone calls from far behind me.

I freeze at the sound. I know that voice. I know that man's voice better than anyone's.

But it's impossible. There's no way he could be here.

I see Dylan shift his eyes to look past me in the direction from where the call came. At the same moment, I begin hearing someone approaching. My breathing grows shallow as I listen to the recognizable cadence of the footsteps. With a gulp, I turn around.

Chad is walking toward me.

For one more moment, I try telling myself it can't be him, but even the way he's dressed is vintage Chad: a long wool coat over a sweater, tapered jeans, and one of his many pairs of nice shoes.

"Chad," I whisper to no one as I stare across the parking lot.

Beside me, Dylan exhales slowly. "So that's Chad."

I press a hand on my churning abdomen. "Yes. That's Chad."

Dylan says nothing more. I also remain quiet; I'm too shocked to do anything but continue staring as Chad comes toward us. There's something strange and almost uncomfortable about seeing Chad in this place. It doesn't make sense, somehow. It doesn't feel right.

"Hi, hon." Chad gets to my side and adopts a smile that doesn't reach his brown eyes, which are shifting between Dylan and me. He pulls me into a hug. "Surprise."

I briefly hug him in return before I step back. "Wh-what are you doing here?"

"I had some days off, so I decided to drive out here to see you." Chad grins proudly. He motions down the street. "I'm staying in the hotel about a block away. Since I got in late last night, I decided not to surprise you until this morning."

I peer down the road, blink a few times, and resume gawking at Chad while I process what's happening. As my shock slowly begins wearing off, memories of my relationship with Chad return to the forefront of my mind. I think about the years we've spent together. I remind myself that I know Chad better than I know anyone else. I realize what a sacrifice it was for Chad to make the cross-country journey to find me. However, all I can think to say is:

"How did you know where I was living?"

"From that text you sent me after you moved in." Chad is still grinning. "You sent me a picture of this building with the address, remember?"

It takes me a second or two, and then I do remember. I remember when I texted him about moving here. That day seems like a lifetime ago.

"The fact that you showed up right now is perfect timing, too," Chad goes on. "I had just walked over here, and I was about to call you when I saw . . . you getting out of the truck." Chad's gaze flicks to Dylan again.

My chest hurts like it's being squeezed in a vice. "I can't believe you're really here."

"Well, I felt that since you and I have such important things to talk about, we should talk about them in person." Chad shows another smile. "Besides, the drive gave me a few days of peace and quiet to sort through my thoughts." He lets his gaze linger on mine before he shifts to face Dylan squarely. He extends a hand. "Chad Abbott. Quinn's very good friend."

Dylan draws himself up to his full height and briefly shakes Chad's hand in return. "Dylan Gillespie."

Chad's eyes narrow as he gives Dylan a once-over. "Med student?"

"Resident." Dylan's expression and tone reveal nothing. "I was driving Quinn home after our overnight shift."

"Ah." Chad slings an arm across my shoulders. "Well, Quinn's here safely now, so feel free to leave."

"Chad!" I shrug off his arm. "Dylan was extremely kind to drive me home, and—"

"You don't need to defend me, Quinn." Dylan's focus hasn't left Chad's face. "I'm capable of doing that myself."

Chad blinks a few times under Dylan's unwavering stare, and then he clears his throat, rolls back his shoulders, and opens his mouth to reply. Before Chad can say anything, however, Dylan turns to me.

"Great work during the shift." Dylan's tone remains measured and restrained. "Goodbye, Quinn."

There's something horribly, crushingly final about Dylan's words, and I'm unable to formulate a response before he starts walking away. I stare after him while a cold, hollow sensation consumes me. Parting ways with Dylan like this isn't right. This isn't how it's supposed to be.

Or is it?

I can't possibly understand Dylan as completely as my heart has me convinced that I do. I only met Dylan a few weeks ago, and it would be reckless for me to get swept up in feelings for him.

In contrast, I've known Chad for years. He drove here because he wants to make things right between us. I've been longing to speak with Chad, and now the chance is right in front of me. I shouldn't pass it up.

At least, that's what my mind is telling me in the split-second I spend trying to sort through my racing thoughts. My heart, however, is telling me something else. My heart is telling me I should go after Dylan. My heart is screaming that letting Dylan go would be the biggest mistake of my life.

"Dylan, wait!" I hear myself yell.

Dylan stops with the door to his truck halfway open. He doesn't turn around.

"Quinn?" Chad is staring at me. "What are you doing?"

Breathing fast, I spin Chad's way. "I'll be right back, okay?"

Chad glances in Dylan's direction, and he puts a hand on my arm. "You can't be serious."

I check over my shoulder. Dylan has gotten into his truck and shut the door.

I pull my arm from Chad's hold. "Give me a couple minutes. Please."

Chad exhales hard. "You do realize I drove all the way across the country to see you, right?"

"Yes, of course I do. I—"

The roar of Dylan's truck engine hits my ears, and my heart lurches. Dylan can't leave before I say something to him. I need to make things right.

I hastily start retreating from Chad. "Just wait here."

I whip around and sprint across the parking lot. Dylan is about to put his truck into gear when he glances up, doing a double take when he notices me. Slowly, he removes his hands from the steering wheel.

I reach the idling truck, tug open the passenger-side door, climb inside, and shut the door behind me. For several seconds, a thick, strained silence fills the cab.

"What are you doing, Quinn?" Dylan finally asks while staring out the windshield.

"I wanted to tell you how much . . . I mean, I wanted to make sure things between us were . . ." I trail off, realizing I have no clue what I'm actually trying to say, let alone how I want to say it. I finally blurt out, "Look, you can't just leave like this."

Dylan arches an eyebrow and peers sideways at me. "I can. And I should."

"I swear I didn't have any idea Chad was coming." I push my hair from my face. "I'm as shocked to see him as you are."

Dylan keeps an empty gaze on mine. "And now that he's here, how do you feel about it?"

"What do you mean?"

"How do you feel about the fact that Chad is here?" Dylan repeats with deliberateness. "More importantly, how do you feel about *him*?"

I stare helplessly into Dylan's eyes. How can I possibly answer his question? How can I make him understand, when I don't understand any of it myself? Everything has become so complicated and confusing that I have no idea what I'm supposed to think or how I'm supposed to feel anymore.

Dylan seems to interpret my drawn-out silence as the answer he needs. Channeling his concentration out the windshield again, he shakes his head.

"You know, this is precisely what I was talking about," he states with an edge to his tone. "This is another example of why it's a mistake to pursue a relationship." He looks at me once more. His expression softens. "Quinn, over these past few weeks, you caused me to want to open my heart again. For the first time in two years, I decided to take a chance on a relationship. And after caring for the Langtons, I was inspired not to wait any longer before telling you how I felt." He motions vaguely in the direction of where Chad remains standing in the middle of the parking lot, and his jaw clenches. "This, however, has only reaffirmed my point. This is precisely why it's a mistake to open one's heart, and it's why I won't ever do so again."

I have to fight the impulse to reach out to him. I can barely breathe. My aching head is growing light. A gnawing, sickening sensation is rising up inside me because I know everything has gotten completely mixed up, but it's too late to fix any of it now.

Dylan puts a cool gaze on me. "It's evident you're not completely over Chad, so whatever I was dumb enough to think might have existed between us means nothing. There isn't anything else we need to discuss."

I realize I'm being dismissed. My throat is thick, and I can hardly see through my tear-filled eyes. There's so much I want to say, but all that comes out of my mouth is:

"Dylan, I'm sorry."

In a fog, I get out of the truck. As soon as I shut the door, Dylan drives away, the roar of his engine fading fast as he disappears from view.

Sixteen

"You don't seem happy to see me," Chad remarks without hiding his tone of annoyance.

I don't reply at first. I can't reply. My emotions are swinging too wildly as the gut-wrenching discussion Dylan and I had replays in my head on a merciless, relentless loop. None of this seems real. Dylan is gone. Chad is here. And in my exhausted-yet-wide-awake haze, I'm left floundering to sort everything out.

I finish filling two glasses of water at the kitchen sink, cross the room, and place them on the table. Taking a seat across from Chad, I finally meet his gaze head-on.

"Of course I'm happy to see you." I sip my water, giving myself time to choose my words. "I'm also extremely surprised."

Chad grins. "Good. I wanted to surprise you. That's why I haven't been calling you lately."

I chug down the rest of my drink.

Chad casually rests an arm over the back of his chair, and he peers around the room. "This apartment is really nice."

"Yes, it is." I place my glass on the table. "I was extremely fortunate Danielle and Savannah let me move in with them. I have no idea what I would have done without their help."

Chad nods but says no more, causing an awkward stop in the conversation. The strained quiet continues while we sometimes make eye contact and other times avert our gazes. I fidget with my water glass, waiting for exhilarating energy to fill the space between Chad and me, like it always does when I'm with Dylan, but instead, the distance across the table feels like a vast, uncomfortable void.

Chad suddenly sits up taller. "So you must know why I'm here."

I flick my eyes in his direction, feeling a little sick to my stomach. Am I ready for this? For weeks, I've desperately wanted to talk to Chad, but now that the opportunity has come, I'm not sure I want it. So much of what I thought I wanted only a few weeks ago—everything I used to believe about relationships—has changed. My understanding of love has grown into something else. Something more.

Yet it doesn't matter if I'm ready. This discussion is clearly going to happen, and it's going to happen right now.

"Yes, I think I know why you're here," I reply, keeping my voice from wavering.

"Good. Then we can get right to it." Chad clears his throat. "Look, after you moved out here, I realized how much I missed having you around. Yes, I got spooked about the idea of a long-distance relationship, and I thought it would be easiest if we weren't officially tied down while living far apart." He reaches a hand across the table and rests it on mine. "But once you left, I realized how badly I still wanted to be with you. I want to be with you more than ever before." His brow furrows. "I know I've promised in the past to commit, but I mean it this time. Please give me another chance."

My mind comes into focus, and I peer directly into Chad's eyes. "So you're fine with long-distance relationships?"

He withdraws his hand. "What do you mean?"

"Well, since you didn't want to do a couples match for residency, we'll soon be living on opposite sides of the country," I calmly point out. "So I obviously need to ask: are you going to get 'spooked' by the long distance again?"

Chad blinks fast. "That's an impossible question to answer. I can't say what it's going to be like while we're doing our residencies. I can't predict the future, Quinn."

I sit back, putting more distance between us. "And when you consider committing to a relationship with me, does it really feel like you're going to be 'tied down,' as you said?"

"What? No." Chad exhales with obvious frustration. "That was only a figure of speech. You're reading way too much into it."

"I see." I gaze out the window. "Then I've got to admit I'm confused. Why do you even want a relationship? What do you believe relationships are all about?"

Chad is staring at me as though he has never seen me before. "Where are all these esoteric questions coming from?"

I don't answer. Instead, I keep studying his face while recalling all the years I spent with him in our emotionally exhausting, on-again-off-again relationship. I almost cringe when I think about everything I sacrificed, explained away, and let myself believe while Chad's commitment rose and fell like the tides. I expected far too little. I tolerated far too much.

As these thoughts go through my head, my heart becomes as calm as my mind. Thank goodness I came out here this month. Because of this journey, I finally discovered what it really means to be in love. At last, I understand what I want, and I know who I want.

"Chad," I begin, my voice not wavering in the slightest, "I don't want to get back together with you. If I'm being honest, I don't think you really want to get back with me, either."

His eyes bug out. "Excuse me?"

"We shared some good times while we supported one another through the challenges of med school," I continue steadily. "But we're not in love now, and in hindsight, I don't think we were ever in love." I show him a gentle smile. "It's time for both of us to move on."

Chad gapes at me, his mouth opening and closing as though he's trying to speak. Eventually, his stunned expression morphs into a scowl. "This is about that Dylan guy, isn't it? He's been some sort of rebound for you, hasn't he?"

I shake my head. "No. This isn't about Dylan. This is about you and me. This is about admitting we have really different beliefs about relationships, commitment, and love. This is about realizing that, because of our differences, we'll never be happy together."

Chad's nostrils flare. He stands up. "Listen to yourself. You're talking about throwing away everything we've shared because some guy you barely know has messed with your emotions."

"No, I'm not throwing anything away. I'm acknowledging that you don't have what I'm looking for, so for both our sakes, I'm telling you goodbye. For good." I get to my feet and draw in a breath. "Chad, I want someone who doesn't run away every time things get hard. I want someone who demonstrates he's committed, not someone who only says he is. I want someone who wants nothing more than to be with me." I go around the table and give Chad a light kiss on the cheek. "You'll fall in love one day. It's just not going to be with me."

Chad takes a stiff step away. "So that's it? You're ending things? You're saying it's over?"

"No, things aren't over." I smile again. "In fact, in a way, I think our lives are only beginning."

Chad clenches his jaw while backing up for the door. "You think you've got things all figured out, but you'll regret this. When you finally come to your senses, though, don't expect me to be waiting for you." He tugs open the door, storms out of the apartment, and slams the door behind him.

Suddenly, the apartment is extremely quiet and still. I peer out the window, amazed by how calm and certain I feel; it's like standing in the eye of an emotional storm. I've grappled with a lot of uncertainty these past few weeks—these past few years, really—but I'm completely certain about this. It may have taken a cross-country trip, an elderly couple in the emergency department, and a wonderful man to help me realize the truth, but finally . . .

Dylan.

His name fills my mind, and a heavy ache presses upon my chest. I go into the main room and collapse onto the chair near the fireplace. Bending forward, I drop my head in my hands while horrible regret consumes me. I was so blind. So stupid. I wasted so much time holding out for a love that didn't exist when a chance at real love was right in front of me. If only I had listened to my heart. If only I had been honest with myself. Instead, in my foolish determination to give Chad another chance, I've lost Dylan. No matter what happens now, he'll never trust me or open up to me again. I've missed out on the chance to share with him a love that would have been more amazing than anything I've ever known.

I jump when I hear the front door being opened. Raising my tear-stained eyes, I see Danielle and Savannah entering the apartment. They're carrying venti-sized cups and breakfast foods from a nearby café. As soon as they see me, they both come to a hard stop.

"Quinn?" Danielle sounds alarmed. "What's wrong?"

I groan. "Chad was here."

Danielle drops her breakfast sandwich. "Chad? Your ex? He was here?"

"Yes." I let my tears fall. "And I've made a complete mess of things."

Savannah and Danielle exchange a stunned look. Without a word, Savannah hastily collects their drinks, scoops Danielle's sandwich off the floor, and takes everything into the kitchen. Meanwhile, Danielle comes into the main room and sits on the couch. Moments later, Savannah emerges from the kitchen and takes a seat beside Danielle. After a time, Danielle softly asks me:

"Do you want to talk about it?"

I sigh exhaustedly. "Chad showed up here this morning completely unannounced."

Danielle almost chokes. "How in the world did he find you?"

"From a text I sent him a long time ago." I look out the window at nothing. "After I moved here, I sent him a picture of this building and included its address. Apparently, Chad decided to use that info to surprise me by driving out here. When I . . . got home from my overnight shift this morning, Chad was in the parking lot." I choose not to share the part about Dylan driving me home after work. That's too personal. Too painful.

Savannah draws in a breath. "If Chad drove all the way across the country to see you,

I'm guessing he wanted to talk about rekindling your relationship?"

I grimace. "Yep."

Danielle's eyes are widening. "So what happened? What did you decide?"

"I told Chad that I finally realized something I should have realized a long time ago: I'm not in love with him, and I don't think I've ever really been in love with him."

"No way!" Danielle claps a hand over her mouth. "How did he react?"

"Unfortunately, he didn't take the news well. I think he's going to have a long, lonely drive home." I pause. "I hope, though, he'll eventually see this was the best for both of us."

Danielle and Savannah share another glance of silent communication. When they turn to me again, they actually both have smiles on their faces.

"What?" My eyes shift between them. "What is it?"

Danielle appears to hesitate. "I realize this might be too soon, but I have to say that I'm glad you gave Chad the boot. From everything you've told us about him, I've never thought Chad sounded as though he came even remotely close to deserving you."

Savannah starts nodding. "I feel the same way. I'm immensely sorry about what happened between you and Chad, because of all the heartache it has caused you to suffer. At the same time, I'm not sorry about what happened because I'm glad Chad is out of your life." She tips her head to one side. "Does that make sense?"

"Yes, it makes sense," I say honestly. "It makes absolute, total sense."

The three of us fall quiet. I look outside again, my heart aching with fresh regret. As before, it's not regret about Chad—it's regret over Dylan. I'll never tell Danielle or Savannah this, though. In fact, I hope no one will ever find out. Since Dylan and I will soon be working together regularly in the ED, and he's the brother of one of my new friends, I won't be able to avoid seeing him. So the best I can hope for is that nobody else will know what transpired between us. It's the only way things won't get even more torturously uncomfortable than they're already going to be. While it's agonizing to think of working alongside Dylan while loving him in silence, I can only hope no one else will ever know how I feel.

Suddenly, the ache in my heart deepens, and the emotional exhaustion of these past several weeks becomes more than I can take. I have to get away. Today. Now. I need to go to a place where I can clear my head, compartmentalize my emotions, and come to terms with what my future holds.

"Quinn?"

I yank my eyes from the window and see Danielle kneeling beside my chair. Her brow is furrowed with concern.

"You really don't look okay." Danielle puts a hand on my arm. "What else can we do for you?"

"You've both been a huge help already, as always." I attempt a smile. "I was just thinking I might ask Doctor Kent if I can rearrange my schedule a little bit." I glance Savannah's way. "If he'll permit, I'll move my shifts for this week to the end of the month."

"I think that's a great idea. You've been through a lot lately, and you should take a few days to recover." Danielle looks over her shoulder at Savannah.

"I agree," Savannah states. "I'm sure Wes will be fine with that, too, especially since you're the only med student on the ED rotation this month, which means the schedule is pretty wide open."

I get to my feet, my thoughts speeding up as my plan continues formulating in my mind. "I'll call Doctor Kent right now." I show them another smile. "Thank you again for everything."

I head to my room and shut the door. Using my phone, I pull up Dr. Kent's number while checking the April calendar to strategize how I can rearrange my schedule. Thankfully, it won't be hard. If I load my schedule with shifts at the end of the month, I can take off a week right now.

And I know exactly where I need to go.

Seventeen

The golden sunlight of late afternoon is filtering through the trees as they sway in the breeze, creating dancing silhouettes of leaves at my feet. I lock my car and zip up my coat, and I begin making my way across the parking lot, headed for the outlook that provides the magnificent view of the south rim of Yellowstone's upper falls.

The area is quiet this afternoon. I don't see many tourists, and all I hear is the wind and the roar of the distant waterfall. As my eyes drift across the familiar scene, I grow pensive. I'm still not sure why I came back here, when every sight and sound vividly reminds me of Dylan. Yet when I left the apartment a few days ago, desperate to get away, I knew I needed to come to this spot. I had to return to the place where my journey of the heart began. I hoped that, somehow, doing so would help me accept what could not be and find the strength to move forward.

I reach the waist-high wall of the outlook and lean against it, gazing at the mighty waterfall on the other side of the canyon. Like it was when

I visited here weeks ago, the panorama from this place is nothing short of majestic. This moment would be serenely perfect, were it not for the hollowness that continues to consume me. I wonder if the pain I feel about what happened with Dylan will ever fade.

As I watch the falls, I inhale and exhale with deliberateness, trying to clear my mind and settle my heart. I then shift my focus to the sounds of the birds chirping in the trees. At last, I close my eyes, allowing the breeze to brush soothingly against my face.

"Miss, do you have authorization to be in the park at this hour?" I hear a man behind me ask.

I jump in surprise, and my eyes spring open. I then become completely still. The man's deep, commanding voice sounded like Dylan's. Exactly like Dylan's.

It can't be him, though. I know this. Even so, my heart has begun pounding wildly. I draw in a breath. Very slowly, I turn around.

Dylan is standing on the other side of the lookout. Dressed in a field jacket over a sweatshirt, dark jeans, and heavy boots, he looks completely at home and meant for this place. His hair is getting rustled by the wind, and the dipping sun is catching his face at an angle, highlighting his strikingly handsome features. And his eyes—his mesmerizing green eyes—are glistening in the sunlight as they focus on mine.

"Dylan," I utter, nearly breathless. "What are you . . . how did you . . ."

Dylan starts striding closer, keeping his gaze locked on me. As he draws near, my body fills with a thrilling sense of anticipation. Dylan finishes closing the gap between us, comes to a stop right in front of me, and searches my face. At last, he breaks the silence:

"Quinn, do you have any idea how many times I've come to this spot over the past couple of days, hoping I would find you here?"

I peer up at him in astonishment, and then my body grows wonderfully warm. "You came all the way out here—all the way to Yellowstone—to try to find me?"

Dylan exhales and looks out at the falls. His brow furrows. "Driving away from you after our last shift, knowing you might get back together with a man who didn't deserve you, was the hardest thing I've ever done." He shakes his head. "I tried telling myself I was making the right choice by leaving you. I tried convincing myself I was being smart to protect my heart. It was no use, though. I knew my heart was yours." He looks at me again, and something in his gaze causes a tingle of delight to rush down my spine. He lowers his voice and goes on, "When Danielle told me what happened between you and Chad, and that you had left to come out here, I knew I had to try to find you. I had to know if I still had a chance."

Tears of joy are brimming in my eyes. "Dylan," I say, the word trembling with emotion, "you've always had that chance with me."

Dylan becomes very still for one long moment. He then slowly—cautiously—reaches out and takes my hands in his. "I've fallen in love with you, Quinn. You've inspired me to open my heart again, and you've let me feel love more fully than ever before. I want nothing more than to be with you, if you'll have me."

My breathing hitches. "I've fallen in love with you, too."

"You have?" Dylan breaks into a smile that makes me weak in the knees. He uses his thumbs to caress my hands. "You really love me?"

His touch is sending thrilling sensations up my arms. "Yes, I really love you." I pause to catch my breath. It feels so elating to be telling him the truth. "I used to think I knew what love was, but I was wrong. I was so, so wrong. Because of you, though, I finally understand what love truly is."

Dylan holds my hands against his chest. "You're the reason I was willing to trust in love again. You gave me my heart back."

"And you helped me feel my heart for the first time," I whisper.

We gaze at one another as if we never want to look away. I then see Dylan's respirations quicken, and I sense my own heart start beating faster. Keeping his eyes on mine, Dylan releases my hands and places his palms on my cheeks, cradling my face. The draw I feel toward him suddenly intensifies, and I lean in closer. Dylan bends down and presses his lips to mine.

My whole body comes alive with an exhilarating sensation that nearly overwhelms me. Dylan continues kissing me with tenderness and passion while his hands drift down my arms and wrap around my waist. I reach up and drape my arms around his neck, returning his kisses with equal desire. This is what it feels like to be in love, and this is what it feels like to be with someone who loves you in return.

When our kiss is finally done, Dylan tips his head to look at me. He shows a grin. "You do realize I've been in love with you since the day I met you, right?"

My eyebrows rise. "You mean, you fell in love with a girl who caused a traffic jam at the park's entrance, spilled luggage all over the road, and locked herself out of her car?"

"Yep." Dylan chuckles. "I was a goner. I couldn't get you out of my mind after that, and it only got worse when we crossed paths again here and helped that man who needed medical care." He looks away, as if lost in the memory. "Still, though, I thought I was safe because I would never see you again." He focuses on me again, and his smile reappears. "So you can imagine how I felt when you were the one who opened the door of the flooding apartment that night."

"I was as shocked as you were," I say with laugh while brushing my hand along the side of his face. "The truth is that I fell head-over-heels for you, too, the moment I laid eyes on you at the park's entrance. Though I tried to convince myself otherwise, you made it impossible for me to deny I was in love with you."

Dylan replies by pulling me in and fervently kissing me again. I become lost in the bliss of his touch. I feel as though I'm soaring, and I never want to come down.

Dylan finishes by letting his lips lightly caress mine before he shows another amused grin. "You certainly got a lot more than you bargained for when signing up for a month-long rotation, didn't you?"

"That's an understatement," I say with another laugh, relishing the sensation of having his arms around me. "I thought my biggest worry was going to be trying not to wreck my reputation at Lakewood before residency even started."

Dylan quirks an eyebrow. "What do you mean?"

"I was afraid I would discover I was a terrible fit for Lakewood," I admit in a quieter tone. "And I thought everyone else would think the same thing."

"Hang on. You've seriously been worried that you're not good enough to work in Lakewood's ED?" Dylan is staring at me. "You've been worried the staff doesn't think well of you?"

"Well . . . yes," I sigh. "I've never worked in such a busy ED before, and . . ." I trail off and put on another smile. "But none of that is important. Not right now."

Dylan takes me by the hands once more. "Yes, it is important, Quinn. You need to know you've been doing a fantastic job in the ED. You're amazing, in fact. And I'm not the only one who thinks so. I've heard Jesse and several staff members say they're looking forward to having you as part of the residency program." He gently tucks one of my curls behind my ear. "You've made a great impression on everyone."

My mouth falls open. "Really?"

"Really." Dylan's expression is so genuine. So earnest. "You're going to be a major asset to the residency program, and you're going to make a difference for the better in the lives of a lot of people." He tenderly brings me into his embrace. "You're incredible, Quinn."

I rest my head against his chest, letting myself drown in the strength and security of his arms. This feels so natural. So right.

"Speaking of residency." Dylan adjusts how he's holding me to meet my gaze again. "I realize trying to navigate a relationship while we're both handling the demands of residency won't be easy, but I want you to know I'm dedicated to making our relationship work." He places a soft kiss on my forehead. "I love you, Quinn."

"I love you, too," I whisper.

While the glow of the setting sun lingers upon us, our lips meet again. When our kiss is done, I sigh with complete and total joy. This journey of the heart has taken me somewhere I never expected, and I know Dylan and I will continue this journey together, strengthened by our true and lasting love.

Epilogue

"Happy birthday, dear Danielle! Happy birthday to you!"

I finish singing along with the crowd, and I join in the boisterous applause that follows. From her seat at the head table, Danielle blushes and waves to her party guests. Joel, who's seated beside her, leans in and gives Danielle a kiss that causes her cheeks to redden with delight even more.

Still clapping, I gaze over the scene with a smile. Joel did a fantastic job planning Danielle's birthday party here at her favorite restaurant, and dining outdoors under the evening sky has been idyllic. Guests are seated at tables adorned with candles and flowers. White string lights are hanging from the trees and glowing against the deepening twilight. Music is drifting through the air, accented by the sounds of clinking glasses and lively conversations. And as for the meal itself, the authentic Italian dinner has been exquisite.

The waiters finish clearing everyone's entrées, and they soon reappear with an assortment of delicious-looking desserts. As the waiters start serving, I continue looking around, trying to impress this beautiful scene on my memory forever. I watch Joel and Danielle gaze adoringly at one another. I see the faces of so many dear people I've met this past month or been introduced to tonight: Savannah, Wes, Rachel, Austin, Tyler, friends Savannah and Danielle have known since they were young, Danielle's parents, Joel's parents, Joel's closest friends, and Savannah's family. As I finish looking over the crowd, I'm struck with gratitude. I didn't know anyone when I drove out here a month ago. Now, I'm fortunate enough to consider these people my friends.

I snuggle closer to Dylan, who's seated next to me and has his arm draped over the back of my chair. It has been about two weeks since we shared our feelings at Yellowstone, and my life has already become far more magical and fulfilling than I ever could have imagined. Each day, in word and deed, Dylan shows me the meaning of true love, and I've never experienced anything more beautiful than striving to show him that same type of love in return. Being with Dylan has expanded my whole existence in an incredible way. It seems so natural and right to be with him that I almost can't remember what my life was like before Dylan was a part of it.

Another great aspect of these past couple of weeks has been the support we've received from our family and friends. They've been nothing short of overjoyed for both of us. Of course, I was particularly worried about explaining everything to Danielle, but she was more elated than anyone when Dylan and I told her our news. In fact, Danielle admitted that ever since she first saw us interact, she had been hoping Dylan and I would "get our acts together and figure out what a perfect match we were."

So these past two weeks—while I've finished my ED rotation, and spent as much time as possible with Dylan and my new friends— have been the best of my life. Although there's no doubt residency will keep Dylan and me extremely busy, I'm even more certain now than I was before that we'll make our relationship work. We love each other, and we understand love is the most important and special thing of all.

In fact, the only bleak spot has been contemplating how much I'll miss Dylan when I leave tomorrow to start my cross-country drive for home. I'm returning to complete the last few weeks of med school and to pack before returning here for residency. Thankfully, Dylan will be flying out for a few days to meet my family and help me pack, so it will make the time we're apart a little easier. Nonetheless, I'll be counting the moments until I return here to start residency and get to be with Dylan regularly once more.

"How are you doing?" Dylan whispers in my ear before placing a tender kiss on my cheek.

I smile at him. "I'm doing extremely well. How are you?"

Dylan's gaze launches fireworks within me. "I've never been better."

We lean in for another kiss, but we both jump when Joel raises his voice and says to the crowd:

"May I have everyone's attention? I have an announcement."

The party guests fall into a hush. I shift in my chair to view the head table. Joel and Danielle are standing up now. He has his arm around her waist and a broad smile on his face. Meanwhile, Danielle is peering at Joel with a perplexed expression.

"You're making an announcement?" she asks. "What announcement?"

There's a smattering of laughter from the group. Joel chuckles before he continues addressing the crowd:

"I wanted everyone to gather tonight to celebrate the birthday of the most wonderful woman on Earth. What you didn't know is that I also wanted you here to witness the most important moment of the life Danielle and I have shared together so far."

I draw in a swift breath, sit up taller, and exchange a wide-eyed glance with Savannah across the audience. Her equally astonished expression confirms she's wondering the same thing: is Joel about to . . . ?

Joel's expression becomes serious. Clearing his throat, he turns to Danielle and gets down on one knee. There are excited, surprised gasps from the guests, the loudest coming from Savannah herself, who's now clutching her hands to her chest and tearfully smiling at her best friend.

Joel's hands are shaking slightly as he removes a small box from the pocket of his suit coat. He opens the box to reveal the gorgeous ring inside. With the ring sparkling underneath the twinkle lights, Joel peers earnestly into Danielle's eyes.

"Danielle Gillespie, I love you with all my heart, and nothing would make me happier than to spend the rest of my life with you. Will you marry me?"

Danielle is crying while gazing at Joel as if there is no one else in the Universe. "Yes, Joel. Yes, I will marry you."

The guests erupt into cheers and applause. Joel breaks into a grin, puts the ring on Danielle's finger, gets to his feet, and wraps her in his embrace.

As I cheer along with the crowd, I sneak a sideways look at Dylan. He's smiling as he claps, and if I'm not mistaken, there's a hint of tears in his eyes.

"I take it you approve?" I ask him.

Dylan nods. "I approve. Joel has treated Danielle like a queen since the day they met, and he has stayed by her side through thick and thin. Not to mention, Danielle is crazy about him. I couldn't think of a better match for my sister."

Smiling happily, I turn to view the head table once more. Danielle and Joel have become surrounded by family members and friends who are enthusiastically offering their congratulations.

"Well, what do you say?" I ask Dylan, playfully tipping my head toward the newly engaged couple. "Shall we venture over there?"

Dylan stands and reaches out a hand to me. "Definitely."

Hand-in-hand, Dylan and I weave through the throng to approach Danielle and Joel. As we get closer, the crowd parts, and I can see Danielle is absolutely beaming—frankly, Joel is, too.

When Danielle notices us, she scurries our way. "Can you believe it?" she exclaims breathlessly. "I'm so happy, I don't even know what to say!"

I give her a hug. "I'm thrilled for you and Joel."

"Thank you!" Danielle puts her hands to her flushed cheeks. "I can still hardly believe this is happening!"

Dylan chuckles, steps forward, and puts his arms around his sister. "I'm really happy for you."

Danielle blinks hard as she returns his embrace. "Thank you, Dyl."

They're both a little teary as they step back from one another. After Danielle wipes her eyes, she adopts a more mischievous expression, wags her eyebrows at her brother, and motions my way.

"Speaking of proposals . . ."

"Whoa." Dylan's deep laugh fills the air as he holds up his hands in a halting gesture. "I think you've got enough to plan for a while without trying to organize other people's weddings."

"True," Danielle giggles. She nudges me. "But hopefully one day."

Joel walks up to join us. His eyes meet Dylan's, and there's a pause. Dylan then smiles and extends a hand.

"Congratulations, Joel," Dylan says. "My sister is getting a great guy."

Joel shakes Dylan's hand in return. "Thank you. I know I'm the luckiest man in the world."

The conversation is interrupted when Joel's parents approach and excitedly begin speaking with the future bride and groom. Dylan and I exchange an amused look and retreat to give them room. Taking me by the hand, Dylan guides me away from the crowd and up a small incline to the base of an oak tree that has twinkle lights gently draped in its branches. With our arms around one another, Dylan and I fall into contented quiet while we watch the celebration.

"I think," I remark after a time, "this has been a perfect night."

"I agree," Dylan says before kissing me.

I unexpectedly hear someone else clear her throat and say, "Oh, um, hey. Sorry to interrupt."

Dylan looks past me and grins. I turn around, snickering when I see Savannah approaching with the corners of her mouth twitching upward.

"Hey," I greet her with a laugh.

Savannah laughs along with me as she reaches my side. "Quinn, before you head out of town tomorrow, I was wondering if you might be able to help me with a problem I suddenly have."

My smile disappears. "Of course. Are you okay?"

"Yep." Savannah is still smiling. "It's just that, if I'm overhearing Mrs. Gillespie correctly, there's going to be a wedding this autumn, which means I'll soon be losing my roommate."

Dylan emits something between a chuckle and a sigh while he shakes his head. "I'm guessing Mom has the entire event planned already."

"That was kind of my impression," Savannah concurs, her smile broadening. She focuses on me again. "So I was wondering: are you still looking for a place to live once you're out here for residency? If so, I would love for you to move in with me. After all, I need someone to join me when I binge on hot chocolate and cookies."

I stare at her. "Are you serious? You're inviting me to live with you?"

"Absolutely." She nods. "I would love it."

"I would love it, too!"

"Hooray! I'm so glad." Savannah gives me a hug. She then looks between Dylan and me with another glimmer of amusement in her eyes. "Now I'll let you two resume, um, whatever it was you were doing."

Savannah winks at us before she strolls away, retracing her path down the incline toward

Wes Kent, who's smiling as he strides across the lawn to join her.

As I turn back to Dylan, I hear the music get louder and a fresh round of applause from the guests. Shifting my eyes to the center of the party, I see Joel leading Danielle to a dance floor that's set up underneath some twinkling string lights. Lost in one another's gazes, the newly engaged couple begins swaying together to the song. Soon, Wes and Savannah join them on the dance floor, and then more couples begin getting up from their tables. It isn't long before the dance floor is filled.

Dylan faces me. Looking right into my eyes, he extends his hand. "Quinn Meyers, would you do me the honor of this dance?"

I place my hand in his. "I would be delighted, Dylan Gillespie."

Dylan wraps one arm around my waist and draws me close. Holding my other hand to his chest, Dylan starts leading me in a slow dance beneath the star-filled sky.

"I love you," he whispers.

"I love you, too."

As we continue to dance, I close my eyes, cherishing this perfect moment. After traveling thousands of miles to a place I had never been before, I found my home because I found love, and I know Dylan and I will dance together for the rest of our lives.

Acknowledgements

This story follows a journey—a journey of the heart—so it's very appropriate that I first thank you, dear readers, for taking this literary journey with me. I thank you from the bottom of my heart for your support and enthusiasm.

Nick, my best friend and companion in this journey we call life, thank you. I love you.

To all the fabulous HBWG ladies—we met on an unforgettable writing journey a couple years ago, and I feel so fortunate we've been friends ever since—thank you your camaraderie, help, and laughter. I can't wait for our next adventure!

I'm also immensely grateful to the members of my pre-release team. Your support during such a crucial phase of the writing journey is appreciated more than I can say.

To my family, who has supported me on the journey from Day One, thank you for everything.

And to Cookie. From little journeys around the neighborhood to bigger journeys beyond, thank you for being my ever-faithful writing buddy.

About the Author

TJ Amberson hails from the Pacific Northwest, where she lives with her husband and nutty cocker spaniel. When she's not writing, TJ might be found enjoying a hot chocolate, pretending to know how to garden, riding her bike, playing the piano, or surfing the Internet for cheap plane tickets.

With a love of several genres, TJ Amberson writes clean romantic comedies for adults, and historical fantasy and contemporary fantasy/sci-fi adventures for teen and mature tween readers.

www.tjamberson.com

She can also be followed on Facebook, Instagram, and Pinterest